Down on the Sidewalk

Down on the Sidewalk

STORIES ABOUT

Children

AND

Childhood

FROM THE
FLANNERY O'CONNOR AWARD
FOR SHORT FICTION

EDITED BY
ETHAN LAUGHMAN

THE UNIVERSITY OF GEORGIA PRESS
ATHENS

© 2020 by the University of Georgia Press
Athens, Georgia 30602
www.ugapress.org
All rights reserved
Designed by Kaelin Chappell Broaddus
Set in 9/13.5 Walbaum

Most University of Georgia Press titles are
available from popular e-book vendors.

Printed digitally

Library of Congress Cataloging-in-Publication Data in process
ISBN: 9780820357621 (pbk.: alk. paper)
ISBN: 9780820357614 (ebook)

CONTENTS

ACKNOWLEDGMENTS

The stories in this volume are from the following award-winning collections published by the University of Georgia Press:

Daniel Curley, *Living with Snakes* (1985); "Reflections in the Ice" first appeared in *Story Quarterly*

Carole L. Glickfeld, *Useful Gifts* (1989)

Antonya Nelson, *The Expendables* (1990); "Cold Places" first appeared in *Quarterly West*

Nancy Zafris, *The People I Know* (1990)

C. M. Mayo, *Sky over El Nido* (1995)

Paul Rawlins, *No Lie Like Love* (1996); "Boys" first appeared in *Prism International*

Dana Johnson, *Break Any Woman Down* (2001)

Kellie Wells, *Compression Scars* (2002)

Barbara Sutton, *The Send-Away Girl* (2004)

Andrew Porter, *The Theory of Light and Matter* (2008); "Hole" first appeared in *Story, Story Competition Winners*

Lori Ostlund, *The Bigness of the World* (2009); "The Bigness of the World" first appeared in *Bellingham Review*

Amina Gautier, *At-Risk* (2011); "Held" first appeared in *Red Rock Review*

ACKNOWLEDGMENTS

Melinda Moustakis, *Bear Down, Bear North* (2011); "Us Kids" first appeared in *Alaska Quarterly Review*

Tom Kealey, *Thieves I've Known* (2013); "The Boots" first appeared in *Story Quarterly*

Anne Raeff, *The Jungle around Us* (2016); "Maximiliano" first appeared in *Antioch Review*

A thank you also goes to the University of Georgia Main Library staff for technical support in preparing the stories for publication.

INTRODUCTION

The Flannery O'Connor Award for Short Fiction was established in 1981 by Paul Zimmer, then the director of the University of Georgia Press, and press acquisitions editor Charles East. East would serve as the first series editor, judging the competition and selecting two collections to publish each year. The inaugural volumes in the series, *Evening Out* by David Walton and *From the Bottom Up* by Leigh Allison Wilson, appeared in 1983 to critical acclaim. Nancy Zafris (herself a Flannery O'Connor Award–winner for her 1990 collection *The People I Know*) was the second series editor, serving in the role from 2008 to 2015. Zafris was succeeded by Lee K. Abbott in 2016, and Roxane Gay then assumed the role, choosing award winners beginning in 2019. Competition for the award has become an important proving ground for writers, and the press has published seventy-four volumes to date, helping to showcase talent and sustain interest in the short story form. These volumes together feature approximately eight hundred stories by authors based across the United States and abroad. It has been my pleasure to have read each and every one.

The idea of undertaking a project that could honor the diversity of the series' stories but also present them in a unified way had been hanging around the press for a few years. What occurred to us first, and what remained the most appealing approach, was to pull the hundreds of stories out of their current packages—volumes of collected stories by individual authors—and regroup them by common themes or subjects. After finishing an editorial internship at the press, I was brought on to the project and began to sort the stories into specific thematic categories. What followed was a deep dive into the award and its history as well as a gratifying acquaintance with the many authors whose works constitute the award's legacy.

Anthologies are not new to the series. A tenth-anniversary collection, published in 1993, showcased one story from each of the volumes published in the award's first decade. A similar collection appeared in 1998, the fifteenth year of the series. In 2013, the year of the series' thirtieth anniversary, the press published two volumes modeled after the tenth- and fifteenth-anniversary volumes. These anthologies together included one story from each of the fifty-five collections published up to that point. One of the 2013 volumes represented the series' early years, under the editorship of Charles East. The other showcased the editorship of Nancy Zafris. In a nod to the times, both thirtieth-anniversary anthologies appeared in e-book form only.

The present project is wholly different in both concept and scale. The press plans to republish more than five hundred stories in more than forty volumes, each focusing on a specific theme— from love to food to homecoming and homesickness. Each volume will aim to collect exemplary treatments of its theme, but with enough variety to give an overview of what the series is about. The stories inside illustrate the varied perspectives multiple authors can have on a single theme.

Each volume, no matter its central theme, includes the work of authors whose stories celebrate the variety of short fiction styles to be found across the history of the award. Just as Flannery O'Connor is more than just a southern writer, the University of Georgia Press, by any number of measures, has been more than a regional publisher for some time. As the first series editor, Charles East, happily reported in his anthology of the O'Connor Award stories, the award "managed to escape [the] pitfall" of becoming a regional stereotype. When Paul Zimmer established the award, he named it after Flannery O'Connor as the writer who best embodied the possibilities of the short-story form. In addition, O'Connor, with her connections to the South and readership across the globe, spoke to the ambitions of the press at a time when it was poised to ramp up both the number and scope of its annual title output. The O'Connor name has always been a help in keeping the series a place where writers strive to be published and where readers and critics look for quality short fiction.

The award has become an internationally recognized institution. The seventy-four (and counting) Flannery O'Connor Award authors come from all parts of the United States and abroad. They have lived in Arizona, Arkansas, California, Colorado, Georgia, Indiana, Maryland, Massachusetts, Texas, Utah, Washington, Canada, Iran, England, and elsewhere. Some have written novels. Most have published stories in a variety of literary quarterlies and popular magazines. They have been awarded numerous fellowships and prizes. They are world-travelers, lecturers, poets, columnists, editors, and screenwriters.

There are risks in the thematic approach we are taking with these anthologies, and we hope that readers will not take our editorial approach as an attempt to draw a circle around certain aspects of a story or in any way close off possibilities for interpretation. Great stories don't have to resolve anything, be set any particular time nor place, or be written in any one way. Great stories don't have to *be* anything. Still, when a story resonates with enough readers in a certain way, it is safe to say that it has spoken to us meaningfully about, for instance, love, death, and certain concerns, issues, pleasures, or life events.

We at the press had our own ideas about how the stories might be gathered, but we were careful to get author input on the process. The process of categorizing their work was not easy for any of them. Some truly agonized. Having their input was invaluable; having their trust was humbling. The goal of this project is to faithfully represent these stories despite the fact that they have been pulled from their original collections and are now bed-mates with stories from a range of authors taken from diverse contexts. Also, just because a single story is included in a particular volume does not mean that that volume is the only place that story could have appropriately been placed. For example, "Sawtelle" from Dennis Hathaway's *The Consequences of Desire* tells the story of a subcontractor in duress when he finds out his partner is the victim of an extramarital affair. We have included it in the volume of stories about love, but it could have been included in those on work, friends, and immigration without seeming out of place.

In *Creating Flannery O'Connor*, Daniel Moran writes that O'Connor first mentioned her infatuation with peacocks in her essay "Living with a Peacock" (later republished as "King of the Birds"). Since the essay's appearance, a proliferation of critics and admirers have linked O'Connor with imagery derived from the bird's distinctive features, and one can now hardly find an O'Connor publication that does not depict or refer to her "favorite fowl" and its association with immortality and layers of symbolic and personal meaning. As Moran notes, "Combining elements of her life on a farm, her religious themes, personal eccentricities, and outsider status, the peacock has proved the perfect icon for O'Connor's readers, critics, and biographers, a form of reputation-shorthand that has only grown more ubiquitous over time."

We are pleased to offer these anthologies as another way of continuing Flannery O'Connor's legacy. Since its conception, thirty-eight years' worth of enthralling, imaginative, and thought-provoking fiction has been published under the name of the Flannery O'Connor Award. The award is just one way that we hope to continue the conversation about O'Connor and her legacy while also circulating and sharing recent authors' work throughout the world.

It is perhaps unprecedented for such a long-standing short fiction award series to republish its works in the manner we are going about it. The idea for the project may be unconventional, but it draws on an established institution—the horn-of-plenty that constitutes the Flannery O'Connor Award series backlist—that is still going strong as it approaches its fortieth year. I am in equal parts intimidated and honored to present you with what I consider to be these exemplars of the Flannery O'Connor Award. Each story speaks to the theme uniquely. Some of these stories were chosen for their experimental nature, others for their unique take on the theme, and still others for exhibiting matchlessness in voice, character, place, time, plot, relevance, humor, timelessness, perspective, or any of the thousand other metrics by which one may measure a piece of literature.

But enough from me. Let the stories speak for themselves.

ETHAN LAUGHMAN

Down on the Sidewalk

Fort Arden

CAROLE L. GLICKFELD

From *Useful Gifts* (1989)

The thing about Glory and Roy Rogers was that they weren't too chicken to play on the roof.

I got the idea when we were at the bottom of the stoop playing Johnny-May-We-Cross-Your-River. I was Johnny and the kids were trying to cross over. "Johnny, may we cross your river?" they yelled out.

Usually I gave them colors. They could cross if they were wearing the color I said, but when I saw a balloon disappear over the top of my building, I said, "Yes you may, if you're willing to come up to the roof."

Right away my friend Glory crossed, and so did her stepbrother, Roy Rogers. The rest of the kids, though, just stood there in front of the little brick wall that separated the stoop from the garden.

"No fair," said Tommy, the eldest of the Shanahan kids.

"What'sa matter?" Glory called out.

"Yeah, what'sa matter?" Roy Rogers said. He was only seven but he always did everything Glory did.

"Too dangerous," said Tommy.

Glory snorted. Roy Rogers tried to snort, but it sounded like he was trying to keep his nose from dripping.

Then Pat Shanahan yelled, "We can't, because our ma wouldn't like it."

"So, don' tell her," Glory said, rolling her dark eyes.

"You don' know nothin'," Tommy said. "We'll have to tell the priest, so nothin' doin'."

"That's rich!" I said, pretending to belly-laugh.

Robin Reinstein was just standing there, next to the Shanahan kids, twirling her brown hair around her finger. I gave her a look.

"Can't. My mother will see I'm gone," she said, letting go of her hair to point to her windows up on the third floor.

I looked up. Mrs. Reinstein was standing at the stove next to the open window in a red and white checked housedress. She waved at us.

Then I remembered what we'd done on Memorial Day. "That didn't stop you from coming to the alley with us to do you know what," I told Robin.

I watched her turn a funny strawberry color, starting with her ears, then spreading over her cheeks like hives.

"She's blushing!" Tommy Shanahan said.

"Am not!"

"Am too!"

"You're all dumb," Robin said, "like Ruthie's mother."

"My mother's not dumb, she's a deaf-mute. So there! You're so dumb you don't even know the difference."

"Awww, she's too chicken to play with anyhow!" said Glory, tossing her head, which made her dark bangs crooked. She linked arms with Roy Rogers. They came over and got me. I linked arms with Glory on her other side. We marched up to the first landing of the stoop, then turned around.

"Big chicken!" Roy Rogers yelled.

We marched up to the second landing, stomping our feet hard on each step.

"Biggest chicken!" Glory yelled.

On the third landing I yelled, "Great biggest chicken in the whole wide world!"

When we got up to the roof the balloon wasn't there. We looked over the edge of the wall. Down on the sidewalk the Shanahan kids were playing Green Light with Iris and Ivy Opals.

"What're we gonna do?" asked Roy Rogers.

"Stop scratching!" said Glory, knocking one of his hands away from his curly head.

"I don't know. What?" I said.

"Let's play Dare You," said Glory. "I'll go first."

"Uh uh, Choosey," I said, meaning we should play Choosey to see who went first.

"Odds!" Glory shouted, before I could pick. She knew odds was my favorite.

Glory and I put our fists behind our backs. Roy Rogers did the calling out. "Once, twice, three, SHOOT!" he said.

Glory stuck out two fingers. I stuck out one. So she got to go first.

It didn't take her long to think of something. She went right to the washlines where clothes were hanging to dry. "You have to make a switch," she said, "from two different lines."

"Ha, ha," I said, switching a black sock on one line with a black sock on another. "No one's gonna know," I said. Then I looked around for something to dare back. I pointed to a pair of blue polka-dot boxer shorts. "That for the bloomers," I said.

Roy Rogers and I almost died when Glory jumped up and pulled the pink bloomers off the line. When she dropped them, we collapsed in hysterics. Glory picked them up and dropped them again, she was laughing so hard. Then she couldn't get them back up on the other line because she was too short, so I held the line down while she stuck the clothespins on the bloomers.

After we did the boxer shorts, she and Roy Rogers started yelling and rolling around on the tar. We didn't hear Mrs. Krakowski open the door, which usually creaked a lot, but we heard her booming voice. "Gott!" she said, seeing the three of us in a big heap. She put a big basket under the washlines. We watched her take off the sheets and fold them, slapping and poking each other when she took down the boxer shorts.

"Ants in her pants!" Glory said. "See them crawling?"

"Ants in her pants!" Roy Rogers said.

I started giggling, pretending I saw the little blue dots moving around.

We could hear Mrs. Krakowski muttering to herself, but we couldn't hear what she was saying. She looked over at us when she took down the bloomers. I could of died. "Such a hot day, no?" she said.

Glory kicked me. I kicked her back. "Real hot," I said.

After that, Mrs. Krakowski talked only to herself. When she left we were hurting so much we couldn't laugh anymore.

"What now?" I asked.

"It's my dare," said Glory, doing a backbend all of a sudden. With her head upside down, she said, "All the wash is gone, so I have to think." She stood back up, then went leaping across the roof, doing jetés, stopping like a statue with her arms out in front of her when she got to the other end. "C'mere," she yelled.

When I got there, she was pointing with her chin to the wall that separated our roof from 26 Arden, which didn't come up as high. Smiling with her lips together, Glory said, "I dare you to jump."

"That's rich," I said, "and if I kill myself . . ."

"Aw-w-w," Glory said.

"Aw-w-w," Roy Rogers said.

I figured that even if I could climb up the wall I'd get all bloody jumping down the other side. I could see my father saying, "I'll break your neck." Then I looked into Glory's dark eyes and got an idea. "Here goes," I said.

I went over and knelt on the stone top of the little wall at the edge of the roof that came halfway up the dividing wall. I kept my head turned away from Arden Street, which was six stories down.

"What're you doing?" Glory asked.

"I can't look, I can't look," said Roy Rogers, putting his hands over his eyes.

"It's my stepladder," I said, standing on the ledge and reaching up to the top of the dividing wall. I kept my back turned to the street. Holding on with all my might, I pulled myself up. Then I sat up there, my feet dangling near where Glory's head was. Roy Rogers was peeking at me through his fingers. When my heart stopped pounding like a drum, I turned so that my feet hung down the other side. But the little wall at the edge of 26 Arden didn't come up as far as I thought.

Roy Rogers was yelling behind me. "She's gonna do it."

"Shut up, stupid," Glory said.

If only someone would come up to the roof now, I thought, even Mrs. Krakowski. I was sorry we'd made fun of her.

"Change your mind?" Glory said.

I held on as I lowered myself down, but I had to let go for the last few inches. As soon as I felt my feet touch the ledge I pushed off toward the roof and went tumbling. I scraped my hands and one knee.

I heard Roy Rogers clapping and yelling. "She did it, she did it!" When I looked up, he and Glory, who were both terrific at climbing, had gotten up on top of the dividing wall. They were in the middle, though—not at the edge.

Glory's almond eyes were like little slits. "So, go ahead," she said to him.

He bent forward, like he was getting ready to jump, but all he did was keep rocking back and forth. "What're you waiting for?" she asked.

"Want me to catch you?" I said. I saw Glory was about to say something. "I dare you to jump into my arms," I said to Roy Rogers, "but you have to sit down first."

5

He plopped down and I got under where his feet were. Then he leaned forward. "T-i-i-m-m-b-e-r-r-r," he shouted, coming at me like a bomber pilot. He knocked me down, with him on top of me, which he thought was real funny. I scraped my other knee.

"Now you," I said to Glory, "but I'm not catching you."

"No fair, no repeats," she said, making up a new rule.

"Chi-i-i—" I bluffed.

Her eyes got like slits again. She started walking on top of the wall toward the edge of the roof. "If you can do it . . ." she said. All of a sudden I knew her feet wouldn't even get close to the ledge on my side, because she was a lot shorter than me.

I ran over to the edge and looked down at the sidewalk. "The Shanahan kids!" I yelled. Just then, Tommy looked up, even though he couldn't of heard me.

"Get him!" I said to Roy Rogers.

"Bang! You're dead," Roy Rogers called out, firing on him.

And that's how Fort Arden was created.

"Keep a lookout for more enemies," I ordered Glory, and then Roy Rogers and I ran down five flights in 26 Arden and six flights back up to the roof of 38 Arden. When we got there, Glory said sarcastically, "What took you so long?"

Right before the Fourth of July I stuck a flag that Glory had made with all forty-eight stars into a hole at the edge of the roof. "Now everyone on Arden Street will know we've taken the fort," I said.

I had learned about the flag when Mrs. Landau took our class to the other two forts in Inwood: Fort Tryon and Fort Washington. She told us about uniforms also, but it was too hot, so we only tied bandannas around ourselves.

That day Glory was on the cannon and I was right next to her, looking out for enemies down below. Roy Rogers was marching back and forth at the other end, carrying his broomstick over his shoulder like a rifle.

"Look!" I said to Glory, as he tried to twirl it. He hit himself in the side of the head and dropped the rifle.

"He's hopeless," Glory said. "Remember when we taught him to say, 'Who goes there?'"

"Yeah," I said, even though I was the one who taught him. He kept giggling until Glory smacked him in the head and said, "Nelson, this is real serious. It's not like playing cowboy, Nelson."

"Don't call me Nelson," Roy Rogers said and then he was okay.

"I hope he doesn't come over," Glory said. "I want to ask you who you think's prettier, Doris Day or June Haver?"

"Doris Day. But she's not as pretty as Jane Powell."

"You think she's pretty?" Glory said. She made a sound like she was trying to throw up.

"Mrs. Reinstein!" I said, pointing down to the sidewalk. "Fire the cannon!"

"BO-OM! BO-OM! BO-OM!" Glory thundered. She was very good with sound effects.

Mrs. Reinstein disappeared up the stoop. Then the Old Clothes wagon pulled up. The Old Clothes man got down from the seat behind the horse.

"Fire the cannon!" I yelled.

"Ruthie, I told you. Not anyone with horses." Her bangs got crooked when she tossed her head. "Soon you'll be telling me to fire on Irish Rose." That's what we called the tenor who came to the back alley to sing for money. Once we threw him down a penny. "And don't tell me to fire on the coal man, neither."

Next thing I knew, Roy Rogers was waving his red bandanna. We signaled him over.

"How come I'm all by myself?" he said, pouting.

Glory mussed his curly hair. "Because you're the sentry."

"Says who?"

"I do," Glory said. I gave her a look. "We do," she said, meaning me and her.

7

"But . . . you're girls," he said. "Only boys can be in the Army."

"Roy Rogers, if you weren't so dumb . . ." Glory started, raising her shoulders to show me how aggravated she was with her step-brother. "First of all, we're bigger than you. Secondly, what do you know about anything? And last but not least, you are a dumb, dumb bunny." She turned her back, but he just stood there.

"There are too girls in the Army," I said. "They're called Waves."

"See?" Glory said, looking at him again. "So git. You can't play Fort today."

Roy Rogers's face scrunched up like he was going to cry. He walked slowly to the other end, picked up his broomstick, and came running back. He pointed his make-believe rifle at her. "Bang! You're dead, dead, dead."

"Oh yeah?" she said, pretending to swing the cannon around.

Roy Rogers leaped at her. "Bang, bang!"

"Bang! I got ya!" said a deep voice behind us. It was the milk-man, coming from the doorway of 42 Arden, in the middle of the roof. He was carrying two crates of empty milk bottles, one on top of the other, so that you couldn't see his face, but you could see his white pants.

"Bang!" Roy Rogers said.

"Bang, bang!" I said.

"BO-OM! BO-OM!" said Glory.

The milkman dropped the boxes down on the roof. The noise was like thunder. "Ehehehehehehehehe," he said, machine-gunning us.

Roy Rogers fell down on the tar.

"I'm dy-ing," Glory said, falling on top of him.

"Good-bye," I said, doubling over, then collapsing.

"See ya," said the milkman, laughing as he picked up his crates and headed across the fort to 38 Arden.

"Ugh! That stuff stinks," I said, about the tar. "It's all mushy, too." That was because of the hot sun.

"Who cares? We have to have a different plan," Glory said.

"An enemy got through our lines. From now on, I'll be General."

The next time we went up, Glory put Roy Rogers on the cannon. I had to laugh because she made her and me sentries at different ends of the fort. We couldn't even talk to each other except by yelling. I was sorry I didn't go to the park with my mother where the pool was. Robin Reinstein had gone right after lunch. It was so hot out I was dripping. Glory was waving her red bandanna.

When I came over she said, "We'll be rovers now."

Together, she and I walked back and forth, guarding the fort. Each time we got to the middle, we talked to Roy Rogers so he wouldn't get lonely. It was so hot our sneakers stuck to the roof as we walked. I was glad when the sky started getting gray.

"Dare you to stay out when the rain comes down," Glory said.

Right away I said okay, since my father was downtown playing cards at his club.

The sky became an even darker gray and then there was a bolt of lightning. Giant drops of rain splashed our clothes and the roof, making big puddles. When we heard the thunder, Roy Rogers ran for the door.

"Go down and get the bucket!" Glory yelled after him.

The rain came down like Niagara Falls. In a few minutes she and I were drenched. I could see Glory's underpants through her dress.

When Roy Rogers came back with the bucket, Glory let it fill up with rain. "The next person who crosses the stoop will get drowned," she said.

There was another roar of thunder. Roy Rogers started running. "Don't drown anyone till I get back!" he yelled.

No one crossed the stoop while he was gone. It was only drizzling when he came back. Then Mrs. Krakowski came up the sidewalk.

"Don't let her see you!" Glory warned.

We ducked down behind the little wall.

"Get the bucket!" she ordered Roy Rogers.

Mrs. Krakowski started up the stoop.

"Ready, aim . . ."

Before Glory could say, "Fire!" Roy Rogers shoved the bucket of water toward the stoop, but then he lost his grip on it. Out sloshed the water, curling like the top of a waterfall, before we heard it go splat on the ground. The bucket came bouncing and crashing after. Face down, we dived onto the tar.

"Is someone crazy?" we heard Mrs. Krakowski shouting. "Vot, have we got lunatics living here now?"

Glory and Roy Rogers kept hugging each other as they lay next to me, giggling into each other's necks and sometimes into mine. I saw the whole front of Glory's pastel green dress was smudged from the black tar. Roy Rogers's face and hands were black. I looked down at my pinafore, because my mother had a thing about dirt, but I couldn't see any on the red and blue flowers.

Then I peeked carefully over the wall. Mrs. Krakowski had gone. The drizzle had stopped. Half the sky was blue again, and over the gray half was a gorgeous rainbow.

"Close your eyes and make a wish," I said, closing my own eyes to wish I'd be as pretty as Doris Day when I grew up.

"What did you wish?" Glory asked Roy Rogers, trying to trick him into telling.

"Give me a nickel and I'll tell."

"Then you won't get your wish," I said.

"I don't care."

"Okay," Glory said. "A nickel."

"A nickel," said Roy Rogers.

"So, what did you wish?"

"Told ya. I wished for a nickel," Roy Rogers said, bursting into hysterics.

Glory's black eyes looked like they were trying to kill him. Then they turned on me. "What's so funny?" she said.

I almost fell down in stitches. She stomped off the fort, leaving Roy Rogers lying at my feet, sloshing around in a puddle.

Soon my side ached from laughing and my teeth were chattering, because it had cooled off and I was still soaked. Roy Rogers and I went downstairs. Glory was in the hallway outside their door. "What are we going to do?" she asked him. "The bucket's not there." She didn't look at me the whole time.

"Ask Mrs. Krakowski?" said Roy Rogers, like he knew it was the wrong answer.

"I dare you," she said.

"Dare *you*," he said.

"You know Dot's gonna get the strap out," Glory said, about their mother. A few times Glory had showed me red welts on her back. My mother said Dot had a really bad temper, even though she was always so nice to me.

"*I'll* ask," I said. I figured Mrs. Krakowski wouldn't say anything to my mother or father because she always told me how she felt sorry for them.

Once Mrs. Krakowski came up to me on the stoop and said, "Too bad."

"What?" I asked her.

"Your parents being deaf-and-dumb."

"They're not dumb," I told her. "They're deaf-mutes. They're used to it because my mother got that way when she was a baby and my father got meningitis when he was eight years old."

She clucked her tongue. "Never to hear your own child . . ." She tried to hand me a dime. "For candy," she said.

"I'm not allowed," I fibbed.

"For something else, then."

"No thanks, Mrs. Krakowski," I said politely.

"Ruthie's gonna ask Mrs.-Ants-in-Her-Pants," Roy Rogers said, jumping up and down.

"Stay here," I told them, afraid they'd make me laugh right in the middle. I went across the stoop.

When she opened the door, Mrs. Krakowski screamed, "Gott! A drowned rat!"

"I dropped the bucket by mistake," I said. "Could I please get it back?"

"You?" She slapped the side of her head. "Vot to expect?" she muttered to herself as she went inside. She came back with the bucket. "Your parents, Gott bless, don't know any better. Such a mess!"

I thought she was a mess, with her blouse hanging half out of her skirt and her stockings bunched around her fat ankles, but all I said was, "Thank you very much, Mrs. Krakowski," and took the bucket. I ran across the stoop to where Glory and Roy Rogers were waiting.

Glory took one look and said, "Oh cripes! We'll have to hammer it!" One side was all bashed in.

Dot wasn't home, so I sat under Dot's hair dryer and Glory started hammering. Then Glory sat under the dryer and I hammered.

"Let me, let me," said Roy Rogers. Glory gave him the hammer. She and I took off our clothes and put on robes so she could iron our things dry. She did her own dress okay but she burned the ruffle on the shoulder of my pinafore. The spaces between the red and blue flowers were brown instead of white. Roy Rogers thought that was hilarious, but he stopped laughing when he hit his foot with the hammer.

When it was time for supper I went upstairs. My shoes squished on each step. It didn't matter, since my mother couldn't hear them, of course, but next time she ironed she would see the burn.

When she saw me, my mother signed, "Like Negro." She stood in the doorway of the bathroom while I washed my face and hands. "Hear happen?" she asked, meaning did I hear what'd happened.

I shook my head, wondering if she meant the bucket. She looked real serious.

"Milkman," she signed, then spelled out "m-u-g-g-e-d" in sign language.

"What m-u-g-g-e-d?" I asked. I'd seen the word in the *Daily News* but didn't know what it meant.

She made signs to show me how the milkman had been knocked over the head and was laying unconscious when Mrs. Shanahan found him. That's what she told my mother after the ambulance came.

My mother and I went into the kitchen and she put a bowl of blueberries and sour cream on the table.

"Where happen?" I asked.

"Up r-o-o-f. D-a-n-g-e-r-o-u-s."

Suddenly I wasn't hungry, even though I loved blueberries. "U-p-s-e-t?" my mother asked, but I pretended I ate at Glory's.

Later Mrs. Shanahan phoned us about the milkman. "Tell your mother Jewish Memorial said it was a concussion," she said. "He'll be okay. But I wonder what the world is coming to when someone almost gets murdered on our own roof."

"Milkman almost k-i-l-l-e-d," I told my mother. "Will b-e all right." I didn't know what a concussion was, so I didn't bother spelling it out.

"N-i-c-e man," my mother said about him. "Feel sorry." She got a hairbrush and started brushing the knots out of my hair. That's when she noticed the burn on the ruffle. "Stupid me, care-less iron," she said.

For a second I almost didn't say anything. But then I said, "G-l-o-r-y iron, b-u-r-n," explaining we got soaked in the rain. I didn't tell her we were on the roof.

When my mother didn't get angry, I put my arms around her

waist and hugged her. Her stomach and breasts were like big soft pillows. She squeezed me and then she let me go. "Sorry spoil dress," she said, smiling so that I could see her dimples. That's when I realized Glory had never told me she was sorry for burning my pinafore. But that was Glory. She hadn't even thanked me for the bucket.

After my mother braided my hair, I got out my library book, but I couldn't concentrate. I wanted to talk to Glory about moving Fort Arden. I figured the brick wall at the top of the stoop would be perfect. There were lots of long, skinny spaces between the bricks, so we could hide behind there and still see who our enemies were.

One thing for sure, I decided: from then on I was going to be General, because Glory and Roy Rogers owed me plenty for saving their lives.

The Boots

TOM KEALEY

From *Thieves I've Known* (2013)

It was a visiting priest, as it often was, and the two altar boys half-listened to the homily and stared out at the small congregation. Snow was falling fast outside, and many of the old people had stayed home, but there was one man—more ancient than any they'd seen—sitting in the back of the church, and he was obviously a homeless man and a little drunk tonight. At least it seemed this way to Omar, the older of the two altar boys, and he watched the man close his eyes and lean forward, almost asleep, then catch himself and listen again to the homily. The priest had moved past grace and love, as if they might be near the bottom of a list, but important to mention nonetheless. When he spoke the words "Lazarus" and "resurrection" the two boys perked up, because that story was often interesting to them. "When his name was called he awakened," the priest said. "Just as our names are called, every day. And we must awake in a similar way." And then the priest went on to some parish announcements. It made Omar frown. He'd been hoping for some new information. He looked over at Lewis, but Lewis did not return the look. The younger boy's head jerked to the side, and then again, as if beyond the priest's homily he could also hear some music that no one else could hear. It was a bad tic and had become worse in the last year. He'd been told he might eventually—when he was older—shake to death, and he'd shared this secret with Omar, who had told him not to worry over it too much, and who'd said, no, he wouldn't tell anyone else.

They went through the rest of mass, ringing the bells when it was called for and taking the gifts back to the altar, and during communion they held the little dishes under the chins of the parishioners, though no one had dropped a host in a long while. It had been a year, and Omar had caught it, and the priest—another visitor, though not this one—had told him that he was a very vigilant young man, and this had delighted both boys, so much so that they'd gone to the dictionary and looked up the word: "watchful and awake, alert to avoid danger." They liked that. When mass was over, they walked down the aisle and waited at the back of the church with the priest as he shook hands with some of the parishioners, and some of the people shook the hands of Omar and Lewis, or patted them on the head, and when this happened the boys smiled though they weren't smiling on the inside. They watched the poor box as some people dropped in dollars and coins, and even the ancient man dropped something in, and when everyone had left the boys took up the box and brought it back to the sacristy and opened it and counted out the money.

It was not much: four dollars and change, plus a candy wrapper, a book of matches, and a little white bone that they picked up and studied. It was just a few inches long and seemed like it might be half the wishbone of a turkey or a chicken, and they wondered about the wish that had been made upon it. Good health maybe, or a change in the weather. They placed it at the top of the stack of money and took it away to the priest, who was preparing himself for confessional.

Once—the year before Omar arrived—there had been a five-dollar bill in the poor box, and Lewis had slipped this into his pocket. He'd bought nine cans of lemon soda with the money and drank them all in one day. He felt bad about it now. He'd felt bad about it for a long time, and he'd been sneaking a quarter into the pile for the last few months. In a few more weeks he'd have it all paid back.

They offered the money to the priest, and the man took it and put it in a drawer, and Lewis stood there with the bone in his open hand. The priest looked at it.

"What the hell is that?" he said.

"It was in the box," said Lewis, and his head jerked to the side.

"Somebody offered it up," said Omar.

"Well, get rid of it," said the priest.

The two boys studied the bone.

"Can we keep it?" said Lewis.

The priest frowned. His expression seemed to indicate that the bone was a great inconvenience to him.

"I don't care," he said, and though there were altar dressings to fold and the chalice and the dishes to wash, and the wine to be poured back into the bottle, the two boys followed the priest out to the confessional where there were two women waiting in the pews just outside. Later, the two boys would try to guess the sins to be confessed: adultery and jealousy and murder and thievery and sloth, the latter of which was the worst as far as Omar was concerned, but now they waited for the priest to open the door to the confessional, and when he saw them standing behind him he said, "What do you want?"

"Can we see in?" said Omar.

The priest looked at his side of the confessional. "In here?" he said.

"Yes."

He seemed to consider that, and he looked over at the two women who were praying with their eyes closed.

"Does Father Ramon let you see in?"

They frowned at that and said that he didn't.

The priest sighed, opened the door, and waved them in, and immediately they asked if they could slide the windows open, and he said to keep their voices down and yes that was all right if they were quick about it.

So, they opened and closed the windows and they each had a seat in the chair. The other leaned outside to see if the little light came on, and when it did he gave the thumbs-up. They asked the priest if one of them could go around and kneel on the other side of the confessional, and the priest said no, go on now, and so they did, back up to the altar and the sacristy where they washed and folded and put things away, and when they were done they put on their coats and scarves and headed out into the snow.

There was a strong and painful windstorm outside, and the two boys headed straight into it, wiping the snow from their eyes and moving from streetlight to streetlight in the dark. The lid of a trashcan blew across the road, and the cars parked near the sidewalk were covered in white, like a long line of sand dunes or mountains in a range. The boys crunched along in the drifts, and Omar thought of his mother, as he often did. He'd not been vigilant enough with her—she'd been a heavy drinker and had died of it—but he tried to put that from his mind, and instead he remembered waiting for her at the laundry in the hospital, watching her sort and weigh the linens that she pulled from baskets and oversized sacks. The room was long and filled with light, and he could hear nothing above the din of the washers and the fifty-gallon tanks filled with bleach water. His mother worked slow and deliberate in her long bib overalls, and every so often she'd motion for him to fold this stack of towels, these pillowcases, and they'd play an unnamed game: a poke to her ribs when she wasn't looking, and a pinch on his ear when he wasn't. Omar kept a tally in his head. He was always way ahead. They took up the sheets together and placed them in the washers.

When the boys arrived at the diner, just past the butcher's shop, they went in and found a booth in the corner. There was some music playing from the jukebox, something slow and bouncy, and the two boys bobbed their heads to the music as they studied the menus. They looked at the pictures of the french toast and the patty melt and the banana pie. There was a line of syrup caked at the top of Lewis' menu, and he scraped it off with the edge of his fingernail. They counted out their money, and figured in for a tip, and while they waited on the waitress they looked out at the snow that was swirling down into the streetlights. Omar imagined the moon and the stars falling to earth.

"What's it going to be?" said the waitress.

"A tea, please," said Omar.

"With two spoons, please," said Lewis.

She looked at them. "That's all you're going to order, isn't it?"

They said that it was, and sorry about that, and she took up their menus and went off into the kitchen.

Lewis took out the bone and placed it on the table halfway between them. His head jerked to the side. It was a strange little bone, they both agreed, and they began to play the football game with it. They slid the bone across the table to each other, trying to score a touchdown by getting the bone to hang off the edge without falling. They tapped it with the ends of their fingers. It was not easy, and they worked at it for a while, and at some point Lewis observed that the table had not been wiped down in a long time. Still, he was the first to score, a lucky shot that ricocheted off the sugar container. Lewis lined the bone up for the extra point, and when he flicked it, it went over Omar's shoulder and into the soup of the man sitting behind them.

"What the hell?" the man said.

They turned to look at him, and the man was dressed in a red Santa Claus suit. He looked very drunk and not very happy about the bone.

"Sorry," said Omar.

"This is a finger bone," said the man.

"Sorry," said Lewis.

"You threw a finger bone in my soup," said the man.

Their tea came then, with two spoons and two little containers of cream.

"What are you yelling at these boys about?" said the waitress.

"Look," said the man. He pointed at his soup. "Finger bone."

The two boys went back out into the wind and the snow. They were filled up with a cup of tea and two refills, and Omar had the bone in his pocket. The man had not given it up easily, and they weren't allowed to play the football game anymore. The snow was coming down sideways now, and they walked into it, back toward the church. Lewis' tic was worse, harder than before and more frequent, so that he began to have trouble walking in a straight line. He took hold of the tail of Omar's coat and followed the boy into the wind.

When they came to the church they could see that there was a strange form under the light by the side door, and they trudged up toward it until they could see that it was a man lying facedown on the steps. The man was bundled in a heavy coat and scarf, and he had no shoes on his stocking feet. The boys circled around him and stopped near the hat lying alone and covered with snow-flakes. Lewis brushed it off and gave it a quick snap against his knee, and he placed it back on the man's head.

They turned the man over and they could see that it was the priest, the visiting one, and he was alive though he seemed fast asleep, and his face was cold to the touch. They found his wallet and the keys to the church in his pocket, and they dragged him inside to the sacristy and closed the door from the cold and the wind.

A cushion was found for his head, and a blanket to put over him. Omar ran warm water over a cloth and wiped the man's face. After a time, the priest opened his eyes and looked up at the boys. He seemed as if he was still half-asleep.

"What happened?" he said.

"Somebody rolled you," said Omar.

"They took your boots," said Lewis.

The man looked down at his socks. "Did they get the wallet?"

Omar held it in his hand, and he opened it so that the priest could see inside. There were many dollars in the wallet.

"Do you want a doctor?" said Omar.

"No. I want you to bring me some wine."

The boys looked to the cabinet where the wine was kept. The key was hanging there in the lock.

"You should go get your boots," said Omar. "I can show you where."

The priest looked up at the two boys. He squinted in the lights. "Leave me alone," he said, and he set his head back on the cushion and closed his eyes.

The boys walked for many miles. When they came to the bridge Omar took Lewis' hand, not for warmth, but because the younger boy was afraid of the water below. They walked carefully over the ice and crossed to the other side.

They found the address they'd been told about—an old foundry building, now falling apart—and they went inside, through a gash in the wall, and they walked past the broken glass and the blocks of old granite and concrete. Behind one of the piles of rocks they found the spiraled staircase. There were little white Christmas lights strung all down the banister, and the boys followed them down. Down and down. The little lights twisted below them like a long, beautiful water snake down into the dark. Both boys had the bad shivers, and they held their collars tight about their necks. Lewis remembered the face of the priest, and his head jerked to the side. It put him in mind of the bodies he'd seen at funerals. The expressions on the faces of the dead: lonely, it seemed to him, and sometimes deep in thought, as if the dead person was about to say something but didn't. He'd asked Father Ramon once could he touch the hand or maybe the feet of a dead man, a parishioner they'd known, and for that Lewis had been sent out to clean the statue of Saint Joseph with soap and water and an old toothbrush. He'd done the work gently, and with some care, because he was Lewis' favorite: not the priest, but Saint Joseph.

When they reached the end of the staircase they came to an open doorway, and the room on the other side seemed warm to them. They looked inside, and there was a large fireplace that was lit with coals. The coals burned orange and blue, and they shed a warm light on the rest of the room. There were candles on the walls and a small desk in the center of the room. A very large man, old and with long, stringy white hair, sat at the desk and was writing quickly in a thick tablet. All around the man were wooden shelves, tall and wide, and they were arranged in some kind of maze, and when the boys entered it they could see, in the firelight, what the shelves held.

Boots and shoes and more boots, of all sizes and makes and all manner of repair that they could imagine. Some were in pairs and some were alone, not set carefully but dropped, it seemed, in some random pattern, some laces tied together and some not. There were men's shoes and women's and many small shoes, so that some of them must have belonged to toddlers or even babies at one time. There were hundreds of them, and as the boys studied the shelves, the large gray man looked up from his ledger and said, "Hey!"

"Hey," said the boys, and they moved closer to the shelves. There was a pair of white sneakers near them, each with a little hole in the tip, as if the big toes had worn them through.

"How did you get in here?" said the man.

"We walked down the stairs," said Omar.

"I liked the lights," added Lewis.

The man frowned at that. He set his pen aside. "Who told you about this place?"

"A child," said Omar.

"And how did he know about it?"

"She," said Omar.

The man's expression didn't change. He looked at them impatiently. "She, then. How did she know about this place?"

"Our friends know a lot of things," said Omar.

The man leaned forward, as if he was trying to bring the two boys into focus.

"Come here," he said.

They walked up to the desk and looked at the man. He was old, though they could not guess the age, and his eyes seemed very tired. He had his hands placed over the writing tablet, and there were other sheets of paper with long lists of names set next to the tablet. A thin film of coal dust covered many of the items on the desk. A lantern was set at the edge of the desk and there were shelves behind the man and two wooden chairs leaning against the shelves.

"What do you want?" the man said.

"The boots," said Omar.

"Whose boots?"

"The priest's," said Lewis, and his head jerked to the side.

"What's wrong with your head?" the man said.

Lewis looked at the floor. "There's nothing wrong with my head."

The man studied them for a moment. He turned the lantern up so that he could see them better.

"What's this priest's name?"

The boys looked at each other. They didn't know the man's name. He hadn't been all that friendly. Omar thought about taking a guess.

"What's your name?" he said instead.

"I can't tell you that," said the man.

"Why not?"

"It's not allowed."

They stood there and studied the man, then the desk. They looked about at the shoes. The boys had stopped their shivers,

23

and the glow from the fireplace was warm. They reached an agreement without saying anything, and they pulled up the two chairs and sat down in front of the desk.

"Hey, now," said the man. "I have work to do."

"What kind of work?" said Lewis.

The man pointed to the tablet. "I have to get all of these names written down tonight."

He still held one hand over the tablet, and the boys looked there. They waited. The man reached over and turned the lantern back down so they couldn't see what he'd written.

"You can't look here," said the man.

"Why not?" said Omar.

"Because it's not allowed."

"There's a lot of things not allowed here," said Lewis.

"That's right," said the man. "There are. And one thing that is not allowed is visitors. So if that's all, I expect you'll be going now."

"Okay," said Omar. "We just need the boots."

The man pointed at the boy. "You're not getting any boots," he said, and when he lifted his hand to point, the boys looked at the names on the tablet. They read as fast as they could, upside down. The man quickly slammed the book shut. It was an old book, and dust blew up across the desk.

"Now you've done it," the man said, and he wiped his fists into his eyes. "There's so much dust here. It comes from the coal." He looked at them. His eyes were filled with tears. "This is your fault."

Lewis got up from his chair. He reached into his pocket and handed his handkerchief to the man.

The man frowned, looked at the boy. Then he took the handkerchief and wiped his eyes. The dust was floating about the lantern, like little bugs in the yellow light.

"Not many people carry a handkerchief anymore," said the man.

"They ought to," said Lewis.

The man nodded. "Yes, they should." He wiped his eyes again, then unfolded the cloth. He held it up in the light. "This is a very nice handkerchief."

"I'll trade you it for the boots," said Lewis.

"No," said the man. "Thank you, though. Why are you concerned about these boots? They're not your boots. How well do you know this priest?"

"Not very well," said Omar.

"Then why do you care?"

The boys thought about that for a while. They looked down at their own shoes, and the man, after a time, looked down at them as well. He studied Omar's quickly, then Lewis'. He studied Lewis' shoes for a long time. A strange expression came over his face, something sad and distant. He sat back in the chair and began to fold the handkerchief.

"We take our responsibilities very seriously," said Omar.

The man smiled at that. He set the cloth aside. "I'm sure you do. That's to be commended. That's also something that's gone out of style. Can I ask you your names?"

They told him, and he picked up his pen. He looked at the ledger. He paused, and then he set his pen back down. "Those are very nice names. I deal often with names, and those are most excellent. I like those very much. I'm sorry, I'm going to have to ask you to leave now. It's been very nice visiting with you. I don't get many visitors here, and you two have been among the finest. Do you think you can find your way out?"

"We'll just follow the lights," said Lewis.

"That's right, just follow the lights."

"They're really nice."

"Do you think so?" said the man. "That was a touch I put on the place. I wasn't sure that anyone would notice. Thank you for saying that. It's been awfully nice to meet you. Lewis. And Omar. I guess this is goodbye, then."

"Goodbye," said Omar.

"Goodbye," said Lewis.

The man picked up his pen. "Goodbye, then."

"There's the matter of the boots, though," said Omar.

"Yes," said Lewis. "We'll still have to settle that."

The man opened the book and began copying names. "I think it's good and settled," he said. "I think that has been well discussed. I'm sorry if you're not satisfied on that matter."

"No," said Omar. "We're not satisfied at all."

"Not even close," said Lewis, and he pointed accusingly toward the man's desk. "I think you were going to steal my handkerchief."

The man looked up. He was quite indignant. "I certainly was not."

Omar shook his head. "If you wanted it you could just have asked for it. I'm sure Lewis would have given it to you."

"I would have," said Lewis. He put his hands on his hips. "If he'd only asked."

"I don't want your stupid handkerchief," said the man. He picked it up and held it out for the boy.

"No," said Lewis. His head jerked to the side. "If you want it that bad you can have it."

"I don't want it at all," said the man. The handkerchief was still there, held out for Lewis.

Omar reached into his pocket then. He took out the bone and placed it on the desk. He slid it forward for the man.

"What's that?" said the man. He pulled back the handkerchief.

"It's a bone," said Omar.

"Finger bone," said Lewis.

The man looked at it. "That's disgusting," he said.

"It's all we have," said Omar.

"Well it's not enough," said the man.

"For what?" said Lewis.

"For the boots."

"So you will trade for them?" said Omar.

The man crossed his arms over his chest. He was looking very cross, and it put the boys in mind of Father Ramon when they asked to see the confessional. "Look, now," the man said. "There's not going to be any trade. I've got work to do here. The boots come in, all right? They come in and I write the names down in this book, and then that's it. All right?"

Lewis' head jerked to the side. "You write the names down?"

"Yes."

"And then that's it?"

"Yes, then that's the end, I'm afraid. I'm sorry. It's not pleasant work, but that's it. Once I write it down."

"Have you written the priest's name down?" said Omar.

The man looked at the ledger. He studied the names. He flipped a page back and studied again. "No," he said. "I haven't yet." He took up his pen and wrote down a name.

"Did you just write it down?" said Lewis.

"No," said the man. "They've got to go in order. It's very important."

"How many names till the priest's name?" said Omar.

The man looked at the boy. He still seemed very cross. He picked up the sheet of paper and studied it. He flipped back a few pages. "A long ways off yet."

"How long till you write it?"

"I don't know."

"Another hour?"

"Yes," said the man. "In another hour. If I'm left in peace, that is. I can't write down the names if I have any distractions."

"Well, we'll stay, then," said Lewis.

"No you won't," said the man.

Lewis looked at the man. "Can I have my handkerchief back?" he said.

The man picked it up and handed it across the desk. Then he set about writing down the names. He copied five names. Then ten, then twenty. The boys sat there and watched him. After a time, Omar took the bone back from the desk.

"Goodbye now," said the man.

"We're not leaving," said the boys.

The man put his pen down. He was very cross this time. More so than before. He looked at Lewis, and then at Omar. He studied the boys. They looked back at him.

"Wait here," he said.

He stood up from his desk and went back into the maze of shelves. They listened to him rummaging around in the shoes. The book was open on the desk, and the boys thought about leaning forward and reading the names again. But they didn't. They sat on the chairs and looked back where the man had gone. Every few moments, Lewis' head jerked to the side.

When the man returned he held a pair of white shoes. Leather, not sneakers. He placed them on the desk and sat down. He turned the lantern up so the boys could see. He placed his elbows on the desk and looked at Omar.

They were Omar's mother's shoes. She'd become a nurse's assistant in her last year, had been studying for it for years before that. The shoes were large and worn, and the laces were still tied up in a bow. They seemed to hover there, in the lantern light, and the boy stood up and picked up the shoes. They were heavy and warm to the touch. He sat down and held them in his lap. Often enough, she couldn't find them at home, and he'd searched under chairs and tables, in closets for them. She'd been a large woman, and he'd liked that about her. The way she might pick him up and he'd disappear.

Lewis held out the handkerchief to him, and Omar shook his head. He wiped his eyes with the sleeve of his jacket. He held the shoes in his lap until they became a white blur. He touched the laces and the rubber soles. There were strings hanging off the edge where the fabric had been worn away and he touched these gently. He thought of her name. Clara. Though he didn't say it aloud. He took the shoes up in his hands and placed them back on the desk. Back exactly where he'd taken them. Then he sat in the chair and looked up at the man.

The man had taken the handkerchief that Lewis had offered, and he was wiping his eyes. He closed the book. He looked behind the boys, as if there might be someone standing there. Someone he knew. When the boys looked, there was only the doorway and the shelves of shoes.

"That was very mean of me," said the man. "I'm very sorry about that." The man picked up the shoes and placed them in a drawer. The boys listened to the drawer shut. "It's just that I need you to leave. I know you came to see your mother's shoes, not to get the boots. I'm terribly sorry about that. It's time for you to go."

Omar looked up at him. He wiped his eyes again with his sleeve. "That's not true," he said. "We came to get the boots."

"Did you?"

"Yes," said the boy.

The man sat back in the chair. He studied the boy for a long while. The fire had ebbed, and the man looked there. It was still warm in the room. The man closed the book.

"Would you like something to drink?"

"Okay," said Omar.

The man opened a box next to the desk. "Do you like soda? Both of you?"

"Yes," they said.

"I have cola and I have lemon."

"Lemon," they said.

"I have just the one can," he said. "You'll have to share."

They said that was all right, and he took out two cups and emptied the can into them. He was very careful with the last drops. He watched the cups carefully, so there would be an equal amount in each. He passed them over to the two boys, and they drank from them. They sipped slowly. That was the polite way to do things.

"I have to go back to my work now," he said.

"How many names before the priest?" said Lewis.

"Many," said the man.

"We'll wait," said Omar.

"I'd rather that you leave," said the man.

"We'll wait," said Lewis, and his head jerked to the side.

The man opened the book. He took up the pen. He began to copy names from the paper into the book. Every few minutes he'd look up at the boys, and there they were, sipping their sodas. He put the names down carefully, and in order. He blocked the boys out of his mind.

"You don't know about waiting," he said. "I've waited here forever. Do you understand that? I've waited here since before you were born, and I'll be waiting here long after you've gone. Here. I've waited here forever. For the shoes and the boots, and especially for the names. And I will continue to wait here forever. Until all of the shoes and boots, and all of the names come in. You can't outwait me. Do you understand that? I've waited the longest. I am the longest waiter."

He looked up from his book at them. The boys stared. They seemed to stare hard at him, as if they were waiting for him to say something else. He wrote down a name, then looked back at the boys. They took a sip of soda. Swallowed. They stared back at him.

"We'll wait," they said.

The priest sat near the window and looked out at the snow. He had the blanket around him, and he pulled it close so that it covered his body up to the neck. He'd been into the wine a bit, and he'd had the shivers all night. When he closed his eyes he had a strange but familiar dream where he was sinking in deep water. There was something heavy in his pockets and it was pulling him down. The water was cold and it was dark below him. There were people above in boats, people he seemed to know, sitting and watching, though no one moved to help. The weight and the cold pulled him down and he struggled to get at the air. He breathed in and was pulled under.

When he woke, he looked out at the snow. Nothing much had changed. Saint Joseph was out there, where he always was, and the statue wore a coat of ice about his shoulders, and there was a tiny white hat of snow on his head.

The priest heard a knock at the door, and he stood up and walked across the sacristy in his stocking feet. On the ledge outside were his boots, set upright and facing the road, as if he could simply step into them. There was a cold wind, and he shivered in the doorway. Two sets of snowy footprints led away from the church. He looked out into the street, and there were two boys passing through the glow of a streetlight. They were walking fast, and their hands were stuck down into their pockets. The head of the shorter boy jerked to the side. The priest picked up the boots and found a note tucked into one of the foot holes. The note was written in small block letters, though it contained no names. It asked him to please put the boots on, and near the bottom was a reminder about a mass at nine-thirty the next morning. It was a feast day, the priest remembered now. Something very important had happened a long time ago.

We didn't ask your name, the note read. *Will you tell it to us tomorrow?* These words were crossed out once and then written again, then crossed out again, then written a third time. It seemed as if there had been a very serious discussion about content between the writers of the note. The priest looked at the bottom of the paper.

We'll be waiting for you, it read. *At nine. If it's convenient. On the back steps.*

Hot Pepper

DANA JOHNSON

From *Break Any Woman Down* (2001)

I guess nobody thought nothing of Uncle Smiley taking up with that girl because he'd already bought two wives out of a catalogue. Nobody say where the wives be now, but anybody who know anything about Uncle Smiley—that he ain't usually one to be smilin'—know that they prolly got they heels to clicking right about the first time he hit them or stuck the tip of his shotgun in they face. Mama always saying that Uncle Smiley beat his women for breakfast, dinner, and supper. But even so, out of all that, at the time she first turned up it seemed like wasn't nobody worried about Uncle Smiley having the girl up in his house. Now, it ain't but three days later and folks talk about "that poor chile" and about how Uncle Smiley should have been ashamed. I didn't think nothing of it myself—not until he threw her out the house, clothes and everything.

We was skipping rope out in the road in front of Uncle Smiley's house that day. It was me, Jonelle, and our cousin from L.A., Vickie, that be sent down South some summers. We was all taking turns turning the rope when the girl come out on the porch and started watching us. We had a little radio with us, and we was singing along with the song, *Diamond in the back, sunroof top, diggin the scene with a gangsta lean whoo whooo.* I thought for a minute she come out to tell us to quit jumping where we was because every now and then some gravel from the road would fly up over the porch. But she didn't tell us nothing. She never said much, and we never said much to her, even though she was always grinning at us when she saw us playing.

I wanted to turn rope some more because I had put some tissue paper down in the front of my halter top. I wanted to see what I'd look like all filled out like Uncle Smiley's girl, and I was afraid the tissue was going to fall out if I did too much jumping, even though it was my favorite thing to do. My arms was getting tired, though, and Jonelle was complaining that I wasn't turning the rope right and she was messing up because of it.

"Y'all let me turn the rope for you," Uncle Smiley's girl said.

We was all surprised she spoke. "If you wont to," I said.

She come out into the road barefoot like us kids with her toenails painted all bright red. Her halter top looked a lot better on her than mine did on me, and she had on these hot pants that had her behind hanging out of them. She couldn't of been more than four years older than me, but she was looking like I wished I did. I saw how all the boys on the hill was always turning they heads and looking at her and I wished they did me like that.

I handed her my end of the rope and she smiled at me when I took it, but I didn't feel like smiling back. I even sort of cut my eyes at her. I don't know why I did it. But she just kept on grinning.

"Let's do a hot pepper, since you want to jump so bad," the girl said to Jonelle.

A hot pepper is when they turn the rope as fast as they can while you try to keep up. Most of the time if you cain't keep up, that rope slapping your skin burn like hot pepper, too.

She and Vickie started turning the rope fast, and Jonelle was jumping as fast as she could. She never got tangled up in the rope once. I couldn't hardly do hot peppers no more because I wasn't as small as Vickie and Jonelle, but I was thinking of trying to until

I remembered the tissue in my halter. Instead I just stood there watching them laugh and clown and carry on. Jonelle got tired after a while, though, and sat down in the middle of the road with all that dust swirling around her.

"Dang. I'm wore out," she said, trying to fan the dust out her way. "You jump," she said to the girl.

"All right. I b'lieve I will jump," the girl said. She handed the rope back to me and was going to start to jump when she saw my cousin, Old Folks, coming up the road.

"Who is that?" she asked, squinting and trying to get a better look at him.

"Oh Lord," Jonelle said. "Here come Old Folks with his slow ass."

Our cousin Old Folks's real name's Nathaniel. He ain't nothing but eighteen, but everybody call him Old Folks because he always move so slow, talk slow, do everything slow. He sweet, though. He sort of liked Uncle Smiley's girl, but the whole three weeks she was with Uncle Smiley, Jonelle and Vickie and them say she never paid no attention to Old Folks until that day. That's what got her in trouble.

Old Folks liked to took all day getting to where we was and sat hisself down on Uncle Smiley's porch. "Whatchall doing?" he said, right slow and all drawled out.

"What it look like?" I said.

"Why you got to be so smart all the time, Bay-Bay?"

I rolled my eyes and put my hands on my hips. I shouldn't of been so mean to Old Folks because I liked him, but I knew he wasn't up on that hill but to see that girl. He hardly ever come round just to talk to us kids. I knew that if my behind was hanging out of my shorts he might of paid more attention to me, though, and it made me mad. I saw him sneaking looks at the girl. She just kept on smiling at him and looking down at those dusty red toenails of hers.

She finally looked Old Folks in the eyes. "You want to jump with us?"

"Ain't that much time in the world," Jonelle said. "What the rope gone do? Wait in the air for Old Folks to jump his slow ass up off the ground?"

We all laughed. Jonelle was younger than me, ten, then come Vickie by a few months, but Jonelle was always cutting up and cussing. She was always saying what was on her mind. Vickie, too, every once in a while, when she got tired of us picking at her and calling her names for not being able to walk around barefoot like the rest of us. But it seemed like it had been a while since I really spoke my mind. Mama said I wasn't no baby no more and I ought to watch what I say to folks and act like a lady.

Uncle Smiley must of heard us laughing and come to his raggedy screen door to see what was going on. I saw him but didn't say nothing, and he didn't speak, either. He just stood there. Nobody else noticed him, and after a while I forgot he was standing there.

"Forget you, Jonelle," Old Folks said, but he was grinning. "You don't want me to show you how it's done. I don't want to show up no little girl."

"Aw, come on," the girl said. "I'll do it with you."

"How I'm gone look, old as I am, jumping rope with y'all?"

She just held out her hand and then waved Old Folks to her.

"Take my end, Vickie," Jonelle said. "My arms is tired."

Me and Vickie was acting stupid with the rope, turning it real slow at first, so slow that Old Folks and the girl could just step over the rope without having to jump. Then we'd try to work in a hot pepper every now and then. Old Folks was a sight. The rope kept slapping his skinny legs after he'd try to jump. He kept getting twisted in the rope with the girl, and we was all laughing and having a good time when Old Folks fell on top of the girl. Thing is, not one of them rushed to get up.

That's when Uncle Smiley opened his screen door. "You chil-ren is skipping rocks on my porch and I want y'all to go on some-where else with that rope, you hear? Tammy Lynn, get your tail in this house."

Uncle Smiley was as mad as he could be but didn't look like it. He didn't have no kind of teeth in his mouth and always looked like he was smiling when he wasn't. The corners of his mouth was always turned up, kind of like the mouth carved on a pump-kin. And he had the highest voice in the world. Instead of sound-ing like the old man he was, he sounded like a little old lady. You wanted to laugh at him, but everybody knew that if you did and he saw you, it was gone be your ass.

"I ain't," the girl said. "We ain't hurting nothing. A few rocks ain't gone hurt your little house."

"Y'all keep turning the rope," she said. "Old Folks?"

"Naw. I b'lieve I'll just watch."

"If you wont to," the girl said, and we started turning the rope for her, even though I was scared of Uncle Smiley. Wasn't that many rocks landing on his porch, but he didn't want us there no-how.

"I ain't gone tell you again, girl," Uncle Smiley said. "You too old to be playing with these kids. Get in this house or I'm gone beat your ass."

"I wish you would," the girl said. "Just because I'm living with you don't mean I'm gone let you run all over me. Your little nasty bed ain't worth all that."

I thought it was gone be all over then. Vickie looked like she was making herself ready to run in case Uncle Smiley went after one of his shotguns, and Jonelle had her hands over her mouth, trying not to laugh. Old Folks was scratching his head, looking everywhere but Uncle Smiley's direction.

Uncle Smiley limped down the porch steps and we all scat-tered. I never seen Old Folks move that fast before. Uncle Smiley grabbed the girl by her pretty little Afro, drug her up the porch stairs, and tossed her into the house. She was fighting him all the way, too, calling him twenty different kinds of bastards. The screen door slammed behind them. We could hear Uncle Smiley cussing and the girl crying, heard some slaps every now and then. Finally, Uncle Smiley kicked open the screen door and threw a handful a clothes out into the road. Right behind the clothes come Tammy Lynn. Uncle Smiley shoved her down the stairs and she went spilling out into the road.

"But where I'm gone go?" the girl was screaming at Uncle Smiley, but he was inside the house. I couldn't even see him. "I ain't got nowhere to go!"

"It ain't gone be here!" Uncle Smiley called out from inside the house. "Should of thought of that when you was showing out for your boyfriend. You better go on away from here before you be worse off."

The girl was covered with dust, crying like a baby. Her halter top was coming down some and you could see some of her chest. I wanted to do something, just didn't know what. She didn't even look at us nohow. She bundled up all her clothes that was in the road and started walking. Old Folks looked like he was gone go after her, but must of thought on it again, because he looked toward Uncle Smiley's screen door and sat right back down. Then he got up and started walking down the road the opposite direction of the girl.

"That's OK, you old nasty motherfucka!" the girl screamed. She was far enough to be out of Uncle Smiley's slapping range, but close enough for him to still hear her. "I did not like being with you, old man! Why do you think I let you slobber all over me!" Her voice broke on them last words, and it hurt my stomach to hear her that way. We watched her until she got smaller and smaller walking down the road and then I couldn't see her no more.

Me and Jonelle and Vickie just sat in the middle of the road after Tammy Lynn got tossed out, not saying nothing for a while.

Then Vickie got up and dusted herself off. "Y'all want to jump some more?" she asked us. Hardly nothing could come between Vickie and playing. I used to be like that, too. Our cousin Shorty fell down one summer when we was playing tag and split her forehead open like a dropped watermelon. I remember we wiped some of the blood off her face with our T-shirts and sent her off to Granny to get stitched so we could finish the game. I didn't think twice about it.

"If we jump," I said, "I'm gone try me a hot pepper."

"You?" Jonelle said. "May as well be Old Folks over here jumping if you gone try it."

"Just watch," I said. But before I started jumping I reached down in my halter and took out all that tissue.

"What you got that for?" Vickie ask me.

"Shut up, Vickie," I said. I didn't feel like explaining nothing to her. She wasn't nothing but a baby. Jonelle was looking at me sly, trying not to grin.

"Let's go," I said. "Get to turning."

We didn't worry about Uncle Smiley coming out the house after us. Even Vickie prolly knew Uncle Smiley didn't whup that girl's behind because of no rocks on his porch.

They tried to turn the rope fast but I jumped rope like they ain't never seen me do. I broke out in a sweat, I was jumping so hard. I didn't mess up once.

Jonelle said I was looking all crazy and mad. Prolly. But it seem like, as hard as I was jumping rope, doing them hot peppers, my heart just wasn't in it.

Boys

PAUL RAWLINS

From *No Lie Like Love* (1996)

If I had a mother, I have told Duke, she would look like Charle-magne, who is sitting now in the hay at the top of the barn where we all can look out the window at the moon. She has hair the color of hay and ditch grass in the fall, and her face and arms are the color of the white moon in the winter. Her legs, too, ex-cept they are covered in scratches like she'd been whipped with a chokecherry branch, and there are little red bites all up her legs and arms from the bugs in the hay. Tonight we've brought her lo-tion for those, and bug spray that Duke thinks will help. Char-lemagne is rubbing it onto her arms and up and down her legs.

"It feels good," she says. She gives us each a smile. "I think it's working."

Duke and I found Charlemagne in the loft yesterday when we climbed up to shoot birds with my uncle's pellet gun. She was standing with a yellow suitcase in her hands like she was wait-ing to catch a train. "Hi, boys," she said. "Who are you?" We told her our names, and she shook our hands. She asked if we thought anybody would mind her sleeping there that night.

"Help me with this," Charlemagne says now. She hands me the lotion bottle and reaches to undo a button at the back of her dress. She folds the dress forward off her shoulders like wings and unhooks the strap back there. Duke and I kneel behind her, each on a side, and smear the lotion up and down her back, which is white and speckled like the rest of her.

Duke wants Charlemagne for his mother, too. Duke's Ma is a fat Indian woman with two long braids and a crooked eyetooth hanging over her lip like a fang. The men she brings home with her sometimes stay on for days, to where Duke mostly lives with me here at my Gran's, and Gran hardly knowing the difference.

While Duke and I rub on the lotion, we tell Charlemagne about Uncle Bob's grave over at the edge of the trees, where the fields end. She's seen it today, from the barn. It's a headstone with a little TV screen built into it. You can see where the power line hangs in the trees.

"He was a hero," I say. "In the war."

"What war?"

"The one in Vietnam."

"Let's go look," she says. She's scooted to where she can see better out the loft window.

"He gets mad sometimes if you do that," I say.

"Who gets mad?" she says.

"Uncle Bob."

"Oh," she says.

Duke is eating what is left of the piecrust from the dinner we brought. If Charlemagne stays long, there'll be nights clouded over and without a moon when she'll be able to see the little light from the screen right at the edge of the trees.

"What's your Uncle Bob get mad about?" Charlemagne says, "the noise from the TV?" She's left the dress open in the back to let the wind cool the bites.

"I don't think that bothers him any," I say.

"What's on it?" Charlemagne says. "What's it about?"

"It's mostly of the Vice President when he gave Uncle Bob's medal to Gran and the funeral they had for him. But there's pictures from the war on it, too," I say. Uncle Bob got his medal for getting his butt shot off in a plane. My other uncle, who we call Waddle and who didn't go to war with Uncle Bob, says this was dumb luck, and Gran tells him, "Shut your mouth."

"Are you on it?" Charlemagne says.

"No," I say. I never knew my Uncle Bob.

She jabs at Duke with her toe. "What about you? Have you seen it?"

I'm watching Duke so he can't lie about it. Gran used to make me lug the flowers she took out for Uncle Bob every couple of days. After she put the TV out there, I remember watching the rockets shooting out from the jungle with flame and smoke streamers like fireworks we go to see in Troy on the Fourth of July. But Duke and I generally steer clear of Uncle Bob's grave.

"Tell me what he gets mad about," Charlemagne says. "What happens?"

I don't want to tell it now. Duke doesn't want to hear it.

"Come on," she says. She's done her dress back up, and she's peeking at the moon through her toes.

I hate to have to tell it. I hate to have to tell it at night when we have to cut across the field back to the house. But Charlemagne wants to hear.

"He yells at you," I say.

"What does he yell?" she says.

Once, after Gran buried the box the Army sent, Uncle Bob's brothers and some friends were arguing about what happened to his medal that was supposed to be epoxied onto the stone under a piece of bulletproof glass. Some of them said it was still there and some said that Gramps had taken it when he'd packed off the spring before. He'd liked it, and before Gran glued it onto the headstone he'd worn it on his suit coat to church.

They went out in a single file line, four of them, through the field to check on Uncle Bob, three of them Uncle Bob's brothers, and my father not with them, him having run off with what Gran calls a hell-bound whore out of Shreveport for a warmer winter on the Gulf of Mexico.

I want to stop here, but Charlemagne won't have it. She'll hear it all. She's got her head propped up in her hands and her eyes opened big and bright.

Sometimes this far up in Montana we see northern lights, not in colors but like a fan of searchlights behind the mountain, like something's going on over there. And the night they went to see, the grave was lit like that, with the four of them trooping out in alfalfa up to their boot tops, tramping down a black snake into the hay, and the lucerne closing up behind them like the jungle to cover up their trail. That's how they told it.

"He was out in the clearing," I say. "They were to the edge of the hay almost, and he was at the clearing, stomping mad. And he had yellow eyes. Then he yelled at them."

"Hogwash" is what Gran says. "Bulldust. Shut your mouths."

"There are stranger things," Charlemagne says. She tells us about a logging track way back in the trees northeast of White Sulphur Springs called Deadman's Road. It's just graded dirt with tire ruts, but there's a sign to warn you. And when you drive it at night you come around a bend down into a hollow, and you better not get out to help the old man in the blue truck there that's got a flat tire.

And the white crosses where people have gone off the highway, you see the ghosts sometimes there at night, coming up out of the barrow pit or standing on the end of a bridge. "And you know what they want?" Charlemagne says, and I don't want to know. I can't move. "They want a ride," she says.

Duke just wants to stay tonight in the barn, but Charlemagne walks us back to the house through the green hay bales lined up in the field. She whistles like a ghost wind through her lips.

"What happened to your husband?" I say.

"Oh," she says, "he got lost in the war, too."

"There isn't any war," I say, not one that I know of.

"The Montana war," Charlemagne says. "The Kalispell bitch and bottle fights."

"That's not a war," I say.

"He's just gone," Charlemagne says.

It's hot out, and Charlemagne's coming with us swimming where Duke and I go. It's a good place, a bend in the river with Russian olives and then bigger trees around and only in the middle too deep to touch bottom. We've brought a big cowboy hat for Charlemagne because she burns red in the sun. She puts it on and says, "Howdy," and Duke and I stretch the barbed-wire fences for her so she can slip through.

At the river Duke and I dog-paddle around in our shorts while Charlemagne sits on the bank and beats puddles in the mud with her heels. The water is slow here but still cold from coming down the mountains, from the Rockies and Canada. We haul up greasy muck from the bottom for wars. We aim for Charlemagne, and she says, "No!" and crabs back away from the water.

When we show her where the rope swing is broken off from where it was on the tree branch, she stands up and says, "Come over here." She grabs us by an arm and a leg, me and then Duke, and twirls us around and bucks us away. She's that strong.

"You're lighter than hay bales," she says. She sends us spinning, sprawled out like bugs, and we scream and fly out over the bright water until she is tired and says, "No more."

"Whose place is this?" she says, resting while Duke spits water in the air like a fountain.

"It's ours," I say. "Mine and Duke's."

"Are we still on your Gran's land?"

I shrug.

She says, "They shoot trespassers around here, you know."

"Nuh uh."

Charlemagne points a finger at Duke and pulls the trigger. He grabs his heart and flies back in the water dead.

"Aren't you afraid of drowning out here by yourselves?" She looks around and finds a long branch she could use to reach us from the bank. "Keep this here from now on," she tells us. "We'll hide it when we go."

Duke and I climb out and shiver in the sunshine to dry, with our arms across our chests. Our jockey shorts are gray and full of grit. Duke is chunky and brown; I am white and can poke my belly out with air like I do to follow Uncle Waddle around behind his back or suck it to my backbone to show Gran my ribs.

"My turn," Charlemagne says. She's scrunching up her hair and looking at her fingernails. "Go sit on the rocks downstream and get warm." She's poking the water with her foot.

Duke and I go, tenderfooting it through the hard grass. Then we double back. Charlemagne sees us before we can duck down to hide.

"Go on," she says. She's on the bank with her dress pulled off. We go and we don't see anymore.

After school starts the next week, Duke and I ride our Schwinn Stingrays down the train tracks to get there, mine with the orange whip flag I can pretend is a CB antenna and Duke's with the Wacky Package stickers all over his banana seat. They're beaters, but we don't have to lock them up not to have them stolen. We push along the rails with our feet down on either side like training wheels. Duke chugs like an engine, until he loses his balance and his bike crashes on the tracks while he rolls down the hill into the weeds. I wait while he climbs back up with his jeans all dusty from the gravel.

Duke rides bumping down the ties this time. He goes, "Ah-hhh," and the sound bounces up and down like in a car on a rough road. We pass behind where Duke lives, and he farts, then spurts ahead from the extra burst of power. We skirt around the four white crosses at the end of the bridge where the dead families hitchhike off the side of the road.

The fourth-grade class meets on the bottom floor, where if there weren't the grating over the windows you could be up on a desk and out while the teacher was writing cursive on the board with her back turned. We pledge allegiance to the flag and sing "My Country 'Tis of Thee." The teacher says, "What is the state bird of Montana?" for a quiz.

Duke shows Elise Pommery his state bird, and she gives him one back, like she's scratching up the side of her nose. During art time we'll drive our flip-off signs around our desks like tanks, our middle fingers making the long gun. We pivot around slow to shoot the enemy. We draw battlefields and curly black explosions while we make growling sounds for the engines and the treads deep in our throats. The teacher only ever says, "That's enough," but doesn't send us to the office.

Everybody cheats during math. Elise helps us because she is the only one who can divide.

Outside at lunch two of the bigger boys walk up on Duke. I'm sitting on the jungle-gym rocket, at the top of the second stage. I fold my arms and hook my feet under the bars to watch.

"What's you got?" one boy is saying to Duke. He wears a muscle shirt with the sides cut out. He has hair under his arms, and his name is Malachi.

"Nothing," Duke says.

"Come on, fat boy," Malachi says. Duke just stands there waiting for what's coming. Malachi snaps, scrapes his fingers across his palm. "Give it here," he says.

Duke turns around to run, and the big boys grab his pants.

They shove their hands in his pockets to worm the change out, a couple of dimes and a quarter, then they dump him under the monkey bars. Duke lies there on his side while the big boys jerk their chins hello at me and go away.

"What do you bring it for?" I say to Duke. He's still lying there, breathing loud, bent double on his side like a dog.

"They'll beat me up if I don't," he says.

"Well what do you bring so much for, then?" I say.

Duke rolls on his back and closes his eyes to the sun. One of these times Duke is going to go crazy. He's going to grab them by the hair and bash their heads bloody against the bars. I'm waiting for it every day now.

Duke sits up to comb his hair with a hard rubber ACE he keeps in his back pocket. I climb the rocket and sprawl across the top. I let my arms and legs hang down like a spider and wait for the snitches on the playground to tell me to get down. It's hot for September, hot for anytime. I drop spit that floats down like dandelion fuzz and try to hit the bars.

"What's for lunch?" Duke says. We share mine that Gran always packs in a big grocery sack. The other kids eat in the lunchroom, but we stay on the playground. Duke hucks a sandwich up to me and raisin cookies. The boiled eggs we throw at third graders. They yell, "You suck!" then run for it. The sun on me makes it too hot to move. I'm a prisoner in a cage. All the bars are molten steel, they're charged with electricity. I'll have to hang from my knees, then drop and do a half flip to land on my feet and escape. The ground is a long way down.

Elise Pommery comes over with same-color carrot and cheese sticks from the lunchroom poking out of her pocket. She dresses like her brother who goes to middle school in greasy green corduroys and a brown plaid shirt.

"Hey, Duke," she says. "Hey, Ray." Elise wore a patch over one eye until she was in the second grade. Her mother tied a scarf around her head, and Elise told everybody in school she was a pirate. Now she's gotten a glass eye, cloudy blue like the short drinking glasses you get free when you buy gas.

Elise doesn't want anything, just to sit with us outside the school till the second bell rings. Duke and I have to go in when it does. We can't cut this early in the year when everybody's still paying too much attention.

Duke says after school we ought to ask Elise if she wants to come smoke with us, but I only got two cigarettes out of Uncle Waddle's pack, so I say no. Duke and I have never had a whole one before, just butts, and once almost an inch off a menthol we found half-crushed in the 7-Eleven parking lot. We're bouncing our front tires up in low wheelies, coasting down the hills with the sun in our eyes. Duke does a siren for me to pull over, then speeds past. We drag our bikes off the road under the bridge over Leman Creek. Duke drops his bike with the back tire dipping in the water.

"The chain's going to rust," I say. Duke is wizzing by the creek, with his back to me.

"Do you have matches?" Duke says.

"Yeah," I say. "I got these." They're in a black book that says in gold "The Blackfoot Lounge." They're the paper kind that were always hard for me to light until Duke showed me how to fold the cover over the sandpaper and rip the match head through.

"You got to be careful doing it that way," he says. He's skipping rocks, the front end tipped up like a fast boat, always three bounces before they plunk. I've got the smokes stashed in a box for Bicycle poker cards that looks closest to Uncle Waddle's hardpacks. I slip one out and pass the box to Duke. Then Charlemagne's behind us.

"Gimme here," she says.

We don't ask. We put the cigarettes in her hand.

"You're too young," she says. She unwinds the white paper in a spiral, and the brown tobacco crumbs float away down the creek. Charlemagne has got her shoes off and her feet muddy from wading. "Why do you come home this way?" she says.

Duke shrugs. He's chewing on a piece of foxtail, sitting on his tipped-over bike.

I am mad at Charlemagne about the smokes. "How come it's your business?" I say. I'm ready to saddle up; I've got my bike swung up against my leg like an open gate.

"Uh, oh," Charlemagne says.

"Go to hell," I say. I'm up the hill for the getaway, but my chain's come off and the pedal slips and drops me onto the bar. "See!" I yell. I throw the bike down the hill and shove out into the creek till I'm up to my waist, but she doesn't say anything. The cold water helps the pinch and burn between my legs and the sick in my stomach till I splash out on the other side. I keep my back turned until I'm sure I'm not going to cry.

Charlemagne sits down on her side of the creek. She gathers her hair up over one shoulder, with her head tipped to the side. The blonde weeds are up to her shoulders, and her legs are still spotted with bites the color of the little red flowers on her dress. Duke's spinning his front wheel, and Charlemagne is raking through the ends of her hair with her fingers, sitting across from me.

I grab a rock I am going to throw to splash her, and quick as I do she jumps up and grabs one of her own. It's bigger, the size of a yeast tin, and she can throw farther. I chuck mine halfway and make a cannonball splash with a waterspout. She hucks hers all the way across, so I have to backpedal up the bank or get splashed.

"I'll give you everything you've got coming," she says. Duke is not on my side in this. I hate Charlemagne.

"I bet you killed your husband," I say.

"Probably," she says.

"You should be in jail."

"Mmhmm," she says. She sits back down in the weeds.

"I'll bet there's a reward," I say. "I'll bet the FBI is looking for you." She's made us bring her the papers before to see if anybody cared she was gone. Now she sticks her fingers in her ears and just stares at me.

When the afternoon is gone, Charlemagne says, "Duke's hungry." It's been hot enough to dry my pants, hot enough to turn Charlemagne's legs pink where they've stuck out under her dress.

"Yeah, come on, Ray," Duke says. He's been dinking around the creek, whistling on grass and bombing water skeeters. He's got his tennis shoes wet and dirty from slipping in.

"How are you going to get back across now you're dry, Ray?" Charlemagne says.

I look at her, then I climb the bank and walk over across the bridge. Duke's put the chain back on my bike.

On the road, Charlemagne fits herself in between my handlebars. "Am I too heavy?" she says.

"I can't see," I say.

"I'll tell you where to steer," she says. "Go slow. Watch for cars." She rides with her feet sticking out, one hand holding her dress between her knees. We pump home and no cars pass and honk.

At Duke's today, his Ma has swatted him with a wooden spoon across his ear.

"Come here," she says. Duke's taken money out of her purse, the black one with the scraggly rabbit-fur trim. Mostly she doesn't miss it when it's the nickels and the pennies, but she's caught him now with a dollar in his fist.

"Hold him," she's screaming. "Get up and catch him." There's a man she's talking to who's lying naked on the bed I can see from the door of the back room. He's resting against the white vinyl headboard, and the yellow blinds are pulled down now in the daytime like it's a sickroom. He pulls a pillow across his privates and motions for me to shut the door.

It's a trailer, Duke's house, not very big, and Duke's Ma has got herself between him and the door. Her braid's swinging like a cow's tail. She's holding her housecoat closed while she goes for Duke with the spoon one-handed. Duke's covered up like a boxer. He catches a swat across the knuckles, and he howls again, but he won't open the fist to give up the dollar.

"Lying," Duke's Ma is yelling, "stealing," swinging with the spoon, most of the time wide while Duke's still got room to move side to side. "Come here," she says, "come here."

The man from the bedroom comes out in his jeans. "Get out," he says to me, and he shoves me at the door with his foot.

I'm outside down the wooden steps, and I can hear Duke's Ma saying, "Get him," and I see the man through the window go for Duke. Then Duke is thrown down the steps and the door slams. He's crying and calling his Ma a name. He gives her both fingers, hard, swinging his arms up like he's starting the music. Then we climb on our bikes. Duke's still got the dollar.

We spend it on Wacky Package stickers, like Duke's plastered all over his bike, that come with wide sticks of chalky pink gum. This time Duke's got "Uncle Bum's Convicted Rice, preferred by panhandlers, freeloaders and hobos in jail" with a cop and a bum on the box, and a "Stingline 45 caliber staple gun." I get "Flysol Spray" for germs to use and "Oscar Moron Bacon" that comes from stupid pigs.

We have stacks we take with us at night to show Charlemagne in the little fort we've built for her in the loft. We bring a flashlight to see better.

"My little brother collected baseball cards," she says. "What are these?"

"Look at this one," Duke says. It's the "Raggedy Ant" doll for baby insects, the one that will bug you.

"Yuck," Charlemagne says.

At the end of the summer we brought scissors and Charlemagne cut her hair short. She wears a bandanna around her neck like a bandit now and sneezes from the dry dust of the hay. She pokes around the rafters with the flashlight after we finish with the stickers, looking for old bird's nests.

"What do you two do all day?" she says. "Who do you play with? Do you have girlfriends?" She's seen the red welt on Duke's ear and asked him how he got it.

I tell her Duke's girlfriend is Elise Pommery, and he shoves me and tells me to shut up.

Charlemagne is calling for the kitten Duke and I stole for her when Gran made Uncle Waddle drown the others in a bucket. She leans back over her heels now and scoops the gray kitty up under its belly. "Come here, love," she says. "Come be Duke's girlfriend."

"Do you know how to kiss?" she says to me. I shake my head. Duke's watching to see if she's going to show me. She walks to me on her knees. It's cool at nights now, and she has on two dresses, one buttoned over the top of the other. She says, "You have to close your eyes." I do, and Charlemagne kisses my lips with a loud pop.

"Just like that," she says. Then she sits down on a blanket in the hay. "It's important to know."

Duke's Ma has gone off somewhere since the first of the month and locked the trailer door. I can get in through a little window in the bathroom. I let Duke in the front door, and we poke around the place like robbers.

Gran always used to tell Duke before he could stay over, "You call your mother. She's a Christian woman." Duke would dial the phone and sit on the stool in the kitchen and pretend to be talking. Now we set another place and Gran just says when he's up at the table, "You're a good eater. You're a good boy."

Gran cooks every time for ten people, even with her sons gone and the wives, too, that sometimes lived here when the sons were out of work. And sometimes it was the sons and not the wives, when the sons were gone off on drunks or kicked out of the house for something. She boils a dozen huge potatoes and makes two quarts of brown gravy, and there's a roast the size of a birthday cake. She sits at the head of the table and tells us to finish what's on our plates, piling more on her own in a big mess that she never eats.

Duke and Uncle Waddle have both dished up double helpings. They watch each other's plates across the table and horse around and spear chunks of each other's food when one isn't looking.

In two weeks is Halloween. Uncle Waddle wants to know what we're going to school as. "Be a hobo," he says. "That's easy."

It's what Duke and I do every year. We each wear one of Uncle Waddle's flannel undershirts with a pillow stuffed underneath. We black-in beards with shoe polish and carry gunnysacks for our loot.

Gran's mashing up her food, thinking of something else.

"Ma," Uncle Waddle says, "I'll have to do up the place." Every year he likes to build something on the porch, a car accident or at least a leg sticking out of the big post box that he can wiggle with a string. "Maybe I could do the headless hobo."

"Hush up," Gran says. "Eat."

Tonight the sky is trying for an early snow. It falls in slivers, but nothing sticks on the ground. The air is full of glass. Duke and I take food from dinner to the barn for Charlemagne, potatoes and bread and meat. We climb to the loft in the dark and call for her.

"She's not here," Duke says. He fishes a piece of bread out of her plate, and we sit down in the hay to wait. Sometimes she goes for a day or two, but she leaves us a note and she always comes back.

"She'll have to find a house or go somewhere where it's warm for the winter," I say to Duke. It's cold in the barn tonight. I've got Charlemagne's horse blanket pulled up around my head.

"Maybe she can live with you and Gran," Duke says.

"I don't know," I say. There are empty rooms in the house. Gran and Uncle Waddle have one apiece; Duke and I share.

"Maybe if your Ma doesn't come back, she could live in the trailer."

"Maybe," Duke says. We sit in the dark, not talking anymore until Duke crawls over to open the window and looks out where the sky is still working to snow. "She's out there," he says, "by the grave." And I hope it's her, the long shadow in the light of the screen and the low clouds.

Charlemagne is covered up with dry leaves when we get there, sitting just under the trees against the headstone. "Stop," she says. On the little TV the Vice President is shaking hands with Gran and then with Gramps and Uncle Waddle. "How do you know it's me? Maybe I'm a ghost."

"You don't look like one," I say.

"What do I look like?" she says.

"You," I say. "Charlemagne."

She nods. "Nothing I can do about that."

The guns are going off for the salute, and the funeral is going to start. At the church where they have the funeral there is a woman with a baby. She has on a blue dress with white knots tied all over on it and a square hat. Her hair is dust-colored, like mine, and she is so skinny her arms look barely bigger than the baby's. I used to think this was my mother.

"It's cold," I say.

"Heaven is hard," Charlemagne says, "very hard. Did you know that?"

"We could build a fire," I say.

Charlemagne moves from under her leaves while Duke and I gather up sticks and the driest twigs you find at the end of branches. We build a little tepee, and Duke lights the match first try.

"Did you see Uncle Bob?" I say. Charlemagne sits down again with her back against the stone and her feet almost in the fire. She's got a ratty gray sweater, one that was Gran's, stretched over her knees, and her kitten is squirming around underneath it. Duke's scrunched up by the flames.

"What did he say?" Duke wants to know.

Charlemagne shrugs. She has leaves in her hair and on her sweater. She picks them off so they won't catch fire.

"Do you know he was twenty-two when he died?" she says.

I shake my head no.

"I'm twenty-two," she says. She dumps a handful of leaves on the fire and they smoke and float up in embers like paper. "You were born. You were almost two years old, still a baby."

"I don't remember," I say.

"Do you know what happened?" she says. "Do you know how the Vietnamese had learned to shoot down airplanes by shooting in front of them? He knew about that, and he thought it was just a story. He thought he had better luck, anyway.

"He was too brave," she says. She reaches out a hand to lay on the stone. "That's what you were, Bob McCrackin." The war will be on next, the rockets coming out of the jungle. While her big shadow waves on the trees and while Duke and I bounce on our toes around the fire, she tells us about it.

"Boys are too brave," she says.

I am not brave now. I am cold. Duke is beating his hands up

and down like wings in the pockets of his coat, and the flames are dying.

"We need more wood," I say.

"We can go," Charlemagne says. "Here." She hands Duke her kitten to put in his pocket, and we stomp out the fire.

"Where are you going to go for the winter?" I say.

"I don't know," Charlemagne says. "Where's a good place? Arizona?" She takes our hands and we walk, crunching the hay stubble in the field. She wears the rubber muck boots we've got her from the house and brown cotton jersey gloves.

"You're going to grow up wild animals," she says. "You're going to be out of control."

"You could stay," I tell her. I don't know where, but we could find someplace. "Or we could go with you."

"We could do that," she says. And while Duke and I make plans, behind us the snowfall covers our tracks.

Majesty

C. M. MAYO

From *Sky over El Nido* (1995)

"It is a long tail certainly," said Alice . . .
"but why do you call it sad?"

Ana Guadalupe María Teresa García Ponçet y Rivera's feet, shod
in the smallest size of purple plastic thongs from the gift and tobacco shop, almost touch the floor. She tugs at the strap of her
black maillot as she studies the breakfast menu, a square of calf's
hide strewn with hand-colored etchings of jojoba and saguaro.

"I will have a triple banana split with extra cherries," she tells
the waitress.

The waitress is a strawberry blonde with an upturned nose.
She smells slightly of coconut. She begins to scribble down the
order, but stops, one arm akimbo, and winks. "Your mother's
gonna go for this?"

"My mother is meeting me at the swimming pool," Ana says,
and stares the girl full in the face. "I would like," she draws the
words out now like saltwater taffy, "a triple banana split with extra cherries."

The waitress scribbles this down.

"And," Ana continues, tucking one ankle under her bottom, "a
double espresso."

"Room number?" The waitress's voice is stony.

Ana claps the room key on the marble table top. "One twenty-three," she says. "García Ponçet y Rivera."

"What García?"

"García. One twenty—"

"Yeah, okay." The waitress bares her teeth.

The swimming pool is cast in shadows until midmorning. The room is a shambles before it's been made up. And there are no cartoons on, only shows where a man with a microphone stalks the aisles of spectators, who stand up and shout things in spurts, who wear strange clothing, pants with elastic waistbands.

Up and down the thickly carpeted sand-colored corridors Ana skips and shuffles, listening for voices, of children complaining, old men, the television. "*Pero ya compraste seis del mismito color, oye,*" "*Watashi no huto momo o monde kudasai—*" "Do we *have* to see the Grand Canyon?" "It was *your* idea!" a man yells at who knows? None of this is the least bit interesting.

On the second floor the ice machine groans, caterwauls, spits cubes into a bin. Ana takes one and draws it along the wallpaper, the closed doors, with one hand, then the other, until it melts to a nub at the end of the corridor.

On the third floor she finds one of the maids' carts, stocked with boxes of purple Kleenex, rolls of three-ply purple toilet paper, sewing kits disguised as matchbooks, jojoba shampoo, a vase crammed with cut orchids. She stands on tiptoe and snatches a handful of foil-wrapped Good Night chocolates.

"*Buenos días,*" she calls out to the maid.

The maid, startled, nearly jumps out of the bathroom, her hands in too-big rubber gloves.

"*Ah, Señorita Ani,*" she says, and her soft brown face breaks with a smile. "*Buenos días.*"

There is grass, lots of grass. Little houses with lush patios ring the grass, and old men in lollipop-colored shirts drive purple covered cans along a winding asphalt path. Ana walks the perimeter, on the lookout for Johnny the bloodhound puppy. She has found him twice now, sitting on the asphalt path just outside his patio, taking the sun. She has never seen his person, only read his dog tag:

MY NAME IS JOHNNY
GENEROUS REWARD
334–0987

"Toot! Toot!" an old man shouts at her from his little cart. She skitters to the side and he whizzes by her, tipping his visor, laughing.

She walks along the path past the duck pond, past a series of amoeba-shaped sand traps, and comes to the patio of Johnny's house. Through the iron bars she can see a white-haired lady squatting down to tend a row of pansies.

"Where's Johnny?" Ana calls to her.

The lady twists her chin around, and then, slowly, as if in great pain, she stands up. She is wearing plaid shorts and an old button-down collar shirt. Her tennis shoes are caked with mud.

"How do you know my Johnny?" she says, approaching the fence. She is very tan, and her skin looks leathery.

"I saw him yesterday," Ana says. "He is nice."

"Yes, well." The woman knocks her trowel against an iron bar, to shake off a dirt clod. "He's having his milk in the kitchen."

"Oh," Ana says. She scrunches her face and scratches the back of one knee with the toe of her thong.

"Where's your mother, dear?" The old lady is squinting.

There are palm trees, lots of palm trees, and a lumpy brown mountain that looks like a camel's back. It is February, a time to be in school. The lobby bar is serving complimentary mugs of chicken bouillon; *nuevo flamenco* bleats from discreetly placed stereo speakers. Ana is perched on a barstool, slurping a cherry-flavored sparkling water with a straw. At one of the tables, a woman in a houndstooth check blazer and a mango Hermès scarf sits curled over her crossword puzzle. A Japanese man works his way towards the glass doors, slowly, using a walker. He hunches his wishbone shoulders as he lets his weight sink with each careful step. Ana pats her thongs against her heels to the clack of castanets; she shreds her purple cocktail napkin into strips thin as pencils, rolled thin as yarn, threads of cotton, fiber-optic hairs maybe.

"*Pues hay todo tipo de escuelas*," Well there are all kinds of schools, someone says in a high voice behind her ear. Ana jerks around, and a man, or a boy—or a woman (for an instant she is not sure)—slides onto the barstool next to hers. His face is the color of molasses, delicate, smooth, but he is too tall, she decides, to be a boy.

"*¿Sabes?*" Do you know, he goes on in a languid, sleepy voice, "there are schools that will teach you to make hats? Or to cut hair? To write sonnets and songs, how to play chess?" He is from Guadalajara, she can tell. His alligator watchband is loose around his hairless wrist. He is wearing a white T-shirt and baggy shorts. He is drinking something that looks like apple soda. "How to trade futures and options even." He has a thick gold rope of a necklace that he pulls out and twists around his thumb.

"What are futures and options?" Ana ventures to ask.

The man opens his eyes wide as walnut shells. He brushes a

strand of lank brown hair behind his ear. "Certainties and may-bes," he says.

They both consider this for a moment. A woman with a tightly pulled chignon leans down to peck the cheek of the woman in the houndstooth blazer. The Japanese man has made it out the door. "*Ike no ishi wa shinwa no tori!*" he says (she thinks), raising one fist towards the swimming pool. "*No yoni yuga de furyu desu.*" The guitars strum softly, madly.

The man puts his elbows on the bar and begins to puff a cheroot, trying to get it lit. The smoke has a cloying smell, like fresh-cut grass. This reminds Ana of her uncles' cigars, Davidoffs they keep in tropical wood boxes in their dining rooms, and clip with metal clippers. She slurps the last of her sparkling water with a noise that sounds like a ribbon of paper caught in an electric fan.

The woman with the chignon is batting her arms now, as if to get out from under a sheet, furiously.

"Sorry, Alex!" the bartender calls over his shoulder. He is polishing a tumbler with a small purple towel. "This is a no smoking bar. You could—"

"Oh," he says, as if charmed, "that's all right." His English is crisp as a toasted biscuit. "It tastes better from a hookah anyway." In one fluid motion he plunges the cheroot into the amber snifter and glides out the glass doors, past the Japanese man (now leaning over the front of his walker, his face tilted stiffly to the sun), past the clay pots of saguaro and aloe, past the croquet lawn still submerged in the shade of the hotel, towards the swimming pool.

From her barstool Ana can see his small figure leap . . . and disappear beneath the shimmering lapis lazuli.

Puddles of pool water flash on the tiles. A waiter scoots by with a tray of bright orange drinks. Alex is lying on a plastic strap chaise longue, leafing through an oversized full-color magazine. He is still wearing his T-shirt, plucking at his chest to help it dry in the sun. His hair is slicked back, and parted down the center. Ana sits crosslegged on the next chaise, slurping a virgin banana daiquiri with a straw. The breeze has raised goose bumps on her legs and arms, and her eyes sting.

Alex says, "I think it's just fabulous that Princess Stephanie had a baby with her bodyguard." He is talking to a much older man who has the bulging eyes of a troll. The old man is slathering lotion on his arms. His flesh hangs in gray, leathery folds. His white hair is thick as a paintbrush and points up straight over his massive forehead.

"I mean, look at his face," Alex says. "Those sloe-eyed smirks."

"He has the face of a turnip," the old man says. He is wearing a zebra stripe bikini. His toes are startlingly long. He may be an American.

"Look!" Alex holds up the open magazine. "Stephanie's put sunglasses on the baby!" Ana recognizes last week's *Hola*. "She's pushing the pram!"

"Hmm," the old man says. He tucks the bottle of lotion under his *Wall Street Journal* and stretches out on the chaise, his back to the sun.

"Hmmmmm," he says again, and closes his eyes.

Ana sucks on her straw, then blocks it with the tip of her tongue. She pulls the straw out, holds it up, one finger on the other end. Banana slush defies gravity.

"*Mi mamá siempre lee* Hola," My mother always reads *Hola*, Ana says. She blinks, hard.

"Hmm," Alex says. He waves at a blonde woman in a parrot-green sarong, who waves back from the other side of the pool, near the clay pots of saguaro, the cabanas. "Alex!" she calls, and blows a kiss.

An airplane passes overhead, then into a tuft of cloud above the camel's-back mountain. The cloud seems bleached, tenuous.

"I like the pictures of Princess Di," Ana says.

The old man has begun to snore, a gentle *click-click*, like muffled castanets. Alex continues leafing through the magazine. He holds it sideways for a better look at something.

A lunch buffet is set up near the cabañas. Ana wraps herself in a sheet-sized purple towel and takes a plate.

"*Buenas tardes*," Good afternoon, the chef says to her. He is from somewhere near the border, she can tell. He is wearing an enormous chef's hat and a starched tunic.

"*Buenas*," Ana says and piles her plate with chocolate pudding.

"Wouldn't you like some lobster salad?" The chef seems concerned. He is waving an unusually long jagged knife. He is standing next to an ice sculpture of a camel. "A slice of roast beef with a little juice?"

"No." Ana is trying to slide a wedge of vanilla cake onto the serving spatula, but it keeps slipping back onto the platter.

The chef purses his lips and grins. "What will your mother say when she sees your plate?"

"I can have whatever I want," Ana says, still struggling with the cake. The chef doesn't seem to have an answer for that. She grabs the wedge of cake with her hand. It lands on the pudding with a *plop*.

"*Atsui. Yogan mitai*," a Japanese woman with a pinched face whispers to herself, apparently. She is wearing a grape-colored Gucci sheath and matching platform sandals. The chef serves her a slab of roast beef and dollop of horseradish sauce, and she minces towards the salads, the jumbles of bell peppers and baby corn, pine nuts and cherry tomatoes.

There is a spa, a very big spa. It has a juice bar where one can snack on chilled carrot sticks and order cocktails: cucumber lemon and carrot; cucumber beet and carrot; papaya; blueberry strawberry squeeze of mandarin orange.

"Cucumber blueberry," Ana says. She is barefoot. She is wearing her black maillot.

"*Fuchi*," Yuck. Alex crinkles his nose. His face is scrubbed fresh, the skin smooth as an olive. He is wrapped in a snow white terrycloth robe; he is wearing purple plastic thongs from the gift and tobacco shop. He is leafing through a large glossy magazine. He smells slightly of Chanel No. 5, or is it Ivoire? Something her mother would wear.

"You smell," Ana says, and bites a carrot stick. The man behind the counter switches on the blender. As it whirrs to a stop, Alex is saying "*you*," with a sneer, jabbing the edge of his magazine at her chest. "And why do *you* follow me around?"

"I'm not following you around," Ana says. "I can sit at the juice bar anytime I like." She slaps her room key on the marble countertop. "I can order anything I like."

"You can't have tequila, or cigarettes," Alex says, staring at the man behind the bar. The man has fully defined biceps. He is wearing a purple T-shirt with the name of the hotel emblazoned across the chest in Times Roman Italic.

"Papaya celery!" Alex calls out.

"Okeydokey," the man says, and switches on a second blender.

Ana waits for the machine to stop. "I can so," she says. Her eyes glitter with outrage. "I can so have tequila and cigarettes and I've had them every night this week." She rests one elbow on the counter and gazes at the man.

"Stop staring, you little nitwit," Alex says, and pulls the collar of his terrycloth robe across his throat. From a stereo speaker near the ceiling, a sitar hums and an old woman's feathery voice begins to chant strange words.

"*¡Alex! ¡Te encontré!*" I found you! It's a short plump girl who may be Venezuelan, or perhaps Colombian. She's doing the cha-cha now, giggling. "Let's go again tonight!" She's halfway through the door to the locker room.

"Ten-thirty?"

The girl seems to be all teeth. Her hair is an unnatural yellow. "Ten-forty-five, ciao!"

Ana snatches his magazine. "*¡Oye!*" Hey! Alex sniffs. He rolls his eyes, crosses his arms across his chest. She moistens her finger with her tongue and turns the page. There is a photograph of a blonde woman, her hipbones jutting out, wearing Ana's same maillot. *Points of interest: a strappy back, a scoop neck.* Ana takes a sip of the cucumber blueberry cocktail. It needs sugar, desperately. *Calvin Klein swimwear*, the small print says. *$163 at Neiman Marcus.*

Alex has moved to the far end of the juice bar and is hunched over a disarranged *Wall Street Journal*. He makes loud rustling noises, going through the paper too quickly. The feathery voice is lower now, the music sweeter, slightly faster, like spindles of afternoon rain.

Gracefully placed details add a soupçon of interest, Ana reads. She sucks in her cheeks, she fans her fingers. But her cheeks are plump with baby fat; her fingernails sadly blunt. She chews her lip. *Have a Hat Attack.* Ana turns the page, and an eye the size of her hand stares back at her, the pupil reflecting a tiger lily. She is about to ask for some sugar when a red-haired man with a mustache pokes his head in the doorway.

"Ms. García Ponçet y Rivera?" he calls out, beaming at Alex. He is wearing a purple T-shirt. His hair is kinky. He looks about forty, but it is hard to tell.

"It's for me," Ana says, tossing down the magazine.

"You!" The red-haired man has a California accent. His laugh sounds like macaroni noodles shaken in a box. He holds open the door to the massage rooms.

"Ciao," Alex says, and gives a *thwat* to the newspaper.

"Is this your first time?" The red-haired man is washing his hands at a small sink in the corner. The voice with the sitar is higher and nasal now, chanting something like "*Oo wah no, oo wah na no.*"

"Nooooooo," Ana says. The lights have been dimmed, and she is sitting with her legs dangling off the side of the massage table. She tugs at the strap of her maillot.

"How do you want to feel today?" he asks.

"Oh, I don't know," Ana says, and lies down on her stomach.

"No, no, no," the man laughs. "First you need to take that bathing suit off. I'll step out for a minute and you lie down on your stomach. You can cover yourself with this." He pulls at the edge of a sheet that has been tucked around the table.

When the man comes back in the room, he announces: "We will do lavender and cucumber."

Ana puts her chin on the backs of her hands. "My mother always has yling ylang and vanilla."

"Oh my God!" the man says. He giggles. "You're much too young for that." He splashes something onto his palm. "Let's do lavender and cucumber. *Trust me.*" He begins to run a fragrant oil across her shoulder blades, then kneads it into the narrow ropes of muscle along her spine. "Cucumber oil is for sunburn, and freckles," the man says quietly. "You look like you're spending a lot of time in the swimming pool."

"Hmmm," Ana says, and squeezes her eyes shut. She feels the oil run across the small of her back, her elbows, wrists, the nape of her neck, like a Cuernavaca morning, like a sitar, something in the shadow.

"You're going to get an extra massage, you're so tiny!" the man chuckles, working her calves now. But Ana doesn't hear anything else he says, because she falls fast asleep, until another sharp and sweeter scent wakes her.

"Lavender," the red-haired man is saying, "is for headaches, for anxiety." And he makes tiny circles with his fingertips behind her ears.

There is steam, really, a lot of steam. It hits Ana in the face like a punch. "Ahg!" she says. She collapses on the tile bench. In a moment she recovers and tries to make out the other figure through the mist. "Hi," she says.

"*Buenas*," Alex says.

"Ha! So you're a girl!"

"I was in the men's steam room yesterday," he says. "So don't draw any conclusions."

"Ha!" Ana says again, weakly.

They sit silently for a while, their limbs limp in the heat.

"Where's your mother?" he says at last. He sounds provoked.

"I'm meeting her by the swimming pool." Ana smooths her towel and stretches out on her back. She adds, "My mother lets me do whatever I want," but senses that this is unnecessary.

"Well . . ." Alex says very slowly. His voice trails off in the heavy air.

A set of nozzles near the ceiling begins to blast in fresh steam. The noise is deafening, then stops with a sudden hiss. A stubby-legged woman in a dolphin-colored bikini comes in and sits with them for a few minutes. She keeps sweeping her hair off her neck and twisting it into a knot, and sighing. Then she leaves.

Alex wraps himself in a towel and shoves open the heavy glass door. As the steam rushes out, Ana can see his face suddenly tense. "Come on out of here," he says. "You shouldn't be in here alone." He reaches down and pulls her up by the arm. "Come on."

A clutch of violinists, a cellist, and a flautist are playing Mozart. Flower arrangements the size of peacocks' tails dot the lobby, in the corners, on pink marble pedestals. An especially large arrangement of parrot tulips, thistle, and red-speckled orchids sits on the mantel, where a gas fire flicks soundlessly in the grate. Ana is wearing her maillot, her purple plastic thongs, and a sheet-sized towel like a poncho.

"No room!" Alex cries from his purple loveseat when he sees her shuffling through the lobby. "No room!"

"There's tons of room," Ana says, eyeing the tufted purple armchair pulled up to one side of the coffee table.

A waiter swishes by with a dish of lemon slices.

"Have a toad's brain," Alex says, and waves an open palm over the low table. There is a silver teapot, two cups on saucers, cream and sugar, a plate of paper-thin finger sandwiches, and a silver bowl of candied chestnuts.

"Those are *marrons glacées*," Ana says and she sticks her tongue out. She climbs into the chair and tucks one ankle under her bottom.

"Have an apple chutney sandwich."

Ana pops a candied chestnut into her mouth. "No thanks," she says, working the sugary mash with her jaws.

Alex is wearing a white double-breasted linen jacket and trousers. A cellophane-wrapped cigar peeks out from his front pocket. He looks as if he would like to reach across the coffee table and slap her, but he says, "Why is Neiman Marcus like a jar of anchovy paste?"

Ana screws up her face, trying to think. She pours herself a cup of tea and stirs in eleven and one-half spoonfuls of sugar. She stares at Alex's shoes, black and cream spectators, exactly like her mother's.

"I don't know," she finally admits. "What?"

"I haven't the slightest idea," he says and he looks at his watch.

"Alex!" It's a woman with platinum hair teased into a poof on top of her head. She's carrying shopping bags in both hands, struggling towards the elevators.

"Ciao!" Alex blows her a kiss as she disappears behind the concierge's desk. "Have a look at this," he says to Ana. He leans over the arm of the loveseat and slips her a glossy magazine with a photograph of Queen Elizabeth in a tam-o'-shanter shaped hat. MAJESTY, it says, in skinny yellow letters.

Ana winces and hands back the magazine. She says, "The Queen has the face of a turnip." She rubs her ear with her towel.

"The Queen must be related to Princess Stephanie's bodyguard, then." Alex balances his saucer on his knee, holding the cup with his pinky out. "Olduvai Gorge," he muses. "Perhaps."

"Princess Di is very nice." Ana rolls her eyes and sinks into the chair. She slips off her thongs and curls her toes around the rim of the coffee table.

"Everything all right for you this afternoon?" A waitress in a black uniform and a white pinafore sets down a pitcher of hot water. There is a surge of violins, a silver trill of flute. "Princess Di is very—" Alex twists his gold chain around his thumb. He pats the cushion of the loveseat. "Come here, I'll show you something," he says. He spreads MAJESTY across their laps. "Look," he commands. "Princess Michael of Kent." He taps a fingernail on the page. "She's wearing that stunning hibiscus raincoat, on her way out of Annabel's. Look, look! at this Serena Stanhope, she's better than a soap opera star! See, she's going to marry Viscount Linley." He leafs through the pages now, quickly. Peachy-skinned women in enormous hats snip ribbons with monstrous scissors, kiss bloated bald children. The Duchess of York leans over the hospital bed of a man whose eyes have shrunk in their sockets. The Queen waves from her seat at a polo match.

At last Alex comes to a photograph of a wizened, square-faced woman. She wears an aquamarine silk scarf knotted at the throat, and simple pearl earrings. Her milky blue eyes squint forthrightly at the camera. She resembles very closely, Ana realizes with a start, Johnny's person.

"And Princess Alice," Alex says breathlessly, sliding an olive hand across the shiny paper. "Have you heard of Princess Alice, Duchess of Gloucester?"

"My mother looks like Isabel Preysler, from *Hola*," Ana volunteers.

The desert sky is the color of a bruise. A handful of stars, widely scattered, wink faintly. From the window of her balcony Ana can see the city and the camel's-back mountain, a gray-brown hulk in the distance. She opens the minibar and takes out a doll-sized bottle of tequila, JOSE CUERVO, it says, HECHO EN MEXICO. She lights a cigarette from the pack her mother has forgotten on the night table. It tastes, as always, like fouled, muddied sand. She pours herself a tumbler of tequila and knocks it back in three gulps without wincing. She holds the cigarette in her teeth. "That's all right," she tells the mirror, "this stuff tastes better from a hookah."

She starts up the jacuzzi and pours in an entire bottle of bubble bath. She makes castles, stalagmites. She sculpts herself a party dress and waltzes across the tiles. She does a plié, an arabesque in front of the sink.

She leaves the shower faucet running and tells the room service waiter that her mother is in the bathroom. As she lets the pecan pie filling melt in her mouth like clear pudding, sips her warm Cherry Coke, and later, as she spears her french fries and pushes them through a pool of ketchup, Ana decides that her mother really does look like Isabel Preysler: a petite sculpted face, shoulder-length chocolate hair, skirts that fall neatly, just above the knee. Isabel Preysler was once married to Julio Iglesias, which Ana finds as improbable as her mother's having been married to her father.

She thinks of the restaurant, the one on the seventh floor where the old men wore dark suits and the women who were not Japanese were blonde, their hair swept up and sprayed, like Princess Di's. There was a view. The waiters brought Ana and her mother mock turtle soup, lobster medallions, fluffy salads of rose petals, nasturtium, frills of chickory in a hazelnut vinaigrette, each plate sheltered under a pewter dome. The domes had tiny knobs on their tops, shaped like pineapples, a strawberry, a pear.

"*Voilà*," the waiter would say, each time.

She had seen Alex and the troll-eyed man sitting along the back wall of the restaurant, squeezed into a purple banquette, under a teardrop chandelier. They looked out at the stars; they watched an airplane fly towards the north. They had ordered an entire vanilla cake. A waiter wheeled it to their table on a glass-paneled cart.

Her Cherry Coke needs ice. But when she thinks of going down to the second floor to the ice machine she has a sudden intuition that she would meet the troll-eyed man, still in his zebra stripe bikini, his flabby gray arms rooting in the bin. Or he might be standing pressed up next to the machine, not necessarily waiting for ice. Moths would flail against the overhead lamp. The maids would be in their sad little apartments, bus stops away. Alex would be in the disco.

Ana bolts the door and draws the chain. She swathes herself in a towel and goes out onto the balcony. The stars twinkle fiercely in the chill. The iron railing is nearly as cold as the tiny bottle of tequila. She drops the bottle over the side, into the thicket of palm, ivy, and fern. She wraps her hands around the railing, arches her back. A breath of breeze sweeps her hair off her forehead; she lifts her chin.

The grass stretches below like an abyss, ringed by the spot-lit path. Clusters of saguaro reach their thick arms to the stars. Near Johnny's house, she can make out a sand trap, dark like a wound. Beyond the grass is the highway. And beyond the highway is the city, shining now like a wonderland.

Us Kids

MELINDA MOUSTAKIS

From *Bear Down, Bear North* (2011)

Us kids smile and wave good riddance when Fox and Uncle Sly roll out one way and we roll another, bruised butts in the seats. We're piled into Big Mary, our station wagon that barely fits us all in and is a miracle for starting up. We're packed in with a huge pot full of frozen moose meat and whatever we have to eat in the back along with a jumbleball of afghans Polar Bear is always knitting. Fox and Uncle Sly go hunting at the homestead and Polar Bear drives us to see Aunt Sheila and Jack and Gracie, our cousins, at their house that Uncle Sly built all googly-eyed drunk. The house has gone through a few names—Slack Shack, Plywood Palace, and the one we all remember and still use is the Tiltin' Hilton.

Aunt Sheila has made gumdrop cookies and she sets a plate of them on the porch. We're pressed to see or taste any gumdrops but Kitty holds up hers. "I see a green one."

Polar Bear takes the pot and afghans into the house and we know to stay put outside. Aunt Sheila draws the curtains but we know what they're doing. Smoking and drinking homemade cranberry lick. We huddle near the side and listen through the cheap-cracked wood.

"The men are good and gone," says Polar Bear.

Ben signs to Rias so he can hear too. Jack shushes Gracie.

"Maybe they'll do us a favor and shoot themselves," says Aunt Sheila.

"Maybe," says Polar Bear. "I'll drink to that." There's the clink of bottles.

J.J. crosses his eyes and raises an imaginary bottle to his lips. Colleen, who has Baby T on her hip, laughs into her hand.

"They talk stars and moonlight in the beginning," says Aunt Sheila.

"And what we get is shit and moonshine," says Polar Bear. Another clink. A smash of glass on the floor.

Kitty gives out a yelp.

"Goddamnit," says Polar Bear.

We huddle closer against the house.

"I hear you out there," Polar Bear says. "You leave us alone. Scram-ola. We'll call you for dinner."

So we scram-ola. In front of the Tiltin' Hilton are two hills, one on each side because Uncle Sly had meant to put the house on one and the shitter on the other. "Nothing better than el-er-vation," he said. But he never got to it, built the house so it was some leaning wobbler between two piles of dirt. He didn't let Fox help him with the house. He did let Fox build the outhouse behind it, near the woods, and it's the only thing that stands up straight. But the hills are perfect for a game of Red Rover, and a rain has started up which puts the mosquitoes to bed for a bit.

". . . we call J.J. over," and he comes mud-slipping down the hill to the arm-linked chain, but Rias and Colleen with Baby T on her hip keep hold. Gracie and Jack and Kitty come to the bottom and join J.J. and they make a wall. The others head up the hill.

". . . we call Rias over," and because he might not see to lip-read with all the rain, J.J. draws an R in the air. Here slides Rias on his belly, and then he gets up and charges the line, breaking through the JackandGracie link. So he steals Kitty and now it's

RiasandKittyandBenandColleenandBabyT at the bottom of the hill.

"... we call Gracie over."

Soon we're all mud creatures which is good because the rain stops and the mosquitoes wake up and swarm around us and the sun streaks through the shiner-eyed clouds.

"Dinner," yells Polar Bear, and she sees us kids all rolled and covered in mud. "Stay off the porch," she says. But she takes Baby T.

We settle on the gravel by the steps with our bowls of moose chili and for once there's something moose about it.

"Colleen, you make sure ... everyone gets hosed ... off ... after everyone eats," says Polar Bear, swimming through her words.

A high-pitched-screaming-wail makes us all stop with our spoons. Aunt Sheila comes wobble-running around the Tiltin' Hilton. She steadies herself on the steps and sits down.

"What is going on?" says Polar Bear.

"There's a bird, or something, in the shitter," Aunt Sheila says, boozy and soft. "And it's trapped and it's dying and I pissed on it." She starts crying her face off. "We have to get it out. We just have to."

"For godssake," says Polar Bear. "It's a bird. What's it matter if the world's shy one?" She waves away the mosquitoes near her face.

"But it's alive," says Aunt Sheila. She's a crying mess.

"ok, ok," says Polar Bear. "Let's go take a look at this bird you pissed on."

"I didn't know it was down there," says Aunt Sheila.

We jump up and follow Polar Bear, the whole mud-covered line of us. Aunt Sheila trails behind, walking zigzag, and Ben falls back to help her.

Polar Bear turns around. "Sheila, that smell."

"I know," says Aunt Sheila.

The shitter smells like a shitter, even from a way off, because of the rain and because they ran out of lye a couple of days before and Uncle Sly kept forgetting to buy some.

Polar Bear gives Baby T to Colleen and goes in to take a look. "It's a dumb buzzard," she says. "That's all."

We take turns, plug our noses, and look down the hole that's surrounded in white Styrofoam so it's warm to sit on in winter. And because Fox made it, it's deep like he made our outhouse at the homestead. There's some flapping and some splashing and a hoarse-whistling-peep of a bird down there. But it's hard to tell what it is because it's dark in the shitter. We got a flashlight in Big Mary so Ben goes to find it and Polar Bear takes Baby T and Aunt Sheila back to the house.

"Promise me you'll get it out," Aunt Sheila says.

"They promise," says Polar Bear.

Ben shines the flashlight and our dried mud faces must scare the bird because it starts squawking. Not that the bird is much to look at either—covered in a slop of years of dirt and piss and shit.

"Get me a shovel," says Ben.

Jack goes to find one that's under the house. By this time we've breathed enough of the smell to get used to it and we've stopped plugging our noses. Ben has J.J. hold the flashlight as he leans in the hole with the shovel, but comes up quick.

"That's not going to do it," he says. "We need something to reach farther."

"I gotta go," says Gracie.

Colleen takes her and Kitty into the woods. Then she goes into the house and brings out a broom and a colander. "Polar Bear and Aunt Sheila and the baby are lying down," she says.

"We need tape," says Ben, and he and Jack and J.J. and Rias crawl underneath the Tiltin' Hilton to look for tape in the scattering of Uncle Sly's tools. Colleen holds the flashlight so Gracie and Kitty can look down the hole.

"He's crying," says Gracie.

"Little bird, don't you cry," sings Kitty.

"He's probably hungry," says Colleen.

Ben comes back holding a dusty roll of duct tape. It's late, but the sun just doesn't quit in July. The mud dries pale and cracked on our skin.

We tape the broom handle to the shovel and Ben holds J.J.'s legs as J.J. goes into the hole and Jack holds the flashlight.

"Pull me out," says J.J. "We need about this much more." He taps the tips of his fingers, uses his arm as a measuring stick. The shovel has reached the bird's head but we need to scoop him out.

"Get that rake," says Ben.

Rakebroomshovel is taped together.

J.J. goes in again, Ben has him by the ankles, and Rias funnels down the tool.

"Stop," yells J.J. "We're losing the shovel."

Ben motions to Rias who brings up the rake.

"Hold right there," says J.J. "I got to hold onto the shovel and you got to bring us both up."

The tape on the joint has come loose.

"Thing about smacked the bird in the head and then got me with it." There's a spot on his forehead where the dry-caked mud is scraped away. "Goddamn shithole."

We tape a stronger wrap.

"This is the last time I'm going," says J.J.

We get J.J. in and then the shovel and the rest.

"I got him," he says. "Pull up. Pull up." There's a squawk and a splash. "He jumped," says J.J. "The stupid bird jumped off." He peers down the hole. "I'm just trying to help you, you piece of shit."

"J.J., calm down," says Colleen.

He slaps the side of the outhouse.

Rias raises his hand.

"ok," says Ben. "You try."

We lower Rias, who is holding the end of the rakebroomshovel, into the hole. He gets the bird on, and we're lifting up, and we hear a bigger squawk and then nothing. The bird's not on the shovel because he's holding it, shit and all, close to his chest, both of them upside down. Ben gets Rias up close to the top and then lifts him and the bird straight up out of the hole. Jack grabs the bird and it's screaming and Rias stands up and takes the bird back, nesting it in the colander and cradling it in the crook of his arm. He pets it on the top of the head and if birds could smile, this bird would have been smiling you're-a-saint lovebeams at Rias.

"That's not a buzzard," says Colleen. "Look at the beak. That's an eagle. An eaglet."

"Still ugly," says J.J.

"Let's wash him up," says Colleen.

We fill a bucket of water at the pump. As long as Rias pets his head, the eaglet sitting in the colander lets us pour small cups of water over him. He's about the size of a chicken, with yellow feet, and yellow at the base of his hooked beak. With the slop off of him, his feathers are grays and browns with white spots on the fringe of his back. All in all, he could be mistaken for a scraggled patch of bear fur, and he wiggles off the water, ruffles up. We find a towel and Rias bundles him. Colleen brings over a half-eaten bowl of moose chili and hands the spoon to Rias.

"See if he's hungry," she says.

He is. He opens his beak and gobbles down the chili. Rias pets his head and then Kitty feeds the eaglet.

"Here you go, little bird," she says.

"Here you go, shitbird," says J.J. His voice pure syrup.

"Shitbird. Shitbird," chimes Jack.

And then Jack and J.J. chant together. "Shitbird. Shitbird. Shitbird."

"That's enough," says Colleen.

"He doesn't know what we're saying," says J.J. "Hey, pretty," he says. "Hey, ugly shit. See."

"Leave him alone," says Kitty. "He's just a baby."

We count and the eaglet sits in the colander on Rias's lap and eats eleven spoonfuls of chili.

"I want to keep him," says Gracie.

"We can't," says Colleen.

"We could teach him to hunt rabbits for us," says Jack.

"Or scratch people's eyes out," says J.J.

"What if he grew up big," says Kitty, "and we could ride him?"

"We'd go up in the sky," says Gracie. "To the mountains."

"You'd still smell the shitter up there," says J.J.

"We have to take him back," says Colleen.

There's a nest in the woods that's been abandoned for three years, but we figure the eagles must have returned, even if Jack says they haven't seen any flying over like they used to.

"Where else could this eagle have come from?" says Ben.

We march past the outhouse, into the woods, Rias carrying the eaglet and the colander. We stand at the base of a tall spruce tree, the tangled nest of branches up high, near the top.

"I see something," says Jack.

And then we all see a white spot of a bald eagle.

"They must be flying in from a different direction," says Ben.

There's no way we can climb the tree and put the eaglet back in the nest. He must have fallen or tried to fly or gotten pushed out, but how he got into the shitter, we don't know.

"We'll leave him here," says Ben. "His parents will hear him."

"But I wanted to keep him," says Gracie, and she buries her face against Rias.

"But he needs to be here, honey," says Colleen.

"I wanted to keep him too," says Kitty.

"But his family will miss him," says Colleen.

Ben gives the signal and Rias unwraps the eaglet and places him on the ground.

"Shouldn't we leave the colander?" says Colleen. "He seemed to like it."

Rias puts the colander on the ground and the eaglet jumps back into it. He strokes the feathers on the eaglet's chest.

"Say goodbye," says Colleen.

Kitty and Gracie kneel down next to Rias. "Goodbye, little bird," they say.

J.J. shakes his head at their sniffling.

Colleen grabs his arm. "Hush," she says.

We walk away, Rias the last one to leave. And when he does, the eaglet starts screeching and it's a good thing Rias can't hear him or anything for that matter or he'd turn back, and we pick up the pace, the sky falling blue through the trees.

We're all still a mudmess but we're tired.

"We'll sleep in Big Mary," says Colleen, so we don't get in trouble for being all mucked up in the Tiltin' Hilton. She sneaks inside and grabs the jumbleball of afghans. We put Gracie and Kitty in the front because they're small and the rest of us cram on the car floor and the seats and the hatch in the back. We pull the afghans over our heads to block out the light that's tricking us into staying awake.

In the late morning, maybe afternoon, we wake up because Jack gets up to go to the outhouse. Big Mary smells like Big Shit. We crawl out of the car dusty and cricked and yawning. No one says anything about what's in front of the porch. The house is quiet, except for the breeze of a snore we know is Polar Bear. What is there to say? J.J. throws a cup of water on Ben. And Ben chases after him. And we all get cups and throw water, splashing off the mud we've been wearing since the night before, dirty rivers trickling down to our toes. And what Polar Bear and Aunt Sheila see bleary-eyed, their hands raised against the glare of the sun, is us kids. Us kids laughing and running over a torn-to-pieces eaglet we bathed and fed and found this morning, brought back to us by birds or dogs or the upside-down nest of the world, stomping what we saved into the ground, an eagle buried under our feet, a flurry of feathers rising up.

From Where I Sit

NANCY ZAFRIS

From *The People I Know* (1990)

In the third grade I appeared on *The Uncle Sylvester Show*, a local program filmed live each afternoon. The show consisted of cartoons and a few games. It featured a studio audience of cheering Cub Scouts, Brownies, Camp Fire Girls, and members of assorted other tribes. I was a Bluebird. The Bluebird friend sitting next to me was Jane.

Uncle Sylvester, the star of the show, retained a goofy sidekick named Private Beanhead. Private Beanhead had the dutiful gangliness of most sidekicks, but in all other ways he was disobedient. At least once during every show Uncle Sylvester was forced to pull Private Beanhead's handlebar mustache to curb his sidekick's incorrigible antics, things like squeezing into a bleacher seat between two giggling Brownies.

Uncle Sylvester was a bit more avuncular, as his name implied. He wore gray hair with bangs, a look that inspired no controversy despite the fact that the Beatles were currently sporting the exact same style. He was rounder and heavier, solid-looking but soft. Someone whose lap a child could sit on. But that was from a distance. Up close I found myself recoiling, hoping he would stay away from my side of the bleachers. There was something else that did not translate onto the home viewer's TV screen and that could only be glimpsed firsthand: Uncle Sylvester's mouth had a tendency to gather saliva when he talked. After a few sentences his lips would glisten greedily. Sometimes a mist would escape his mouth as he spouted directions during the commercials and cartoons, referring to us often as "good boys and girls." His hands opened and closed at us with the rapacity of a miser being held back from his coins. Once on screen, however, he kept his hands locked inside his belt at the small of his back. As he faced the camera, those of us behind him watched the fabric of his pants dance in and out like piano keys. This was what interested me most—all the things the camera could not catch.

At the end of every *Uncle Sylvester Show* the kids were rewarded for their enthusiasm with the Round-Up. The Round-Up was when the camera caressed each face individually. Large TVs were positioned at each end of the bleachers so the children could see themselves as they appeared. The jolt of their own faces on a TV screen sent the girls into a one-syllable giggle before straightening quickly into the friendly wave and smile they had been practicing for days. With the boys it was a different story, muggings and antics, the kinds of things that get knowing, long-suffering nods from elementary school teachers.

Meanwhile the mothers stood offstage watching another TV; their dark outlines could be seen fluttering in the recess of the studio. With no such invention as the video cassette recorder to immortalize their babies, the mothers crammed together and grabbed at the moment as if it were champagne gulped from the bottle.

After every face had been panned, the boys and girls began a restless thumping. Everyone knew what happened next. At the conclusion of Round-Up, the camera flew about for several seconds and then alighted upon a single face. The owner of the face received a prize and the show ended.

I sat quietly and waited. Of all the people there, I was probably the only one who didn't want to win. I willed the long neck of the camera lens to turn away. But it kept swinging back, alighting upon me in brief teases. When the camera finally stopped moving, there I was, encircled on the television screen. Uncle Sylvester and Private Beanhead came running around to my seat. In the distance I saw the fluttering of mothers turn inward. They were searching out my mother as though they would know her instantly, the same way you would know the single black mother belonging to the single black child. I'm handicapped, and people expected my mother to match.

After the show Jane's mother offered me a hug. I liked Mrs. Gilbert but I was not ready for another adult's touch, having still on me the gooiness of Uncle Sylvester's wiggling fingers while he asked my name. His grip on the back of my neck grew tighter with each question. I had squirmed to escape but he had immobilized me.

As we filed offstage Private Beanhead and Uncle Sylvester mustered the last light of their star personae to shuffle us out of the studio. A bored limpness soaked Private Beanhead's comic, rubbery body. Beside him Uncle Sylvester appeared to be biting a bullet. The tension provided the first angles to his spongy face. But he used his clamped jaw to good effect: the expression of holding back pain also passed as concern for the children as he nodded silently. His cupped hands moved up and down like someone calmly redirecting a water leak; it was, I assume, to keep the spurting children at bay. One of the departing Cub Scouts jumped to honk Private Beanhead's enormous nose, and Private Beanhead tilted his head heavenward with a grimace of imprecation. His nose, reared back, revealed two cavernous pyramids. Later my mother told me Private Beanhead was also the news weatherman, and I began following the weather just to glimpse those impressive nostrils again.

On the way home we went to McDonald's. Jane and her mother went with us. We parked and walked up to the takeout window. I wore braces on my legs and when I walked I bounced up and down. My sister said I looked like I was riding one of those horse sticks. Often my arms flew up with the effort, but that was controllable if I concentrated. Otherwise I looked fine. I was described as having a very pretty face, although the compliment is such an established insincerity that even a third grader develops an anxiety about just the opposite being true. But sometimes when I was lined up next to their own daughters, mothers bent toward my mom, and with a bit of confidential surprise remarked upon my delicate features. I would feel slightly more reassured.

My mother, who usually balked at paying the extra three cents for a tiny cup of ketchup, sprang for two. We gathered up our sandwiches, French fries, drinks, and extra ketchup, and settled down on a picnic bench. I opened up my hamburger and looked at the pickles. Just looking at them, their diaphanous green texture coagulated with ketchup, was a great pleasure of mine. My embarrassment at having been roped in by the Round-Up was over. I was happy. I turned around to check the arches. The numbers hadn't changed since my last visit—over 9 million hamburgers had been sold.

"It's still the same," Jane said.

"I wonder if we're the next millionth hamburger," I said. "Maybe they'll change the numbers while we're here."

"That would be fun," Jane said.

Next to us, the two adults had begun a soft undercurrent of conversation that I recognized as mother talk. A French fry slid up and down Mrs. Gilbert's lip as she nodded vigorously to my mother's remarks. My mother, for her part, seemed to have carved out several sentences, a whole speech it seemed to me, or at least a paragraph. I had never seen her speak so long without being interrupted. Having friends, I suddenly realized, was different from having a family.

The soothing chords of their conversation glided to a close.

Though I couldn't distinguish the words, the glissade at the end indicated a question. Mrs. Gilbert's eyes widened in thought. A ringlet dropping by her temple formed the curve of a question mark. My own eyes grew large in imitation. I felt at my hair and came up against thin straight bangs.

I had always noticed Mrs. Gilbert's coiffure. The styles mothers chose were such a consistent source of disappointment that I had come to view marriage as something to avoid for fear of what it would do to my hair. Mrs. Gilbert's blondish hair was a particular tragedy, I thought. Sectioned out by a home perm, it had taken on a plaid effect. Some swatches hung loosely, fuzzily straight; other swatches had been conscripted into maladroit dollops. Yet her hair so easily could have been beautiful.

My mother's hair, a uniform brown bob, was less startling, with less potential, but neither had she ruined it. It was not the style I would have chosen for me or for my Barbie dolls, but it was a lot better than Mrs. Gilbert's.

I moved up to their faces. It was no contest. There was nothing to say. My mother was beautiful. Mrs. Gilbert was not. She had a pert nose with a slight gully at its tip, and a small chin that trembled when she was excited, as she often was. She was cute, cute enough for jobs in the support services, secretarial, nursing—but not cute enough to strike out on her own. My mother, however, could strike out on her own. That was what I liked to think.

As we got into our cars to go home, I heard Jane telling her mom that we had been hoping to be the next millionth hamburger so we could see them change the sign. It was a long explanation. At the end of it Mrs. Gilbert exclaimed, "That would have been fun!"

They were a team, I saw, a mother-daughter team. I looked over at my own mother. We were a team too. A better team. On the way home my mother told me that the nickname for Sylvester is Sly. "As in sly like a fox," she added.

"Oh," I said. I took this bit of information to heart.

When we pulled into the driveway my dad was under the hood of our second car. His head lifted to view our arrival. Then it dropped down to the engine. Tricked into believing I was safe, I tried to hurry away. But the beam of his flashlight caught me. I didn't know if this was torture or solicitude. I got to watch the gawky hitch of my shadow all the way into the house. Was he playing? Did he want a hug? Was he angry? I was never sure. Angry or in a good mood, it was about the same. Freeze tag, Catch, Hopscotch. He would suggest these games to me in a good mood and when I demurred he would suggest them to me in a bad mood.

The same sort of mercury fluctuated through my sister's veins. She was in the seventh grade and she and her girlfriend Dale DuKane spent all their time in the bedroom, dancing to Beatle records. My mother and I were consigned to eavesdropping through the door. They danced until they stunk up the room with body odor—Dale DuKane body odor, for there was nothing of the smell I could associate with my sister. When it was particularly bad my sister would open the door and call us in to smell it. Dale DuKane would stand in the corner, shyly proud of her accomplishment.

The shyness was deceptive. At least it deceived me; without exactly understanding, I associated shyness with innocence and so, when Dale DuKane became pregnant two years later, I was incredulous. "Shy like a fox," my mother explained. But I refused to believe it. I couldn't fathom it. This so angered my sister that she went after Dale DuKane (they were estranged by this time), found her, and dragged us face to face for a confrontation. With that same expression of shy proudness she had accorded her body odor, she admitted she was pregnant. More importantly, she admitted she wasn't a virgin. I refused to believe either one, so my sister slapped me across the face and pulled me home. In our front yard she ripped off my braces and went inside to throw them at my mother's feet and announce I was several miles away.

My mother went screaming through the back door, squealed out the driveway, and spied me standing expressionlessly on the front porch. She didn't say a word, but her face was muscular and taut. My sister ran out singing, "She's been had, she's been had, she's been had!!"

A few nights after my appearance on *The Uncle Sylvester Show*, my sister invited my mother and me into her bedroom. A wild dancing session had left the room incredibly smelly. "Look what Dale Evans DuKane has done!" my sister screeched by way of invitation. She swung out the door like an impresario and a rank blast greeted us.

My mother, not one to waste her opportunities, took advantage of one of the few invitations to enter the inner sanctum. She strode in with clothesline rope and proceeded to tie my sister to the bed in order to cut her bangs. She had me throw my body over her on the bed, counting on my sister's basic good heart to prevent her from kicking me, and thus make the job of hog-tying that much easier. Dale DuKane retreated to a corner and howled. Once my sister was tied up, my mother came at her with the scissors, but my sister twitched her head so violently that poking out her eye became a real possibility and my mother had to desist from her bang-cutting venture. My sister shoved us out the door and threatened to kill us.

In five or ten minutes we crept back to their door and returned to eavesdropping. A fight had erupted over why Dale Du-Kane hadn't helped my sister when my mother was tying her up. Dale DuKane explained that she was laughing too hard because she thought it was just a joke; when she recovered and saw the danger of the situation, she became afraid for her own bangs. This led to another argument about whose hair was more important and whose bangs were better, meaning straighter (they spent most of their nondancing time taping their bangs with special bang tape).

After leaving them to their bangs argument, my mother chuckled to herself all through the dinner preparations. When Dale DuKane and my sister finally emerged from the bedroom, it was in the heat of battle. They confronted my mother and demanded to know whose bangs were straighter. My mother turned around with a serious face, a neutral face, the kind of face I imagine actors shaking into before the camera rolls—hold it, wait a minute wait a minute, give me a second. Okay. She looked at them and said she thought both sets of bangs were horrible and had made their foreheads all pimply, and then she returned to mashing the potatoes. Both Dale DuKane and my sister screamed with delight. Their shrieks melted right into the whine of the mixer until you couldn't tell machine or human apart. My mother went right on mashing.

When the screams rolled to a finish, I asked my sister why she had cut the bangs off all my Barbie dolls and she and Dale DuKane renewed their shrieks of delight.

But their relationship was not to last long. For people who seemed to enjoy each other so much, they constantly bickered. Their arguments, always hysterical, usually centered around the Beatles. The Beatles were not entirely unrelated to the subject of bangs, however, since Jane Asher—Paul's girlfriend—had an enviable set of straight bangs to go with her straight long hair. Dale DuKane and my sister were filled with venomous jealousy. They wrote letters to Jane Asher calling her a slut, and many more letters to Paul McCartney himself, warning him about the slatternly Jane. They were in agreement about this particular business, but their peace didn't last long. There was the little matter of Beatles lyrics.

In the song "I Want To Hold Your Hand" Dale DuKane claimed the line on the refrain was *I can't hide I can't hide I can't hide!!* My sister, on the other hand, argued that the line was *I get had I get had I get had!!*

My sister, having the strength of her convictions even when

wrong, shoved Dale DuKane against the wall. Dale DuKane responded by slapping my sister in the face. A clean crisp shot that left finger marks. Then they proceeded to rip each other's blouses off until they stood in nothing but bras and skirts.

Unfortunately this fight took place in the hallway of our elementary school. Dale DuKane got suspended for three days, while my sister got off with writing a 500-word essay. The topic was "Why Girls Should Not Fight."

Her first sentence was *Girls should not fight in a physical manner because they are younger members of the race known as women.* Every sentence that followed began *Girls also should not fight in a physical manner because in addition to the fact that they are younger members of the race known as women . . .*

In this way the 500-word essay only required about ten sentences. My sister read it aloud to us. Her conclusion was this:

> *Girls also should not fight in a physical manner because in addition to the fact that they are younger members of the race known as women, they could be having their periods and then their cramps might get worse and they would have to go to the nurse and lie down all day and miss important classes such as English, and they would have to call up someone on the phone and get the homework assignment after they got home. Also their period pad could get ripped off, and things might drop out between their legs.*

That was the end of the essay. My mother had shrunk her mouth and appeared to be munching on it as she listened. My sister was especially pleased with her lenient punishment when she found out Dale DuKane had been right all along about the lyrics.

"How do you like it?" she asked my mom.

My mother said, "Mm-hmm."

"What else?" my sister asked.

"Nothing else," my mother said.

"What else?" my sister demanded.

"Get rid of the dropping-out stuff," my mother said.

"Why!" my sister shouted, laughing hysterically. "Stuff drops out between your legs!"

"Hmm," my mother said dryly. She was ready to turn her attention elsewhere. She was not going to give my sister the response she wanted. But I had started giggling and was bent over trying to hide it, and when my mother saw me, a bubble of laughter blew through her lips. Then she stood up to do something official.

My sister followed her. She told her Dale DuKane had hair under her arms and everyone had seen it, that's why she got suspended and not her. My mother didn't react but began filling the sink with clean dishwater. Then my sister turned to me. She demonstrated how Dale DuKane had ripped her blouse to shreds.

"That was an expensive blouse," my mother added, her back to us at the sink.

"The sleeve ripped right off," my sister explained. And for the rest of the day she had been forced to wear her blouse with the sleeve missing.

"They sent you home," my mother corrected.

There was also a ripped front pocket, my sister added, that left a hole just the right size for her boob to go through. She cupped her tiny breast and demonstrated for me. I saw my mother's head turn slightly to take it in. She pruned her mouth to prevent any amusement from showing.

Then my sister told us Dale DuKane had started her period and now she could get pregnant if she kept screwing around with Doug Snow.

My mother said, "Don't use that word."

"What word do you want me to use?" my sister challenged. "You know what I mean."

I was trying to think of Jane and her mother having this conversation. Then I tried to think of Jane's mother and my sister having this conversation. I couldn't imagine it.

My father walked through the room and we fell silent. Although I had been quiet all along, he chose me to look at. He said, "What are you up to?" and I said, "Nothing." He said, "I can't walk in here without someone trying to stir things up," and continued out the door.

My mother started to chase after him, but my sister stopped her and screamed, "You know what word I mean!! Don't pretend you're so innocent!!"

My sister kept bothering her and my mother kept trying to clear her off her shoulder and do the dishes until finally she gave up and stepped outside and called my father's name. Panic creased my sister's face and she ran down the hallway and slammed the door to her bedroom. My mother asked my father to go put gas in the car. My father yelled that he wasn't going to put gas in the car until she stopped stirring things up, and if she didn't stop stirring things up she could run out of gas and then maybe she'd learn.

My mother replied she hadn't been stirring things up, what did he mean by that, and what exactly would she learn if she ran out of gas, how cruel, and he said it wasn't cruelty it was a lesson, and she said, "Oh a cruel lesson!" So began another argument that never had a clear beginning or end.

After my sister turned in her essay with its musings on menstruation, she was reprimanded and punished again. This time she was not given another essay that might allow her creative juices to flood. She was made to write this sentence five hundred times: *If I continue this pattern of disobedience, I will subsequently become a juvenile delinquent.*

My sister diagrammed the assignment in columns and colors. She drew the first column and penciled *If* on every line. Then she drew a second column, took a red pencil, and wrote *I*. She used blue ink for *continue*. By the time she reached the seventh column and the word *disobedience*, it was clear she would not be able to get the whole sentence on one line, something she should have thought of had she bothered to think ahead.

Undaunted, she scotch-taped extra sheaves of paper and widened her margins. By the time she was done, she had something that looked like a road map, words that were interstate-divided, multicolored, and accordion-creased from its mystifying system of folding.

Now that her friendship with Dale DuKane was over, she found a new friend with a rapidity that over the years would never cease to amaze me, especially when it involved men. One of the initiations her new friend had to undergo was learning the sentence *If I continue this pattern of disobedience, I will subsequently become a juvenile delinquent* and repeating it often for my mother's benefit.

The friend's name was Elizabeth Browning and one day her name was Liz, the next week Eliza, then Betsy, Beth, and so on. Each day, as we drove her home, my mother seemed to take pleasure in addressing her at every opportunity by her current name of choice. Elizabeth had tiny sharp features and her face as a whole drew back from its center point, the nose. It was an effect my mother called fox-faced, continuing her fixation with fox analogies. She was anxious to meet Elizabeth's mother, to see if they looked alike.

When they did meet, on a Saturday when my mother was taking the girls to the skating rink, I saw my mother kind of staring at Mrs. Browning and smiling in that hidden way of hers, as if she could already see the beginning, middle, and end of this person's whole rather amusing life. She asked the mother if she had named her daughter after Elizabeth Barrett Browning. Mrs. Browning said she didn't know; her husband had chosen the name.

With this the husband magically appeared at the doorway. He had on a white T-shirt and was holding a beer and did a good job of filling up the whole doorway. My mother turned and asked him if he had named his daughter after Elizabeth Barrett Browning. The husband gave her a blank, beery, not too kindly stare, which slowly rotated and settled on me, and my mother said, "You know, the famous poem, 'How do I love thee let me count the ways.'" After intoning this first line my mother closed her recitation of the poem, not out of fear of Mr. Browning but because she didn't know the rest.

My mother's obliviousness to this frightening hulk in the doorway caused a look of admiration to cross over Mrs. Browning's face, so noticeable that Mr. Browning thundered a warning. "I'm just impressed with her knowledge of books," Mrs. Browning explained, her hands sweeping us like dust balls toward our car. When we left them, I knew my mother had managed to start a big fight in her wake.

On the way to the skating rink my sister asked her to recite the rest of the poem.

"How do I love thee let me count the ways," my mother said.

"That's all you know!" my sister squawked gleefully.

My mother feigned boredom at my sister's screaming. In the backseat my sister jabbed Elizabeth into joining in. From the front seat I watched the impassive face of my mother, the only glimmer of movement the eye muscles moving back and forth to the rearview mirror.

"What do you expect from someone who has stuff dropping from her legs?"

"Stop it."

"Do you deny it?"

"Oh stop it," my mother said wearily, "or I'm dropping you home with Daddy."

"Oh stop it stop it," my sister mimicked. "And if you continue this pattern of disobedience, you will subsequently become a juvenile delinquent and I will subsequently drop you home with Daddy."

"Very funny," my mother said, though I sat beside her giggling. "Somebody thinks so."

Then my sister prodded Elizabeth into saying, "Don't you think it was mean of Mrs. Latimer to make her write that?"

"No, Betsy," my mother said. "Because that's what she is. She's going to be a juvenile delinquent."

"My name isn't Betsy," Elizabeth said. "It's Beth."

"And I would thank you for addressing me by that name," my sister prompted.

"And I would thank you for addressing me by that name," Elizabeth repeated.

"How do I name thee, let me count the ways," my mother said.

"Very funny in case you were wondering."

"You asked me to recite the poem," my mother said.

"Could you speed it up?" my sister demanded.

During these first few rides, as I was getting to know Elizabeth, my sister often browbeat her into exclaiming enthusiasm over my appearance on *The Uncle Sylvester Show*. She herself hadn't bothered to watch the show, due to lack of interest, yet she was inordinately proud of my appearance on it. Years later when I graduated from law school, she swelled with pride but neither attended the ceremony nor watched a single minute of the videotape. My college graduation she showed up for but left during the A's. Just as "Appelbaum" was being called, she bolted up from her chair with a shock of realization on her face. "Oh my God!" I could almost hear her saying. "They're calling every fucking name in alphabetical order!" Appelbaum, who was kind of a nut, grabbed the diploma and ran off like a maniac, escaping almost as fast as my sister. My mother remained blissfully ignorant, having learned by then never to sit near her daughter.

Pinned in the backseat, Elizabeth did her best to praise *The Uncle Sylvester Show*. My sister asked her if she thought I had won the Round-Up prize because I'm crippled, and Elizabeth said no. Then she asked my mother and my mother said no. Then she asked me and I said yes. My sister shrieked wildly at this. Then she asked Elizabeth if she thought I was funny and Elizabeth said she didn't know. My sister repeated this question until Elizabeth said yes. Then my sister asked, "Are you sure?" and Elizabeth said yes to this too. Then my sister told me that Dale DuKane hadn't liked me because I was crippled and this was the real reason she had ripped her blouse off. After a few seconds my sister said, "Just kidding. It was really over the Beatles. Dale DuKane really likes you." And she asked me if I believed her and I said yes. Then she said, "Are you sure?" and my mother said, "Yes, she's sure. We're all sure. Now shut up." My sister started shrieking again and asked my mom why she had done that, didn't she like her? and my mother said, "Oh yes yes yes, now PLEASE."

As usual my sister had worked herself out of control and as the ride ended she was shouting her 500-word essay, which she had memorized and was currently teaching to Elizabeth. *Also their period pad could get ripped off, and things might drop out between their legs!*

My mother swung into the parking lot of the skating rink. "Out," she said.

My sister jammed her up against the steering wheel and shoved her way out. She slammed the car door, almost taking off my mother's hand. Despite this, she turned to wave goodbye. My mother emphasized a wide *H* as she pulled the steering column gearshift into first and aimed the wheels at the two girls. My sister's mouth formed a round donut of terror and delight, and she and Elizabeth Browning took off through the parking lot with our car steadily behind.

"I'm worn out," my mother said. "How does she get like this?"

I was privy to these conversational asides since she had no one else to listen to her. "Did you notice Elizabeth's mother is fox-faced like her?" she asked me as we continued chasing them through the parking lot. I watched my sister laughing so hard she constantly stumbled in her running. I never felt so happy. I loved getting to ride along in the front seat and listen to things I shouldn't be hearing. Whenever my mother was driving them anywhere I would grab my braces like others grab their coats and flounder toward the car in a panic, braces half on half off, afraid they wouldn't wait. "Go horsey go!" my sister would yell out the window, constantly trying to get my mother to pull out of the driveway as though she were really leaving without me. During these times I felt no need to have a friend of my own along; in fact, without one, there was more of a reason for me to cling to the shadow of my sister and Elizabeth.

On a Saturday when the weather was warming up, my mother planned a trip to the Morgan Horse Farm. The drive was more than two hours long; all week I found myself anxiously looking forward to the trip, to the more than four hours I would spend in the car with Elizabeth and my sister, and I purposely neglected to invite any friend of my own.

We started early in the morning with picnic food my mother had prepared the night before. By the time we got to the edge of the city, my sister and Elizabeth had already decimated the sandwiches; however, my mother, anticipating this, had the real bag hidden away.

Once at the horse farm, my mother issued warnings to behave to both my sister and Elizabeth. But it was too late. Now that we were already here, they were going to do anything they wanted. Which they did. Even before the tour began it became apparent that the studhorse would garner all their attention; my mother, also anticipating this, had passed on our first tour guide, an older woman, and opted for a tough-looking cowboy. I heard her speak to him in a low voice while we waited for the right number of people to assemble. One of his cheeks popped in and out as he nodded to my mother. To my mother his voice was quiet and respectful, but with my sister and Elizabeth he was a tyrant with a twang. "I don't want to hear it from you two," he warned. His hand pointed to them in the shape of a pistol. They looked to my mother for salvation from this abuse, but she ignored them.

The end of the tour brought us into the museum. I wandered from there into the gift shop, where my heart sank in disbelief. Jane and her mother stood over a counter of souvenirs. My instinctive reaction was escape. I didn't want to share my sister and her friend. Of all the places in a two-hour radius, why were they here?

I turned to leave but the braces and the hitch in my stride created just enough metal clicking to turn their heads. "Hello the Boat!" Mrs. Gilbert called excitedly. This was supposed to be kind of a joke, because I had just loaned Jane a book called *Hello the Boat* and it was about early settlers floating down the Ohio River on flatboats while Indians lined up along the shore and shot arrows at them. At the sound of her voice I felt like one of their arrows had pierced me in the back. "Why hello, hello there!" I turned around with a painful smile.

A large crisp butterfly was pinned to the lapel of Mrs. Gilbert's jacket. She and Jane wore matching jumpers with ruffles. Immediately my pain vanished in the urge to hide them before my sister and Elizabeth caught sight of their sugary clothing.

I felt torn between two worlds, embarrassed to have my friendship with Jane revealed to my sister and Elizabeth; afraid for Jane, on the other hand, and the comments my sister might deliver to her directly instead of saving them for the ride home.

Then my mother walked in and greeted them without hesitation. Now it was Mrs. Gilbert who seemed overtaken by embarrassment. An untamed curl swung recklessly on her temple as she issued breathless excuses about having relatives in the area, otherwise she would have certainly extended an invitation. Her forehead began to shine. It never crossed my mind that they should have invited us to come along on their outing, but seeing an adult break into a mist of perspiration over her social lapse made me feel all the more guilty, not just for neglecting to ask Jane but for not wanting to ask her, for being so overwrought with my sister's and Elizabeth's presence I would have gladly lied to keep her away.

And so I agreed when Mrs. Gilbert mentioned what a delight it would be for Jane and me if I rode home with them in their car. Jane smiled shyly. And though I admired Jane, there was something missing. Looking at Mrs. Gilbert's butterfly, I felt the deadliness of trying to arrange oneself in a pleasing manner, but I managed nonetheless to prop myself in their backseat, pretty as a picture, and wave a pleasant farewell to my mother. I was miserable. I was with a friend and a very nice mother, and yet I had never been so unhappy.

Mrs. Gilbert stood in the parking lot enjoying a final few words with my mother. When she saw Jane and me waiting for her, her fingers toodled good-bye and she broke into a sort of a run, a mother's trot, elbows digging into her ribs and hands flapping aimlessly. My mother immediately turned to hush my sister and Elizabeth before they had even a chance to comment.

A girlish excitement shone on Mrs. Gilbert's face. She stuck her head briefly into the backseat to make sure we felt it too. Her chin trembled slightly. I wondered if Jane could have kissed her now had she asked. Would the hint of perspiration on her forehead repel Jane too? For a moment I looked over at Jane and wondered how she could stand it, how she could stand living with her own mother.

For the first part of the trip my mother's car was just in front of us as we wound along country roads. It seemed so bulky and slow, like a huge gorged scarab. I tried to picture my sister and Elizabeth screaming at my mother to speed it up. Were they talking about us? I wondered. I wished I were there to listen.

Surprisingly, Mrs. Gilbert drove with only one hand, except on curves. Her free hand roamed her body, from hairline to eyes to upper lip. Her fingers nibbled at the buttons of her blouse, ironing the front placket, toying especially at the area between her breast. All this nervous movement I held against her.

From the vantage point of the backseat I had a new angle and unlimited freedom to stare. Once again I studied the particular tragedy of her hair. It could have been so lovely. It was a brownish golden color with actual yellow streaks, thick and shiny. Many times I imagined myself having that hair and the ways I would style it once it was mine. I'd let it hang long and straight and luxurious. I would not, as Mrs. Gilbert had done, reel it in like so much tangled fishing wire. I was sick just thinking about it.

"Oh look," Mrs. Gilbert said.

Up ahead my sister and Elizabeth had turned around and were pressing their faces to the back window. Mrs. Gilbert chuckled. "Hello!" she called as though they could hear her. Then my sister started pumping the finger of one hand through the ring the other hand formed. Mrs. Gilbert put her hand close to the windshield and waved back.

The road twisted around the contour of the Appalachian Mountains. We began climbing, and my mother's car crawled more slowly. I saw my sister and Elizabeth bouncing crazily, obviously yelling at my mother to speed up. Around one of the corners appeared a sign: SCENIC VIEW AHEAD. My mother's car turned into the half circle and stopped. We pulled in behind. When she opened the car door, it was as if a volcano had been unsealed from a vacuum. Instantly there was the shrill explosion of voices. Both Jane and Mrs. Gilbert jumped.

The mothers met at the edge of the half circle and looked out over the valley. They made appreciative remarks to each other about its beauty. My sister and Elizabeth refused to get out of the car. Instead they stayed inside, screeching things like "Scenic View Ahead! Oh my God! Scenic View! The most scenic view of horse wicks in the world!!" Jane had stopped midway between the car and the edge of the escarpment. Each time she edged farther toward the view, the raucous laughter spun her head back to the car and the two people who inspired a strange kind of fear and a strange kind of attraction.

I was more decisive than Jane. I ignored the view completely and walked over to them. "Faster faster!" my sister screamed and I turned around to Jane with a knowing laugh. They may be frightening but I can handle them. I know these people was the message I was trying to send. Feeling proud and adult, aware of Jane watching me, I plopped my forearms on the open window and peered in to chatter.

"Having fun with Jane the slut?" my sister asked me. I didn't know what a slut was, but I knew it was the word she used to describe Paul McCartney's girlfriend, Jane Asher.

"Yes," I said.

"So you admit she's a slut?" my sister said.

I looked around. "What's a slut?" I asked. "Just tell me."

"A slut is someone who's crippled," Elizabeth said.

"Watch it," my sister said and slapped her, or tried to. They locked horns and were suddenly grappled and intertwined. Their bodies ground into the floor space and they disappeared. Was this the end of another friendship?

I called to my mother, who was enjoying her respite of mother talk with Mrs. Gilbert. I pointed to the car. "They're fighting," I said. With an almost motionless nod, she managed to convey her weary dismay. Then she went back to talking with Mrs. Gilbert. I joined Jane in our no-man's land, midway toward either group.

The fight must have resolved itself, for in a few minutes they began to recite my sister's 500-word essay. *Girls should not fight in a physical manner because they are younger members of the race known as women.*

"All right," my mother quickly said. "We'd better go."

"They're getting restless," Mrs. Gilbert encouraged, though it was her own face that was dropping little by little as their recitation chipped away at her genial expression. My mother stood briefly by the driver's side, and I gave her what I hoped was a longing look. *Take me with you.* I wanted my face to shout its message.

I saw a response in my mother's face.

But Mrs. Gilbert's voice innocently chirped in. "We're having a grand old time," she said.

The chanting of my sister and Elizabeth grew louder. They were fast coming to the final, obscene part of the essay. My mother flung me an italicized look, a quick look that said I'm sorry I've got to go now and you know why. I searched for a twinge to her eyes that would mirror my own sadness at being left behind. But it could hardly matter so much to her that I was stuck with Jane and Mrs. Gilbert since I would be home in two hours' time. Perhaps she even believed I was having fun, just as Mrs. Gilbert did. Would I always be thought of as having a grand old time when I was really so miserable?

I watched them drive away, trouble and wild moods and frantic adolescent love on the horizon for my sister, and what for me? Could I sense already that my future contained a procession of humble pleasures which would give more joy to others than to me? That I would be expected to feel my reward from their small kindnesses, to blush tearfully at their prizes or compliments? That warm regard and gratitude were my province, and that the more alarming passions would not be mine?

Hole

ANDREW PORTER

From *The Theory of Light and Matter* (2008)

The hole was at the end of Tal Walker's driveway. It's paved over now. But twelve summers ago Tal climbed into it and never came up again.

Weeks afterward, my mother would hug me for no reason, pulling me tight against her each time I left the house and later, at night, before I went to bed, she'd run her fingers through the bristles of my crew cut and lean close to me, whispering my name.

Tal was ten when this happened, and I was eleven. The backs of our yards touched through a row of forsythia bushes, and we had been neighbors and best friends since my parents had moved to Virginia three years before. We rode the bus together, sat next to each other in school, even slept at each other's houses, except in the summer when we slept out in the plywood fort we'd built under the Chinese elm in Tal's backyard.

Tal liked having the hole on his property. It was something no one else in the neighborhood had and he liked to talk about it when we camped out in the fort. The opening was a manhole that Tal's dad had illegally pried open, and it led to an abandoned sewer underneath their driveway. Rather than collecting their grass clippings and weeds in plastic bags as everyone else on the street did, the Walkers would lift the steel lid and dump theirs into the hole. It seemed like a secret, something illicit. We never actually knew what was in there. It was just a large empty space, so murky you could not see the bottom. Sometimes Tal would try to convince me that a family of lizard creatures lived there, just like the ones he swore he'd seen late at night by the swamp— six-foot-tall lizard people that could live on just about anything, twigs or grass, and had special vision that enabled them to see in the dark.

That was twelve years ago. My family no longer lives in Virginia and Tal is no longer alive. But this is what I tell my girlfriend when I wake at night and imagine Tal talking to me again:

It is mid-July, twelve summers ago, and Tal is yelling to me over the roar of the lawn mower less than an hour before his death. His mouth is moving but I can't hear him. Tal is ten years old and should not be mowing the lawn, but there he is. His parents are away for the day on a fishing trip at Eagle Lake, and Kyle, his older brother, has offered him fifty cents to finish the backyard for him. Tal and I are at the age when responsibility is an attractive thing, and Kyle has been nice enough on a few occasions to let us try out the mower, the same way my father has let us sit on his lap and drive his truck.

It's drought season in Virginia. No rain in two weeks and the temperature is in triple digits, predicted to top out at 105 by evening. The late afternoon air is gauzy, so thick you can feel yourself moving through it and when I squint, I can actually see the heat rising in ripples above the macadam driveway.

Tal is hurrying to finish, struggling through the shaggy grass, taking the old rusted mower in long sweeping ovals around the yard. The back of his T-shirt is soaked with sweat, and from time to time a cloud of dust billows behind him as he runs over an anthill or mud wasps' nest. It is the last hour of his life, but he doesn't know that. He is smiling. The mower chokes and spits and sometimes stalls and Tal kicks at it with his bare feet. In the shade of the Walkers' back porch, I am listening to the Top 40 countdown on the radio, already wearing my bathing suit, waiting for Tal to empty the final bag of clippings into the hole so we can go swimming at the Bradshaws' pool.

The Bradshaws are the last of the rich families in our neighborhood. Their children have all grown up and moved away, and this summer they are letting Tal and me use their pool two or three times a week. They don't mind that we curse and make a lot of noise or that we come over in just our underwear sometimes. They stay in their large, air-conditioned house, glancing out the windows from time to time to wave. We swim there naked all the time and they never know.

It's strange. Even now, I sometimes picture Tal at the end of the driveway just after he has let the mowing bag slip into the hole. He is crying and this time I tell him not to worry about it.

"Let it slide," I say. "Who cares?"

And sometimes he listens to me and we start walking down the street to the Bradshaws'. But when we reach their house, he is gone. And when I turn I realize he has started back toward the hole and it is too late.

In the retelling, the story always changes. Sometimes it's the heat of the driveway on Tal's bare feet that causes him to let the bag slip. Other times it's anxiousness—he is already thinking how the icy water is going to feel on his skin as he cannonballs off the Bradshaws' diving board. But even now, twelve years later, I am not sure about these things. And I am not sure why the bag becomes so important to him at that moment.

It is said that when you are older you can remember events that occurred years before more vividly than you could even a day or two after you experienced them. It seems true. I can no longer remember the exact moment I started writing this. But I can remember, in precise detail, the expression on Tal's face the moment he lost the mowing bag. It was partially a look of frustration, but mostly fear. Perhaps he was worried that his father would find out and take it out on him or Kyle as he'd done before, or maybe he was scared because Kyle had told him not to screw up and he'd let him down, proven he could not be trusted.

In the newspaper article, the hole is only twelve feet deep; they'd had it measured afterward. But in my memory it is deeper. The bag is at the very bottom, we know that, but even on our bellies Tal and I cannot make out its shape in the darkness. Warm fumes leak from the hole, making us a little dizzy and our eyes water, a dank odor, the scent of black syrupy grass that has been decomposing for more than a decade. Tal has a flashlight and I am holding the ladder we've carried from his garage. If Tal is nervous or even hesitant as we slide the ladder into the hole, he does not show it—he is not thinking about the lizard creatures from the swamp or anything else that might be down there. Perhaps he imagines there is nothing below but ten summers' worth of grass, waiting like a soft bed of hay.

We both stare into the hole for a moment, then Tal mounts the ladder carefully, the flashlight clamped between his teeth, and just before his mop of blond hair disappears, he glances at me and smiles—almost like he knows what is going to happen next.

A few seconds later I hear him say, "It smells like shit down here!" He says something else and laughs, but I can't hear what it is.

The flashlight never goes on. Not after I yell to him. Not after I throw sticks and tiny stones into the hole and tell him to stop fooling around. Not even after I stand in the light of the opening and threaten to take a whiz on him—even pull down my bathing suit to show him I am serious—not even then does it go on.

Later, in the tenth grade, a few years after my family had moved to Pennsylvania, I received a letter from Kyle Walker. He was living and working in Raleigh since high school. In the letter, he said he wanted to know what had happened that day. He'd always meant to ask me, but could never bring himself to do it. There was no one else who had actually been there, and it would help him out if he knew the details.

A few days later I wrote him a long letter in which I described everything in detail. I even included my own thoughts and a little bit about the dreams I had. At the end I said I would like to see him sometime if he ever made it to Pennsylvania. The letter sat on my bureau for a few weeks, but I never mailed it. I just looked at it as I went in and out of my room. After a month I put it back in my desk drawer.

Two firemen die in the attempt to rescue Tal. Two others end up with severe brain damage before the fire chief decides that they are looking at some seriously toxic fumes and are going to have to use oxygen masks and dig their way in from the sides. Later the local newspaper will say that Tal and the two firemen had probably lived about half an hour down there, that the carbon dioxide had only knocked them out at first, but that the suffocation had probably been gradual.

There is a crowd of people watching by the time the young firemen carry out Tal's body and strap it onto the stretcher. He no longer seems like someone I know. The skin on his face is a grayish blue color, and his eyes are closed like he's taking a nap. Seeing Tal this way sends Kyle into the small patch of woods on the other side of the house. Later that night Kyle will have to tell his parents, just back from their fishing trip at Eagle Lake, what has happened. There will be some screaming on the back porch and then Kyle will go into his room and not come out. For years everyone will talk about how hard it must have been on him, having to carry that type of weight so early in life.

When the last of the ambulances leave, my mother takes me home and I don't cry until late that night after everyone has gone to sleep, and then it doesn't stop. Tal's parents never speak to me again. Not even at the funeral. If they had, I might have told them what I sometimes know to be the truth in my dream: that it was me, and not Tal, who let the mowing bag slip into the hole. Or other times, that I pushed him in. Or once: that I forced him down on a dare.

That is the real story, I might say to them. But I will not tell them about the other part of my dream. The part where I go into the hole, and Tal lives.

The Bigness of the World

LORI OSTLUND

From *The Bigness of the World* (2009)

The year that Ilsa Maria Lumpkin took care of us, Martin was ten going on eleven and I, eleven going on twelve. We considered ourselves almost adults, on the cusp of no longer requiring supervision, but because our days were far more interesting with Ilsa in them, we did not force the issue. Her job was to be there waiting when we arrived home from school, to prepare snacks and help with homework and ask about our days, for our parents were deeply involved at that time with what they referred to as their "careers," both of them spending long hours engaged in activities that seemed to Martin and me nebulous at best. We understood, of course, that our mother did something at our grandfather's bank, but when our father overheard us describing her job in this way to Ilsa, he admonished us later, saying, "Your mother is vice president of the bank. That is not just *something.*"

Then, perhaps suspecting that his job seemed to us equally vague, he took out his wallet and handed Martin and me one of his business cards, on which was inscribed his name, Matthew Koeppe, and the words PR *Czar*. For several long seconds, Martin and I stared down at the card, and our father stared at us. I believe that he wanted to understand us, wanted to know, for example, how we viewed the world, what interested or frightened or perplexed us, but this required patience, something that our father lacked, for he simply did not have enough time at his disposal to be patient, to stand there and puzzle out what it was about his business card that we did not understand. Instead, he went quietly off to his study to make telephone calls, and the next day, I asked Ilsa what a *czar* was, spelling the word out because I could not imagine how to pronounce a *c* and *z* together, but she said that they were people who lived in Russia, royalty, which made no sense.

Ilsa often spent evenings with us as well, for our parents kept an intense social calendar, attending dinners that were, my mother explained, an extension of what she did all day long, but in more elegant clothing. Ilsa wore perfume when she came at night, and while neither Martin nor I liked the smell, we appreciated the gesture, the implication that she thought of being with us as an evening out. She also brought popsicles, which she hid in her purse because our parents did not approve of popsicles, though often she forgot about them until long after they had melted, and when she finally did remember and pulled them out, the seams of the packages oozing blue or red, our two favorite flavors, she would look dismayed for just a moment before announcing, "Not to worry, my young charges. We shall pop them in the freezer, and they will be as good as new." Of course, they never were as good as new but were instead like popsicles that had melted and been refrozen—shapeless with a thick, gummy coating. We ate them anyway because we did not want to hurt Ilsa's feelings, which we thought of as more real, more fragile, than other people's feelings.

Most afternoons, the three of us visited the park near our house. Though it was only four blocks away, Ilsa inevitably began to cry at some point during the walk, her emotions stirred by any number of things, which she loosely identified as *death*, *beauty*, and *inhumanity*: the bugs caught in the grilles of the cars that we passed (death); two loose dogs humping on the sidewalk across our path (beauty); and the owners who finally caught up with them and forced them apart before they were finished (inhumanity). We were not used to adults who cried freely or openly, for this was Minnesota, where people guarded their emotions, a tradition in which Martin and I had been well schooled. Ilsa, while she was from here, was not, as my mother was fond of saying, *of* here, which meant that she did not become impatient or embarrassed when we occasionally cried as well. In fact, she encouraged it. Still, I was never comfortable when it happened and did not want attention paid me over it—unlike Ilsa, who sank to the ground and sobbed while Martin and I sat on either side of her, holding her hands or resting ours on her back.

We also liked Ilsa because she was afraid of things, though not the normal things that we expected adults to be afraid of and certainly not the kinds of things that Martin and I had been taught to fear—strangers, candy found on the ground, accidentally poking out an eye. We kept careful track of her fears and divided them into two categories, the first comprising things of which she claimed to be "absolutely petrified," her euphemism for those things that she deeply disliked, among them abbreviated language of any sort. Ilsa frequently professed her disdain for what she called "the American compulsion toward brevity." She did not use contractions and scolded us when we did, claiming that they brought down the level of the conversation. Furthermore, when referring to people, she employed their full names: the first, what she called the "Christian" name although she was not, to my knowledge, actively religious; the middle, which she once described as a person's essence; and the surname, the name that, for better or worse, bound them to their families.

Ilsa eschewed all acronyms and initialisms, even those so entrenched in our vocabularies that we could not recall what the initials stood for. She once left the following message on my parents' answering machine: "I am very sorry that I will be unavailable to stay with the children Saturday evening, October 24, as I have been invited by a dear friend to spend the weekend in Washington, District of Columbia." My parents listened to this message repeatedly, always maintaining a breathless silence until the very end, at which point they exploded into laughter. I did not understand what was funny about the message, but when I asked my mother to explain, she gave one of her typically vague responses. "That Ilsa," she said. "She's just such a pistol." Something else must have occurred to her then, for a moment later she turned back to add, "We shouldn't mention this to Ilsa, Veronica. Sometimes families have their little jokes." Of course, I had no intention of telling Ilsa, a decision based not on family allegiance but on my growing sense that laughter was rarely a straightforward matter.

My mother and Ilsa first met at Weight Brigade, to which my mother had belonged for years, certainly as long as I could remember, though she had never been fat, not even plump. She was fond of saying that she had no "love relationship" with food, lingo that she had picked up at her meetings, sitting amidst women who had not just love relationships with food but desperate, passionate affairs on the side. My mother, who kept track of numbers for a living, liked that Weight Brigade promoted a strict policy of calorie counting and exercise, which she thought of in terms of debits and credits, though I suspect that what she liked most of all was the easy sense of achievement that she felt there among women who struggled terribly, and often unsuccessfully, with their weight.

She rarely missed the weekly meetings, but because she preferred to compartmentalize the various areas of her life, she disapproved greatly of Weight Brigade's phone-buddy system, under which she was paired with another member who might call her at any time, day or night, to discuss temptation. I once heard her tell my father that these conversations, mostly breathy descriptions of ice cream that only served to work her phone partner into a frenzy of desire, were akin to phone sex. After several minutes of listening to her phone buddy's chatter, she would hear the freezer door open and the rattle of a cutlery drawer, and then her phone buddy would bid her an unintelligible goodbye, speaking through, as my mother liked to put it, "a mouthful of shame."

Over the years, my mother was paired with numerous women (as well as one man), all of whom she alienated quickly, unable to sympathize with their constant cravings or the ease with which they capitulated. Furthermore, when they sobbed hysterically during weigh-ins, she dealt with them sternly, even harshly, explaining that they knew the consequences of gorging themselves on potato chips and cookies, which made their responses to the weight gain disingenuous as far as she was concerned. My mother was always very clear in her opinions; she said that in banking one had to be, that she needed to be able to size people up quickly and then carry through on her assessment without hesitation or regret, a policy that she applied at home as well, which meant that if I failed to unload the dishwasher within two hours after it finished running or lied about completing a school assignment, she moved swiftly into punishment mode and became indignant when I feigned surprise. Among the members of Weight Brigade, her approach won her no few enemies. Eventually, she was no longer assigned phone buddies, and by the time she met Ilsa, the other members were refusing even to sit near my mother at meetings, though she claimed to be unbothered by this, citing envy as their sole motivation.

Ilsa was plump when we knew her but had not always been. This we learned from photographs of her holding animals from the pound where she volunteered, a variety of cats and dogs and birds for which she had provided temporary care. She went to Weight Brigade only that one time, the time that she met my mother, and never went back because she said that she could not bear to listen to the vilification of butter and sugar, but Martin and I had seen the lists that our mother kept of her own daily caloric intake, and we suspected that Ilsa had simply been overwhelmed by the math that belonging to Weight Brigade involved, for math was another thing that "absolutely petrified" Ilsa. When my parents asked how much they owed her, she always replied, "I am sure that you must know far better than I, for I have not the remotest idea." And when Martin or I required help with our math homework, she answered in the high, quivery voice that she used when she sang opera: "Mathematics is an entirely useless subject, and we shall not waste our precious time on it." Perhaps we appeared skeptical, for she often added, "Really, my dear children, I cannot remember the last time that I used mathematics."

Ilsa's fear of math stemmed, I suspect, from the fact that she seemed unable to grasp even the basic tenets upon which math rested. Once, for example, after we had made a pizza together and taken it from the oven, she suggested that we cut it into very small pieces because she was ravenous and that way, she said, there would be more of it to go around.

"More pieces you mean?" we clarified tentatively.

"No, my silly billies. More pizza," she replied confidently, and though we tried to convince her of the impossibility of such a thing, explaining that the pizza *was* the size it was, she had laughed in a way that suggested that she was charmed by our ignorance.

Ilsa wore colorful, flowing dresses and large hats that she did not take off, even when she opened the oven door to slide a pizza inside or sat eating refrozen popsicles with us on the back deck. Her evening hats were more complicated than the daytime hats, involving not just bows but flowers and actual feathers and even, on the hat that Martin and I privately referred to as "Noah's Ark," a simple diorama of three-dimensional animals made of pressed felt. Martin and I considered Ilsa's hats extremely *tasteful*, a word that we had heard our parents use often enough to have developed a feel for. That is, she did not wear holiday-themed hats decked with Christmas tree balls or blinking Halloween pumpkins, although she did favor pastels at Easter. Still, Ilsa's hats really only seemed appropriate on the nights that she sang opera, belting out arias while we sat on the sofa and listened. Once, she performed Chinese opera for us, which was like nothing that we had ever heard before and which we both found startling and a little frightening.

Later, when we told our parents that Ilsa had sung Chinese opera for us, our mother looked perplexed and said, "I didn't know that Ilsa knew Chinese."

"She doesn't," we replied. "She just makes it up." And then Martin and I proceeded to demonstrate, imitating the sounds that Ilsa had made, high-pitched, nasally sounds that resembled the word *sure*. Our parents looked troubled by this and said that they did not want us making fun of Chinese opera, which they called an ancient and respected art form.

"But we aren't making fun of it," I replied. "We like it." This was true, but they explained that if we really liked it, we wouldn't feel compelled to imitate it, which Martin and I later agreed made no sense. We did not say so to my parents because about some things there was simply no arguing. We knew that they had spoken to Ilsa as well, for she did not sing Chinese opera again, sticking instead with Puccini and Wagner though she did not know Italian or German either.

My mother, in sartorial contrast to Ilsa, favored tailored trousers, blazers, and crisply ironed shirts, and when my father occasionally teased her about her wardrobe, pointing out that it was possible to look vice presidential without completely hiding her figure, my mother sternly reminded him that the only figures she wanted her clients thinking about were the ones that she calculated for their loans. My mother liked clothes well enough but shopped mainly by catalog in order to save time, which meant that the UPS driver visited our house frequently. His name was Bruce, and Martin and I had always known him as a sullen man who did not respond to questions about his well-being, the weather, or his day, which were the sorts of questions that our parents and the babysitters prior to Ilsa tended to ask. Ilsa, however, was not interested in such things. Rather, she offered him milk on overcast days and pomegranate juice, which my parents stocked for her, on sunny, and then, as Bruce stood on the front step drinking his milk or pomegranate juice, she asked him whether he had ever stolen a package (no) and whether he had ever opened a package out of curiosity (yes, one time, but the contents had disappointed him greatly).

Martin and I generally stood behind Ilsa during these conversations, peering around her and staring at Bruce, in awe of his transformation into a pleasant human being, but when we heard her soliciting tips on how to pack her hats so that they would not be damaged during shipping, we both stepped forward, alarmed. "Are you moving?" we asked, for we lived in fear of losing Ilsa, believing, I suppose, that we did not really deserve her.

"No, my dears. I'm simply gathering information." She clasped her hands in front of her as she did when she sang opera, the right one curled down over the left as though her fingers were engaged in a tug-of-war. "It is a very sad thing that nowadays there is so little useless information," she declaimed, affecting even more of a British accent than she normally did. "That is our beloved Oscar, of course," she added, referring to Oscar Wilde, whom she was fond of quoting.

When Bruce left, she first washed his glass and then phoned my mother at work to let her know of the package's arrival, despite the fact that packages were delivered almost daily. My mother, who was fond of prefacing comments with the words, "I'm a busy woman," rarely took these calls. Instead, Ilsa left messages with my mother's secretary, Kenneth Bloomquist, their conversation generally evolving as follows: "Hello, Mr. Bloomquist. This is Ilsa Maria Lumpkin. Would you be so kind as to let

Mrs. Koeppe know that the United Parcel Service driver has left a package?" She ended each call with neither a *goodbye* nor a *thank you* but with a statement of the time. "It is precisely 4:17 post meridiem," she would say, for even when it came to time, abbreviations were unacceptable.

Then there were the things of which Ilsa truly was afraid, but they, too, were things that I had never known adults to be afraid of. One night, as Martin and I sat at the dining room table completing our homework while Ilsa prepared grilled cheese sandwiches with pickles, she began to scream from the kitchen, a loud, continuous ejection of sound not unlike the honking of a car horn. Martin and I leapt up as one and rushed to her, both of us, I suspect, secretly wanting to be the one to calm her, though in those days he and I were rarely competitive.

"What is it?" we cried out in unison, and she pointed mutely to the bread, but when Martin examined the loaf, he found nothing odd save for a bit of green mold that had formed along the top crust. Ilsa would not go near the bread and begged him to take it into the garage and dispose of it immediately. He did not, for we both knew that my parents would not approve of such wastefulness, not when the mold could be scraped off and the bread eaten. I do not mean to suggest that my parents were in any way stingy, for they were not. However, they did not want money to stand between us and common sense, did not want us growing up under what my father was fond of calling "the tutelage of wastefulness." They were no longer churchgoers, either one of them, but Martin and I were raised according to the tenets of their residual Protestantism.

Ilsa was also deeply afraid to ride in cars with power windows, which both of ours had and which meant that she would not accept a ride home, even at the end of a very late evening. "What would happen if you were to drive into a lake?" she asked my father each time he suggested it. "However would we escape?" When my father explained to her that there were no lakes, no bodies of water of any sort, along the twelve blocks that lay between our house and her apartment, which was actually a tiny guest cottage behind another house, she laughed at him the way that she had laughed at Martin and me when we tried to explain about the pizza.

Our neighborhood was quite safe, but my father still felt obligated to walk Ilsa home, and while he complained mightily about having to do so, he always returned disheveled and laughing, and eventually my mother suggested that she walk Ilsa home sometimes instead, not because she distrusted my father, for she did not, but because she too wanted to return humming and laughing, her clothing wrinkled and covered with twigs. Martin and I encouraged this as well because we were worried about our mother, who had become increasingly distracted and often yelled at us for small things, for counting too slowly when she asked us to check how many eggs were left in the carton or forgetting to throw both dirty socks into the hamper. Of course most people will hear "twigs" and "clothing wrinkled" and think sex, and while I cannot absolutely rule this out, I am fairly sure that these outings did not involve anything as mundane as sex in the park. My certainty is based not on the child's inability to imagine her parents engaged in such things; they were probably not swingers in the classic sense of the word, but they were products of the time and just conservative enough on the surface to suggest the possibility. No, my conviction lies entirely with Ilsa.

It was my fault that things with Ilsa came to an end. One evening, after my father returned from walking her home, he went into the bathroom to brush his teeth and noticed that his toothbrush was wet. "Has one of you been playing with my toothbrush?" he asked from the hallway outside our bedrooms.

"No, Ilsa used it," I said at last, but only after he had come into my bedroom and turned on the light. "We had carrots, and she needs to brush her teeth immediately after she eats colorful foods."

My father stared at me for a moment. "Does Ilsa always use my toothbrush?"

"No," I said patiently. "Only when we have colorful foods." This was true. She had not used it since we had radishes the week before.

The next morning behind closed doors, he and my mother discussed Ilsa while Martin and I attempted, unsuccessfully, to eavesdrop. In the end, neither of them wanted to confront Ilsa about the toothbrush because they found it embarrassing. Instead, they decided to tell Ilsa that Martin and I had become old enough to supervise ourselves. We protested, suggesting that we simply buy Ilsa her own toothbrush, but my father and mother said that it was more than the toothbrush and that we really were old enough to stay alone. We insisted that we were not, but the call to Ilsa was made.

Nonetheless, for the next several weeks, my father was there waiting for us when we returned from school each day. He told us that he had made some scheduling changes at work, called in some favors, but we did not know what this meant because we still did not understand what our father did. He spent most afternoons on the telephone, talking in a jovial voice that became louder when he wanted something and louder again when the other party agreed. He did not make snacks for us, so Martin and I usually peeled carrots and then sat on my bed eating them as we talked about Ilsa, primarily concerning ourselves with two questions: whether she missed us and how we might manage to see her again. The latter was answered soon enough, for during the third week of this new arrangement, my father announced that he and my mother needed to go somewhere the next afternoon and that we would be left alone in order to prove our maturity.

The next day, we watched our parents drive away. Once they were out of sight, I began counting to two hundred and eighty, for that, Ilsa had once explained, was the amount of time that it took the average person to realize that he or she had left something behind. "Two hundred and eighty," I announced several minutes later, and since our parents had not reappeared, we went into our bedrooms and put on our dress clothes, Martin a suit and tie, which he loved having the opportunity to wear, and I, a pair of dress slacks and a sweater, which is what I generally wore for holidays and events that my parents deemed worthy of something beyond jeans. Then, because we did not have a key, we locked the door of the house from the inside and climbed out a side window, leaving it slightly ajar behind us. We knew where Ilsa lived, for our parents had pointed it out on numerous occasions, and we set off running toward her in our dress shoes, but when we were halfway there, Martin stopped suddenly.

"We don't have anything for her," he said. "We can't go without something. It wouldn't be right."

Martin was what some of the boys in his class called a *sissy* because he did not like games that involved pushing or hitting, preferring to jump rope during recess, and because he always considered the feelings of others. Though I wanted to think that I too considered the feelings of others, I often fell short, particularly when it was not convenient to do so or when my temper dictated otherwise. When it came to pushing and hitting, Martin and I fully parted ways, for I was fond of both activities. Thus, several months earlier, when I heard that three of Martin's classmates had called him a sissy, I waited for them after school and threatened to punch the next one who used the word. I should mention that while Martin had inherited my mother's slender build, I took after my father, a man who had once picked up our old refrigerator by himself and carried it out to the garage, and so the three boys had looked down at the ground for a moment and then, one by one, slunk away. When we got home, I told Ilsa what had happened, and Martin stood nearby, listening to me relate the story with a thoughtful expression on his face. He had a habit of standing erectly, like a dancer, and when I finished, she turned to him and said, "Why, it is a marvelous thing to be a sissy, Martin. You will enjoy your life much more than those boys. You will be able to cook and enjoy flowers and appreciate all sorts of music. I absolutely adore sissies."

Thus, when Martin insisted that we could not visit Ilsa without a gift, I did not argue, for I trusted Martin about such things. We turned and ran back home, re-entering through the window, and Martin went into the kitchen and put together a variety of spices—cloves, a stick of cinnamon, and a large nutmeg pit— which he wrapped in cheesecloth and tied carefully with a piece of ribbon.

"That's not a gift," I said, but Martin explained to me patiently that it was, was, in fact, the sort of gift Ilsa would love.

Fifteen minutes later, we stood on the porch of Ilsa's cottage, waiting for her to answer the door. We had already knocked three times, and I knocked twice more before I finally turned to Martin and asked fretfully, "What if she's not home?" To be honest, it had never occurred to us that Ilsa might not be home, for we could only think of Ilsa in regard to ourselves, which meant that when she was not with us, she was here, at her cottage, because we were incapable of imagining her elsewhere—certainly not with another family, caring for children who were not us.

"She must be at the pound," I said suddenly and with great relief. But Ilsa was home. As we were about to leave, she opened her door and stared at us for several distressing seconds before pulling us to her tightly. "My bunnies!" she cried out, and we thought that she meant us, but she pulled us inside and shut the door, saying, "Quickly now, before their simple little minds plot an escape," and we realized then that she truly meant rabbits.

"Martin," she said, looking him up and down, her voice low and unsteady, and then she turned and scrutinized me as well.

Her hair was pulled back in a very loose French braid, and she was not wearing a hat, the first time that either of us had seen her without one. It felt strange to be standing there in her tiny cottage, stranger yet to be seeing her without a hat, intimate in a way that seemed almost unbearable.

"You're not wearing a hat," Martin said matter-of-factly.

"I was just taking a wee nap," she replied. I could see that this was true, for her face was flushed and deeply creased from the pillow, her eyes dull with slumber, as though she had been sleeping for some time.

"We brought you something," said Martin, holding up the knotted cheesecloth.

"How lovely," she exclaimed, clapping her hands together clumsily before taking the ball of spices and holding it to her nose with both hands. She closed her eyes and inhaled deeply, but the moment went on and on, becoming uncomfortable.

"Kikes!" screamed a voice from a corner of the room, and Ilsa's eyes snapped open. "Kikes and dykes!" screamed the voice again.

"Martin, I will not tolerate such language," Ilsa said firmly.

"It wasn't me," said Martin, horrified, for we both knew what the words meant.

"I think it was him," I said, pointing to the corner where a large cage hung, inside of which perched a shabby-looking green parrot. The bird regarded us for a moment, screeched, "Ass pirates and muff divers!" leaned over, and tossed a beakful of seeds into the air like confetti.

"Of course it was him," said Ilsa. "The foul-mouthed rascal. I saved his life, but he hardly seems grateful. His name is Martin."

"Martin?" said Martin happily. "Like me?"

"Yes, I named him after you, my dear, though it was wishful thinking on my part. I dare say you could teach him a thing or two about manners."

"Why does he say those things?" asked Martin.

"Martin ended up at the pound a few months ago after his former owner, a thoroughly odious man, died in a house fire—he fell asleep smoking a cigar. Martin escaped through a window, but it seems there is no undoing the former owner's work, which made adoption terribly unlikely. They were going to put him down, so I have taken him instead." She sighed. "The bunnies—poor souls— are absolutely terrified of him."

Martin and I looked around Ilsa's living room, trying to spot the bunnies, but the only indication of them lay in the fact that Ilsa had covered her small sofa and arm chair with plastic wrap as though she were about to paint the walls. "Where are the bunnies?" I asked. I did not say so, but I was afraid of rabbits, for I had been bitten by one at an Easter event at the shopping mall several years earlier. In truth, it had been nothing more than a nibble, but it had startled me enough that I had dropped the rabbit and then been scolded by the teenage attendant for my carelessness.

"I should imagine that they are in the escritoire," she said, and Martin nodded as though he knew what the escritoire was.

"Come," said Ilsa. "Let us go into the kitchen, away from this bad-mannered fellow. We shall mull some cider using your extraordinarily thoughtful gift."

We huddled at a square yellow table inside her small, dreary kitchen, watching her pour cider from a jug into a saucepan, focusing as deeply on this task as someone charged with splitting a neutron. "How are you, Ilsa?" asked Martin, sounding strangely grown up. She dropped the spice ball into the pan, adjusted the flame, and only then turned to answer.

"I am positively exuberant," she replied. "Indeed, Martin, things could not be better here at 53 Ridgecrest Drive." She paused, as though considering what topic we might discuss next, and then she asked how we were and, after we had both answered that we were well, she asked about our parents. We were in the habit of answering Ilsa honestly, and so I told her that our parents seemed strange lately.

"Strange?" she said, her mouth curling up as though the word had a taste attached to it that she did not care for.

"Yes," I said. "For one thing, our father is home every day when we arrive from school"—Martin looked at me, for on the way over we had agreed that we would not tell Ilsa this, lest it hurt her feelings to know that our parents had lied, so I went on quickly—"and our mother is gone until very late most nights, and when she is home, she hardly speaks, even to our father."

"I see," said Ilsa, but not as though she really did, and then she stood and ladled up three cups of cider, which she placed on saucers and carried to the table, one cup at a time. She fished out the soggy bundle of spices and placed that on a fourth saucer, which she set in the middle of the table as though it were a centerpiece, something aesthetically pleasing for us to consider as we sipped our cider.

"I may presume that your parents are aware of your visit to me?" she said, and we both held our cups to our mouths and blew across the surface of the cider, watching as it rippled slightly, and finally Martin replied that they were not.

"Children," Ilsa said, "that will not do." This was the closest that Ilsa had ever come to actually scolding us, though her tone spoke more of exhaustion than disapproval, and we both looked up at her sadly.

"I shall ring them immediately," she said.

"They aren't home," I told her.

Ilsa consulted her watch, holding it up very close to her eyes in order to make out the numbers because the watch was tiny, the face no larger than a dime. Once I had asked Ilsa why she did not get a bigger watch, one that she could simply glance at the way that other people did, but she said that that was precisely the reason—that one should never get into the habit of glancing at one's watch. "Please excuse me, my dears. I see that it is time to visit my apothecary," she said, and she stood and left the room.

"What is her apothecary?" I asked Martin, whispering, and he whispered back that he did not know but that perhaps she was referring to the bathroom.

We were quiet then, studying Ilsa's kitchen in a way that we had not been able to do when she was present. There was only one window, a single pane that faced a cement wall. This accounted for the dreariness, this and the fact that the room was tiny, three or even four times smaller than our kitchen. When I commented on this to Martin, he said, "I think that Ilsa's kitchen is the perfect size. You know what she always says—that she gets lost in our kitchen." But his tone was defensive, and I knew that he was disappointed as well.

"There's no island," I said suddenly. Our parents' kitchen had not one island but two, which Ilsa had given names. The one nearest the stove she called Jamaica and the other, Haiti, and when we helped her cook, she would hand us things, saying, "Ferry this cutting board over to Haiti," and "Tomatoes at the south end of Jamaica, please." Once, during a period when she had been enamored of religious dietary restrictions, she had announced, "Dairy on Jamaica, my young sous chefs. Meat on Haiti," and we had cooked the entire meal according to her notions of kosher, though when it came time to eat, she had forgotten about the rules, stacking cheese and bacon on our hamburgers and pouring us each a large glass of milk.

From the other room, we heard a sound like maracas being rattled, which made me think of our birthdays because our parents always took us to Mexican Village, where a mariachi band came to our table and sang "Happy Birthday" in Spanish. We heard water running and then the parrot screaming obscenities again as Ilsa passed through the living room and back into the kitchen. She had put on a hat, one that we had not seen before, white with a bit of peacock feather glued to one side.

"This has been an absolutely splendid visit, but I must be getting the two of you home," she said. "Gather your things, my goslings." But we had come with nothing save the spices, which now sat in a pool of brown liquid, and so we had no things to gather.

When we arrived home that afternoon, our father was already there, waiting for us at the dining room table, where he sat with the tips of his hands pressed together forming a peak. He did not ask where we had been but instead told us to sit down because he needed to explain something to us, something about our mother, who would not be coming home that day. "You know that your mother works for your grandfather?" he began, and we nodded and waited. "Well, your grandfather has done something wrong. He's taken money from the bank."

"But it's his bank," I replied.

"Yes," said my father. "But the money is not his. It belongs to the people who use the bank, who put their money there so that it will be safe."

Again, we nodded, for we understood this about banks. In fact, we both had our own accounts at the bank, where we kept the money that we received for our birthdays. "He stole money?" I asked, for that is how it sounded, and I wanted to be sure.

"Well," said my father. "It's called embezzling." But when I looked up embezzling that evening, I discovered that our grandfather had indeed stolen money.

"And what about our mother?" Martin asked.

"It's complicated," said our father, "but they've arrested her also."

"Arrested?" I said, for there had been no talk of arresting before this.

"Yes," said my father, and then he began to cry.

We had never seen our father cry. He was, I learned that day, a silent crier. He laid his head on the table, his arms forming a nest around it, and we knew that he was crying only because his shoulders heaved up and down. I sat very still, not looking at him because I did not know how to think of him as anything but my father, instead focusing on the overhead light, waiting for it to click, which it generally did every thirty seconds or so. The sound was actually somewhere between a click and a scratch, easy to hear but apparently difficult to fix, for numerous electricians had been called in to do so and had failed. I had always complained mightily about the clicking, which prevented me from concentrating on my homework, but that day as I sat at the table with my weeping father and Martin, the light was silent, unexpectedly and overwhelmingly silent.

Then, without first consulting me with his eyes, our custom in matters relating to our parents, Martin slipped from his chair and stood next to my father, and, after a moment, placed a hand on my father's shoulder. In those days, Martin's hands were unusually plump, at odds with the rest of his body, and from where I sat, directly across from my father, Martin's hand looked like a fat, white bullfrog perched on my father's shoulder. My father's sobbing turned audible, a high-pitched whimper like a dog makes when left alone in a car, and then quickly flattened out and stopped.

"It will be okay," Martin said, rubbing my father's shoulder with his fat, white hand, and my father sat up and nodded several times in rapid succession, gulping as though he had been underwater.

But it would not be okay. After a very long trial, my mother went to jail, eight years with the possibility of parole after six. My grandfather was put on trial as well, but he died of a heart attack on the second day, leaving my mother to face the jury and crowded courtroom alone. Her lawyers wanted to blame everything on him, arguing that he was dead and thus unable to deny the charges or be punished, advice that my mother resisted until it became clear that she might be facing an even longer sentence. Martin and I learned all of this from the newspaper, which we were not supposed to read but did, and from the taunts hurled at us by children who used to be our friends but were no longer allowed to play with us because many of their parents had money in my grandfather's bank and even those who didn't felt that my mother had betrayed the entire community.

We missed her terribly in the beginning, my father most of all, though I believe that he grieved not at being separated from her but because the person she was, or that he had thought she was, no longer existed, which meant that he grieved almost as though she were dead. There was some speculation in the newspaper about my father, about what was referred to as his "possible complicity," but I remain convinced to this day that my father knew nothing about what had been going on at the bank, though whether it was true that it was all my grandfather's doing, that my mother had been nothing more than a loyal daughter as her lawyers claimed—this I will never know. Martin was of the opinion that it shouldn't matter, not to us, but I felt otherwise, particularly when he came home from school with scratches and bruises and black eyes that I knew were given to him because of her, though he always shrugged his shoulders when my father asked what had happened to him and, with a small smile, gave the same reply: "Such is the life of a fairy." My father did not know how to respond to words like *sissy* and *fairy*, nor to the matter-of-fact manner in which Martin uttered them, and so he said nothing, rubbing his ear vigorously for a moment and then turning away, as was his habit when presented with something that he would rather not hear.

Of course, as Ilsa walked us home from her cottage that day, we had no inkling of what lay ahead, no way of knowing that the familiar terrain of our childhoods would soon become a vast, unmarked landscape in which we would be left to wander, motherless and, it seemed to us at times, fatherless as well. Rather, as we walked along holding hands with Ilsa, our concerns were immediate. I fretted aloud that our parents would be angry, but Ilsa assured me that they were more likely to be worried, and though I did not like the idea of worrying them, it seemed far preferable to their anger. There was also the matter of Ilsa herself, Ilsa, who, even with her hat on, seemed unfamiliar, and so Martin and I worked desperately to interest her in the things that we saw around us, things that would have normally moved her to tears but which she now seemed hardly to notice. Across our path was a snail that had presumably been wooed out onto the sidewalk during the previous day's rain and crushed to bits by passersby. I stopped and pointed to it, waiting for her to cry out, "Death, be not proud!" and then to squeeze her eyes shut while allowing us to lead her safely past it, but she glanced at the crushed bits with no more interest than she would have shown a discarded candy wrapper.

As we neared our house, I could see my father's car in the driveway. "Can we visit you again, Ilsa?" I asked, turning to her.

"I am afraid that that will not be possible, children," she said. "You see, I will be setting off very soon—really any day now—on a long journey. I suspect that I may be gone for quite some time."

"Are you going to see the ocean?" I asked. At that time in my life I could not imagine anything more terrifying than the ocean, which I knew about only from maps and school and movies.

"Yes," she said after giving the question some thought. "As a matter of fact, I believe that I will see the ocean. Have you ever seen the ocean, children?" Martin and I replied that we had not.

"But you must," she said gravely. "You absolutely must see the ocean."

"Why?" I asked, both frightened and encouraged by her tone. "Why must we?"

"Well," she said after a moment. "However can you expect to understand the bigness of the world if you do not see the ocean?"

"Is there no other way?" Martin asked.

"I suppose there are other ways," Ilsa conceded. "Though certainly the ocean is the most effective."

"But why must we understand the bigness of the world?" I asked.

We were in front of our house by then, and Ilsa stopped and looked at us. "My dear Martin and Veronica," she said in the high, quivery voice that we had been longing for. "I know it may sound frightening, yet I assure you that there have been times in my life when the bigness of the world was my only consolation."

Then, she gave us each a small kiss on the forehead, and we watched her go, her gait unsteady like that of someone thinking too much about the simple act of walking, her white hat bobbing like a sail. At the corner she stopped and turned, and seeing us there still, called, "In you go, children. Your parents will be waiting," so that these were Ilsa's final words to us—ordinary and rushed and, as we would soon discover, untrue.

Held

AMINA GAUTIER

From *At-Risk* (2011)

Kim knew better than to ask for a favor while her mother's shows were on. Her mother sat on the love seat, positioned directly in front of the TV, with newspaper spread out across her lap. She was peeling potatoes to make french fries, routinely dropping peelings onto the newspaper without ever looking at her hands or the knife. She kept her eyes glued on the television, watching *Hawaii Five-O*. She ignored Kim. When Kim crossed in front of the TV, her mother didn't even blink. All she said was, "You not made of glass."

"Ma, please?" Kim whined. "She's your only granddaughter."

Kim's mother turned to face her. She was still young. Thirty-five. But she was the mother of three and her face showed it. "Don't even look at me like that," her mother said. "I already told you no. Don't make me repeat myself."

Ever since she'd had the baby, Kim had been expecting something different from her own mother. Something more along the lines of guidance and advice. She expected her mother to give her pointers and tips, to provide free babysitting, to help her along as if she was an apprentice learning under a master. She hadn't expected the quiet censure her mother gave off without trying, the way she prefaced everything she said to Kim with "Now that you're a mother" or "Now that you think you grown." That was before she realized that her mother was most likely just jealous of her. After all, she had gotten her figure back quickly and naturally without having to exercise. She had rubbed cocoa butter onto her swollen belly every day of her pregnancy once her friend told her about it, and now she had no stretch marks. Kim had seen her mother walking around the house in a bra and slip, had seen the light brown streaks across her stomach stretching like a hand upwards towards her breasts. No wonder she was jealous.

A loud cry came from the bedroom Kim shared with her younger sister.

Her mother looked past her to the television and said, "You better go see to the baby. I don't know why you left her alone in there with only Asha anyway."

Kim didn't run; the baby was always crying and it was never over anything important. She crossed the crowded bedroom, walking past the two twin beds and toward the baby's crib, stepping over Asha, who was lying on the floor reading comic books, oblivious. "What happened?" Kim asked her. "What'd you do?"

"Nothing." Asha looked up from her comic book. She had the look of her father about her, deep brown skin and owlish eyes. "What did Ma say?"

"What you think?"

"Told you."

"Shut up." Kim looked down at the baby. She was lying on her back, staring up at Kim as she cried, naked except for her diaper.

"When are you gonna do my hair?" Asha asked. Her thick hair was wild around her head, making her look like she'd just woken up.

"Later."

"You already said that twice today."

"I'm saying it again," Kim said, looking down at the baby without really seeing her, her eyes blurring with tears. Let either of her two sisters need something, and her mother would no doubt break her neck falling all over herself. But let Kim ask for one little thing, and all of a sudden it was a federal case. "Why she gotta be like that?" she whispered.

"Who?" Asha asked. "Be like what?"

"Mind your business," Kim said. "Does she need to be changed?"

Asha shrugged, turning the page. "Do I look like her nanny?"

"Don't get smart." Kim rolled her eyes. She couldn't figure out how such a small infant could be so loud. She reached into the crib and tugged gently on the baby's fat brown leg. "Come on, now. Stop crying," she begged the infant. "Shush, baby. Hush now for Mommy?"

"I'm trying to read here," Asha said.

"Shut up," Kim snapped, checking the baby to see if maybe she was wet. The baby was dry and well fed. Kim didn't know why she got like this, why she cried for no reason. And she didn't know what to do to make her stop.

"What's the matter with Mommy's baby?" she asked, annoyed at how babies seemed to cry for no reason at all. There were many nights when the baby cried and Kim didn't go to her. She would just lie on the bottom of the bunk, listening to Asha snore and the baby cry. If Asha didn't wake up and complain, then Kim would let the baby go on until she got tired of crying and her breath got all huffed out like crying was a hard day's work. Asha would usually wake up by then. She would kick her foot against the mattress over Kim's head and say, "Can't you hear? You better get up."

And Kim would say, "Let her go on. She'll tire herself out."

Then Asha would kick some more and say, "I'ma tell Ma."

Kim would get up then because Asha was the youngest daughter, the baby of the family, and the apple of their mother's eye. Kim was only the middle child and not even the smart one—that was her older sister, Rashida.

Just when Kim's sleep would start getting good the baby would start crying to wake her up, uncaring that it was the middle of the night. The baby acted as if she was the only one that mattered. No one or nothing counted but her. Kim was sure she did it on purpose, just to prove she could.

On the nights when Kim did get up, the baby wouldn't even be wet or hungry. As soon as Kim peered over into the crib at her, the baby would stop and smile while her brown eyes were saying, *Look what I can make you do*. Neither Kim's mother nor her sisters had ever told her that babies were sneaky that way.

Kim rummaged around the crib and found the pacifier bundled up in the thin cotton blanket. She rubbed the lint off of it and tried to stick it in the baby's mouth, but she wouldn't take it. The baby cried with her mouth open so wide that Kim could see the back of her throat. Kim decided to be firm with her. "You gotta stop this noise right now," she said, but the baby continued.

"I hope she get laryngitis," Asha muttered, trying to turn her pages as loudly as possible.

"You be quiet," Kim said. "Nobody asked you."

Kim wondered if what Asha said was true, if the baby really could cry her voice away. "Please don't do that," she whispered so that Asha wouldn't hear. "Just stop crying for a minute. Just one minute, okay, please?" She took her daughter out of the crib and bounced her on her knee to see if that would work. The child stopped for a moment, then began anew in another fresh bout of squalling.

Asha said, "Maybe she's hungry."

"I already fed her. I did everything. Fed her. Burped her. Changed her. It's like she don't never stop." Kim looked at her daughter. "You don't never stop, do you?"

"If she answer you, I'm calling *Ripley's Believe It or Not!*" Asha said, no help at all to anyone.

Kim took the baby down the hallway and called to her mother.

"Ma! What am I supposed to do?"

Her mother shouted from the living room, "I know you not asking me nothing. You ain't want my advice this time last year, don't ask me nothing now." Then she turned the volume of the TV up louder to drown out the crying. The show was ending. Kim heard McGarrett say, "Book 'em, Danno. Murder one."

"Ma, can't you just watch her for two hours? Just this once? Please?"

"Two hours here, two hours there. Next thing you know I'll be running a day care center. I already raised my kids," she said.

"Yeah. What a fine job," Kim muttered.

"And don't think I can't hear you!" her mother shouted back.

"Dang. Don't have a heart attack," Kim said softly, making sure her mother couldn't hear this time. Why did it always have to be a federal case when she asked her mother to watch the baby?

Kim brought the baby back into her bedroom and put her into the crib. She retrieved the pacifier and forced it into the baby's mouth. Then she curled her hair and changed her clothes for the third time, switching from her cutoff denim shorts to a tight skirt and a shirt that left her stomach bare, glad that her old clothes finally fit her right. She looked at her watch and wondered if she would ever be able to get out of the house today.

None of her girlfriends had this problem. Their mothers were always willing to help out. They were supportive. But no, she had to live with a bunch of selfish people. Ever since she had the baby she hardly ever went out. By the time she'd dressed the baby and combed her hair just so, something would come up. Or if she actually made it out the door, little Danielle would cry or fuss or spit up before Kim could even get three blocks and she'd have to bring her right back. Kim's sister Asha was too young to watch the baby and Rashida was always too busy studying for her CUNY courses. And whenever someone did take the baby off her hands, they acted like they were doing her a favor. Like she should bow down and kiss the ground they walked on. They tried to make her feel bad every time she left the house, as if she was abandoning the baby. Like she was wrong to want to go and see Malik. Was she out of line to still want to go out and have some fun every now and then? They acted like she was dead and buried. No one wanted to help her. No one wanted her to have any fun. She was only sixteen.

Asha lifted her head up. "Rashida can watch her when she gets home."

"What you think I'm waiting for?" Kim snapped.

Asha rolled her eyes and reached for another comic book. She had a stack of them at her left elbow. She spent all of the money their mother gave her buying comic books. She could sit still for hours reading about the Riverdale High gang. Kim couldn't understand why someone would want to be cooped up all day reading about fake people when you could be outside with real ones.

Rashida was a bookworm, too. Only she didn't read comic books. She read thick textbooks with words so small they gave Kim a headache just to see them. Rashida worked part-time and took classes at the city college. She talked numbers—balance sheets and income statements and journal entries—she wanted to be an accountant. She was the only person Kim knew taking courses during the summer. The girls Kim's age went to summer school because they had to and most of the older girls that were Rashida's age had jobs. Rashida said it would help her get her degree faster. Kim thought it was a waste of both a good summer and good looks. Kim had never seen Rashida with a boyfriend and she blamed it all on her sister's attitude and not her looks. She was pretty without having to do much, but she wouldn't take advantage of it. When the two of them went out to the supermarket or to the pizza shop, the boys watched Rashida and spoke to her, but she never answered. When cars honked at her, she pretended not to hear. Unlike Kim, she never slowed her walk to a saunter or smiled out of the corner of her mouth. Kim secretly believed that Rashida was a twenty-year-old virgin.

Kim pulled a folding chair up to the window so that she could keep an eye on what was going on outside. It was still early enough in the day that only children and old folks were outside. Harsh sunlight glinted off the awnings of the corner store across the street. Young girls with strollers walked to the park. Boys in baggy jeans despite the heat guarded the corners and pay phones. The sun rocked off of the brown bricks of her housing project. She looked down below. A boy was riding a bike, his father chasing behind him, holding the training wheels in one hand. Four girls formed a square, clapping their hands against each other and singing:

> *We're going to Kentucky*
> *We're going to the fair*
> *To see the señorita*
> *With flowers in her hair*
> *Oh shake it shake it shake it*
> *Shake it if you can*
> *Shake it like a milkshake*
> *And do the best you can*
> *Oh rumble to the bottom*
> *Rumble to the top*
> *Then turn around and turn around*
> *Until you make a stop!*

Kids her own age weren't there. They were out working their summer jobs. Or they were taking care of their children. Or they were at the park. A girl from upstairs was sitting outside on one of the benches, braiding her boyfriend's hair. At night-time, the courtyard would be filled with kids Kim's own age. Her mother would complain about the noise and say she couldn't sleep. Rashida would say she couldn't study. But Kim would love it. At night, they brought the music out. It was always like a block party with everyone outside chilling, joking, laughing, flirting, enjoying the coolness of a breeze in the few hours they had to cool down and kick back and be real before having to start all over again tomorrow.

The baby began to cry insistently. Kim went to the crib and tapped the mobile, hoping to create a distraction. Then she heard the front door unlock.

Kim didn't even let Rashida get halfway down the hallway before she grabbed her. "Your niece misses you," she said.

"Where is she?"

Kim nodded in the direction of her bedroom.

Rashida shook her head. She dropped her heavy book bag in the hallway and followed Kim into the room. She reached down into the crib and tickled the baby's stomach. "Hey, good looking."

"Hey," Kim answered.

"Not you. The baby."

"You know you're my favorite sister, right?" Kim said.

"What about me?" Asha said.

"Be quiet!" Kim hissed.

Rashida said, "I don't have any money."

"No, not money. I just need you to watch her for a little while. I gotta go see Malik." Just then, a fresh bout of crying began.

Rashida said, "I've got an accounting test tomorrow morning."

"It's not going to take long," Kim said. "I'm just going over there to get some money."

"How long?"

"Forever!" Asha piped in.

"Be quiet!" both Kim and Rashida said.

"Like two hours."

"Just some money?" Rashida held her gaze. "Why is she crying? Is she wet?"

"No she ain't wet. You think I don't know if she wet?" Kim said.

"Let me hold her." Rashida reached for the baby. She smiled at the baby and rubbed noses with her. "Hey Danielle. Hey pretty brown eyes," she sang as the baby gurgled, then grew quiet.

"How'd you do that?" Kim asked, awed.

"I didn't *do* anything."

"Maybe I can start singing like that to keep her quiet."

"You could just hold her," Rashida said. "Maybe you should give it a try."

It was just the type of thing she expected Rashida to say. Rashida would pop up with things out of the blue. She had a knack for saying things that had nothing to do with the conversation at hand. And their mother called Rashida the smart one.

"I ain't trying to raise no spoiled brat," Kim said. "I can't be holding her all the time."

"I'm not saying for you to pick her up every minute of the day, but sometimes you should just hold her so she knows she's loved and cared for."

"Can't nobody care for her more than I do," Kim said.

"I'm not talking about maintenance," Rashida said. Her voice took on that sad slow quality that it always did when she started explaining things. It made Kim feel like she was missing something important. It made her feel like a moron.

"How long has she been lying down?" Rashida asked.

"All day," Asha supplied.

"That's not true!" Kim argued.

"You never hold her," Rashida said. "I've hardly ever seen you do it."

"I do," Kim defended.

"Like when?"

"You want to know when?"

"When."

Kim couldn't think of a single time right off the top of her head, but she knew she could come up with plenty of examples if she had time to think. Besides, she spent plenty of time with the baby. She made sure to keep her hair brushed and oiled so that it would continue to grow. She kept her child clean. Now that it was summer and hot and sticky, she constantly made sure the child was covered in baby powder to keep her cool and dry. She didn't overfeed her. She was vigilant on diaper changing. She didn't see what else she could do.

"All of the time," Kim answered.

"Well then, she shouldn't be crying. She should be used to you holding her," Rashida said. She handed the baby back to Kim. "Here you go."

Kim snatched her baby back. She took the quieted child in her arms and smirked at her sister. "See? I hold her plenty." A moment later, the baby started to cry again. "Something must be wrong with her. She must be wet."

"You said she wasn't wet," Rashida said, shaking her head soberly.

"Well, maybe a tooth then. Anyway, she knows she's loved." She jiggled the crying baby. "You know you're loved, don't you?" she asked. Then she held the baby tighter and her voice became desperate. "Don't you?" she asked, shaking her.

She didn't like the way Rashida was watching her, or the way Asha was pretending not to. "I don't know why you think you can be all in my business, trying to tell me how to raise my child. Just 'cause I ask you a favor don't mean you all that. I didn't ask you for all that. I just asked you to look after her for like two hours, that's all. Dag. Think you better than somebody all the time. Forget it. I'll watch my own child. I don't need you or all of your advice."

Kim watched as her words made Rashida's face fall.

"I'm sorry," Rashida said, her eyes so round and full of wounded hurt that they reminded Kim of a deer. "I didn't mean to make you feel that way. I wasn't trying to usurp. I just don't want you to raise her like we were."

Kim knew what she meant. Their mother had barely raised them. Rashida woke them in the mornings and made them breakfast, getting out three bowls and pouring instant oatmeal and hot water into each one. All they needed to do was stir. Rashida sat them at the kitchen table and turned off the cartoons and made them do their schoolwork while she slid pans of french fries or fish sticks in the oven to bake or boiled a pot of rice. The one thing their mother did do was attempt to keep the house clean. But no matter how hard she tried, she couldn't do anything about the shabbiness. Crocheted doilies covered the coffee tables and the arms and backs of couches to hide their age. The sofa and matching love seat were old and worn; the turntable on their stereo set unit had been broken for over two years. They had three TVs, but only one worked. A nineteen-inch set sat on top of a floor model TV whose tube had blown and never been replaced. Kim didn't want her baby to grow up living like that.

"Yeah, well, you did usurp," Kim said, wondering what *usurp* meant. "And you don't have to worry about that. It'd be a cold day in hell before I ever raise my baby like that."

"If you say so."

"I do say so," Kim said. "Besides, you act like I'm a bad mother or something. I do everything I'm supposed to for her."

"Sometimes you have to do more than that," Rashida said.

"Oh?" Kim tightened her hold on the baby. "And how many children do you have?" she asked. Rashida swore somebody had died and made her an expert on every subject known to man, but for once, Kim could put her in her place. Kim waited for an answer. When Rashida didn't respond, she said, "I thought so."

Their mother came down the hallway and rapped on the door. "That baby still crying? What's going on in there?" she asked.

"Nothing," Kim said. She turned to Rashida. "So are you going to watch her or what?"

"All right. Just let me recopy my notes. Then I'll take her and you can go."

"You can study and watch her at the same time."

"No, I think I'll take her out to the park so she can get some fresh air. She likes that. You're not the only one who needs to get out every now and then," she said pointedly.

"Fine. Have fun. Don't blame me if you fail that test."

"I won't fail," Rashida said. She went back to her own room and closed the door to study.

"I won't fail," Kim mumbled in a snippy voice that she thought was a fair imitation of Rashida's. "I won't. No, not me. I never fail. I'm perfect. And I'm a better mother than you, Kim."

"Who are you talking to?" Asha asked when Kim came back in the room.

"Nobody."

"Are you about to leave?"

"Yeah."

"But you said you would braid my hair. I've been waiting for you all day."

"I'll do it later."

"What am I supposed to do until then? Walk around looking like this? You never come right back," Asha complained. Kim looked her over and felt sorry for her. Her hair was a mess. Asha must have washed it earlier in the day because it now stood out around her head in a tight tangled bush.

"Get the grease."

"It's finished."

"Then get the Vaseline."

When Asha came back with the Vaseline, Kim sat down on the edge of her bed and motioned for her little sister to position herself on the floor. Asha sat down between Kim's knees and leaned her head back so that Kim could line the part in her hair up with her nose to make it straight.

"It's not going to be nothing fancy now. I don't have time for all of that."

"I know," Asha said. "I just want you to do it and make it look nice."

"I don't have time to be making it look nice."

Kim began to part and grease sections of her sister's hair. Asha closed her eyes and said, "You always make it look nice."

Kim smiled and started to cornrow her sister's hair quickly upward into a high crown. It wasn't everyday that somebody gave her a compliment. Kim had never thought of Asha as attractive, but as she looked at her sister's smiling face, she saw the potential in Asha's good bone structure, thick brows, and curly lashes. If only she wouldn't stare at people all the time, guys might look at her twice. Maybe it was good that they didn't look at her. It meant that Asha had more time to herself. More time to read those silly comic books. The innocent and trusting ease on her face made Kim think her beautiful. She only hoped Asha stayed that way.

Kim paused at the front door before she left. Her mother was watching another show now. She had already peeled the potatoes. Now she was quartering them. Asha had already gone outside and Rashida was getting the baby ready for their trip to the park, and so it should have been easy to talk to her mother without the extra ears around. But it wasn't.

"You find somebody to watch her?" her mother asked without looking at her.

"Yeah." She started to leave. Then she turned back. "Ma?"

"Mmm?"

"Did you ever hold me?"

"What are you talking about?" she asked, looking up at Kim, her expression blank.

"I mean, when I was a baby, you know? Did you—did you used to pick me up a lot?"

"Well, you never cried a lot like your sisters. Never put up too much of a fuss—"

"I mean when I wasn't crying. When you didn't have a reason." Kim wanted to take her questions back and fly out the door. Even to her own ears, it sounded as if her life depended on the answer.

Her mother laid the knife down on the newspaper and smiled as if amused. "Yes, Kim I did hold you," she said. "I always had a reason. You were my baby. That was reason enough." When she said it and smiled as if in remembrance, with her head leaning to the side as if she was hearing a distant sound, Kim could see the pretty woman her mother had been before her kids and life had caught up to her.

Kim nodded. She felt silly for remaining in the doorway, yet she wanted to climb onto the couch. She wanted to be held again. She left the apartment quickly, knowing that if she remained she would only embarrass herself.

Kim got on the local and switched at Broadway East New York to the express. There was nowhere for her to sit on the train. She leaned against the doors, bracing herself, and read the same ads above the rail. Half of them were in Spanish. The other half were offers for invisible braces, good foot doctors, chiropractors, and legal attorneys offering to sue for malpractice. A Chinese man selling batteries, gum, and whistles moved through the car soliciting customers.

During the train ride, she made a mental promise not to get into a fight with Malik. She hated fighting in his tiny room with the thin walls, knowing that everyone in his house could hear. He wasn't a bad father. He loved to spoil the baby when he had the money. Already Danielle had two pairs of tiny gold earrings, one pair of small hoops and one pair of studs. She had a small gold bracelet. He'd even had her and the baby's name tattooed on his arm. But he was no good when it came to making steady payments or bringing routine supplies. He couldn't seem to figure out why one box of Pampers was not enough for the summer or seem to understand how fast a baby's feet could grow.

Malik kissed her and complimented her outfit. He led her past his siblings seated around the living room and drew her into his bedroom. He had a tiny box fan in his window; it hummed and blew hot air into the room. Before she sat down on the bed, Kim glanced at the mirror above his bureau. Taped to the upper left corner of it was a snapshot he had the nurses take of him, her, and the baby in the delivery room. Kim was holding the baby in her arms and Malik was leaning down beside her with an arm draped over her shoulder. Kim looked past the chubbiness of her oily face and focused on the way the three of them looked complete, like a real family, in that picture.

"I see you've still got that picture up," Kim said.

"My two ladies," Malik said. "Always." He showed off his right arm, flexing it for her, making the dark ink and cursive letters that were her and the baby's names jump. He always did it to make her laugh.

For a while, they talked as they listened to songs on the radio. He talked about work. Then he asked about the baby. He grunted when Kim told him about all the crying, but when she started to ask for money, he rolled over on the bed and closed his eyes. He said, "You're always coming over here for money."

"Where else I'm supposed to go?"

"Don't start, Kim."

"Why I gotta be starting when I ask you to take care of your daughter?"

He turned back around to face her. "You think I don't want to take care of her? Do you even see all the people living in this damn house? How you think they eat, Kim? How you think they pay the rent? How you think I get to stay here? I got to put money into this right here to make sure I got a roof over my head before I can go throw some money at you."

She hated how he did that, took her words and talked them into a way that made it seem like she was the selfish one. "She's your daughter," she said.

"I know that. And this is my family. If I say I ain't got it, I ain't got it. What, Kim? Do you think I got a stash of money lying around here and I'm hiding it from you? I ain't got it, and I wish you stop coming over here asking for shit I ain't got!"

She got off the bed. "Fine, then I won't come no more! You don't never have to worry about us!"

There were tears in her eyes that she didn't want him to see. She turned her head and smoothed out the creases in her skirt.

"Don't get like that," he said. Malik stood up and went to her. "But how you think I feel, knowing you coming on over here, knowing what you gonna ask me, knowing I got to say no again and have you look at me like I ain't shit?"

"I didn't say all that," she protested, sitting now on a corner of his bed, far away from him, tucking her hands under her thighs. "I just can't do it by myself." She could force him to pay. Her mother and sister had told her about her options. She could take him to court, garnish his checks, have him be ordered to pay child support. But then she would lose him. She'd have money coming in for her daughter, but Danielle would lose her father. If he felt all he had to do was pay, then that was all he would do. He wouldn't be in their lives. Kim had seen her friends take that route and the kids were the ones that really lost out. Besides, she didn't want any bad feelings between them. She hadn't thought about how it would make him feel to have to say no. She only knew what it felt like to hear it, then have to go back home and face the knowing eyes of her mother and sisters.

"We could get our own place," she whispered. "Then it would just be our bills. Nobody else's."

He didn't try to hide his amusement. "You not even eighteen. Can't put your name on nobody's lease."

Kim nodded. She bit her lip and fixed one of her curls that had begun to wilt.

"Look, can we just not think of this for a while?" he asked, tugging on her leg.

"No," Kim said. "I ain't come here for that."

"Okay." He took her hand and drew light circles on her palm. "Okay." Then he moved closer to her and began to kiss her until she forgot why she had originally come.

Kim got off the train and changed her mind about heading home. Without knowing she was going there, she found herself at the park.

Rashida was seated on a bench across from the kiddie swings reading out loud from a small white book. She held the baby on her lap; the stroller stood nearby. For once, the baby wasn't crying.

"Hi."

Rashida looked up from the book. "What are you doing here? Don't tell me that after all that Malik wasn't home?"

"He was there," Kim said. "I just came to get Danielle so you could study."

"I told you it was all right. I have my notes—"

"I just wanted her."

Rashida faltered for a moment, sitting stock still with the baby. Then she smiled brightly and said, "Hey. That's fine. I mean, she's yours, right? You can have her whenever you want." Rashida handed the baby over and gathered her belongings. As soon as Kim held her, the baby started to cry.

Now that she was alone with the child, Kim didn't know what to do. Most of the time, someone else was always around, watching her. Now the pressure was off of her for just a moment. No one was looking over her shoulder.

Kim changed the baby's position and held her under the arms, lifting her high. Kim wiggled her a little so that her tiny feet swung in the air. The crying stopped.

"You like that," Kim said. "Hey."

She realized that she was holding the baby incorrectly and brought her back down. She put her hands around the baby's waist and lifted her back into the air. She did it swiftly and the baby began to gurgle and make nonsense noises.

Kim brought the baby back down and held her out at arm's length so that she could look her over. All this time she had thought there was more of Malik in the child than herself. But now she could see traces of her features shining through. It was the eyes. They were hers. A dark, dark brown that made the pupils hard to see. There was a little bit of her in her daughter. She could see herself. Kim touched her daughter's cheek with a finger and smiled into the eyes that were like polished black mirrors.

The baby was quiet now, but curious. Rapt. Her eyes followed Kim's every movement. She brought the infant closer and inhaled, smelling the warm baby scent of powder and new, new skin. The baby reached for her hair and Kim laughed, feeling like the two of them were the only two people that had ever been in the world. And they were only now just meeting.

Maximiliano

ANNE RAEFF

From *The Jungle around Us* (2016)

When Simone arrived at the airport in Asunción, she was met by a sullen taxi driver sent by her sister Juliet, who had not been able to get off early from her job teaching English to pick Simone up herself. The taxi driver insisted on carrying both of her bags, and she felt somewhat ridiculous walking behind him, bagless. He had to stop twice to catch his breath, but each time Simone offered to help he shook his head angrily. Simone suspected he had a heart condition of which he was not aware.

Simone was a home health care worker. She had begun working in this field part-time for an organization called Student Help for the Elderly when she was in college, and when she graduated, she was still working for Mrs. Levinson. Mrs. Levinson's son paid her well, above the going rate, since Simone was the only health care worker that his mother would tolerate. The job was meant to be a stopgap measure while she figured out what she was going to do with her life, so when Mrs. Levinson died two years later and Simone had still not figured out what her next step would be, she decided to go to Paraguay to visit her sister, for whom seeing the world was, at least for now, far more important than figuring out what she was going to do with her life.

Simone was surprised when the taxi driver pulled into a long driveway that led to a large, white Spanish colonial house. She supposed she had expected a hut or a garret, which was more Juliet's style. Simone knew that Juliet was living with a man named Raúl. Juliet had written to her about him. Simone imagined that this was his house. He had recently returned to Paraguay. He had been in what Juliet had termed *self-imposed exile* in Madrid for years but had returned for his father's funeral, and then he had not gone back into exile. His father had been a traveling sales-man who had had children all over the country. Rumor had it that he even had one child with a Mennonite woman. According to Juliet, Raúl had not liked his father, and now that his father was dead, he had no reason to be far away from home.

The taxi driver brought her bags all the way to the front door, where he waited with her—though Simone had already given him a generous tip—until Juliet, who had just gotten back from work, answered the door. It had been only a year since Simone had seen her sister, but Simone's first thought was that she seemed thin, too thin. When they embraced, Juliet's arms felt brittle and limp. She looked as though she hadn't been outside in a long time. She looked, Simone thought, like a young version of one of her home health care clients.

Juliet led her from the foyer into a big living room that con-tained only one sofa and a few metal folding chairs. There were no decorations on the walls and no curtains on the windows. Ju-liet sat down on the sofa, so Simone sat on one of the folding chairs. They talked about Simone's trip, about how she had had to change planes three times, about their father. He was well. Juliet said that he wrote to her every week but that she did not write as regularly because she did not have much to report. "Par-aguay is not very interesting," she said, a statement that Simone found odd because Juliet had once told her that she could not imagine a place in the world that was not interesting, that every place had its strangeness. For Juliet strangeness in itself was interesting.

A small, plump woman entered the room carrying a tray with two tall glasses of fresh grapefruit juice. They drank the juice, and Juliet told Simone that there were more grapefruits in Paraguay than anyone knew what to do with. "After it rains it smells of rotten grapefruit, and you always have to watch for fallen grapefruits when you're walking through the city." She paused before adding, "I have come to hate grapefruit juice."

"Then why are you drinking it?" Simone asked, and Juliet laughed, but she did not offer an explanation.

Without warning Juliet jumped up and grabbed Simone's bags. "Let me show you your room. You must be tired. Do you want to take a nap? Are you hungry? Do you want to take a bath?"

Juliet was not usually jumpy. On the contrary, she was the calm one, the one who was always telling Simone to relax, to play it by ear, but Simone was too tired to give her sister's behavior much thought. After all, they had not seen each other in a year. It would take some time for them to get into the rhythm of things with each other.

"Perhaps a shower will do me good. Maybe afterward we could go for a walk," she said. Once she was clean, she would be able to think about other things, she thought. Once she'd had a shower, they would be able to talk.

"Maybe," Juliet said. "Let's see how you feel."

Simone's room was large—as large as a classroom. In it there was a single bed and one metal folding chair. Again there were no curtains and nothing on the walls, which were painted a light mint green. "There's no closet," Juliet said, and Simone told her it didn't matter, that she could keep her things in her bags.

"Are you sure?"

"I'm sure," Simone said.

There was a bathroom down the hall with a big claw-foot bathtub and no showerhead. "Everyone here takes baths," Juliet said and laughed, though Simone did not know what was funny about this either. The bathroom smelled of mildew, and the bathtub was not filthy but definitely not clean. "Do you have some Ajax or something?" Simone asked.

"What for?"

"To clean the tub."

Juliet smiled as if Simone were asking her for something completely ridiculous, like a marionette or a shoehorn, but she went and got some Ajax. "Here," she said.

Simone scrubbed the tub and then took a long bath. The bath water smelled slightly of metal, like a bagful of pennies. She was not in the habit of taking baths and was certainly not the type to take long baths, but she was tired and wasn't yet ready for what was to come next.

When they were children, Juliet and Simone did not need to talk much. They could sit on the floor in one of their bedrooms and read or draw for hours without saying a word, but they liked the fact that the other one was present, sharing the air, thinking her own thoughts. Sometimes they would lie on their stomachs listening to records for an entire rainy afternoon. Now what Simone needed was a little more time alone. She let more hot water into the bath, sank down deeper into the water. Just a little more time and she would feel revived, ready to catch up, to make plans.

In her letter, Juliet had said that she was very interested in taking a trip up north to the Chaco to see the Mennonite communities and suggested that the three of them—she, Simone, and Raúl—could do that together when Simone came to visit. In her response, Simone had mentioned that she was also quite interested in seeing the Iguazú Falls, and Juliet had replied that everyone wanted to see the Iguazú Falls. "The Iguazú Falls are not what they are cracked up to be," she wrote. Simone figured she could go on her own if Juliet did not want to accompany her. Simone did not mention that she would prefer to make the journey to the Chaco without Raúl, but that is what she thought, though of course she had not even met him yet, and it was possible that she would like him very much and that the three of them would have a great time together driving up north to see the Mennonites.

When Simone came downstairs after her bath, Juliet was not there. She found the small plump woman in the kitchen peeling potatoes. "Juliet?" she asked.

The woman said something that she did not understand.

"*Gracias*," Simone said. She explored the house. There were four more bedrooms upstairs, two of which were completely empty. The bedroom that she assumed was Juliet and Raul's was furnished like hers, only their bed was a double and in the far corner of the room was an old armoire with a mirror built into the doors. Of course, she did not enter the room. She always respected people's privacy. In her line of work that was very important. There were many live-in health care workers who snooped around—rifled through the drawers of their frail charges, read their letters, looked through photo albums, stole—but not Simone.

She sat on the sofa in the living room and waited for Juliet to return. The bath had made her even more tired, so she lay down on the sofa and closed her eyes. When she woke up, it was getting dark. She could hear the sounds of something frying coming from the kitchen, and a radio was on somewhere in the house. "Juliet," she called from the couch. "Juliet."

The small plump woman came into the living room, wiping her hands on her skirt. She said something and Simone thanked her again, and she went back to the kitchen. Simone got up and turned on the light, thinking that Juliet might have left her a note. She sat down on the couch and began crying quietly so the woman in the kitchen would not hear her, though it might have been comforting to have the woman come in, speak some words, sit down next to her. Crying was not something she did often, and she felt that she should get up from the sofa, take a walk, a run even, but she could not rouse herself. Eventually, she dozed off, jerking awake every so often only to drop off again. Finally, after what seemed like a long time but turned out to have been only an hour, she was awakened by the sound of a child singing.

"This is Maximiliano, Raúl's son," Juliet said. She and a boy of about six who was dressed in a school uniform—navy blue shorts and a white shirt and navy blue blazer—were standing very close to her in front of the couch. They were holding hands.

"Hello, Maximiliano," Simone said. "You have a beautiful name."

"He doesn't speak English," Juliet said, and then she translated what Simone had said into Spanish.

He smiled and said *"gracias"* and something else, which she did not understand. Juliet translated. "He says that it's not a name for a small child."

"But some day you will be grown up," Simone said.

"That is a long time from now," he said sadly.

"It is not as long as you think," Simone said. "Before you know it, you will be a man."

"Like my father," Maximiliano said.

"Yes, like your father," Simone said.

"But I will be different from my father," Maximiliano said.

"Of course you will be different, but you will be grown up like him," Simone said.

"And his mother?" Simone asked, turning to Juliet.

"His mother's Spanish," Juliet said. "She couldn't stand living here, so she went back to Madrid. The agreement is that Maximiliano will spend the summers in Spain. But she hardly makes an effort to call him, so it's not like she's dying to see him. Raúl's plan is to do nothing when summertime comes, to wait and see whether she'll ask for him or just let it go."

"Maybe it's not that she doesn't want to see him. Maybe she's just feeling guilty because she left," Simone said.

Juliet shrugged. "Maybe."

"You didn't tell me there was a child," Simone said.

"There's nothing to tell. He's very good, like we were when we were children. He's my very patient Spanish teacher. He gives me lists of words to memorize and tests me on them every morning at breakfast. He reads a lot and draws birds. Do you want to see the drawings?"

"Sure," Simone said. Juliet spoke to Maximiliano, and he ran out of the living room and up the stairs, returning with a large album, which he set down on the sofa next to Simone. Then he ran off to get another one. He repeated this process until there was a pile of five albums on the sofa. He sat down next to her and showed her each drawing, pointing out various features. He did not seem to mind that she did not really understand what he was saying. The drawings were almost perfect. They looked like faded photographs but were, in fact, color pencil drawings done with a light and steady hand.

After they finished looking at the drawings, the three of them ate avocado omelets and boiled potatoes. Again they drank tall glasses of grapefruit juice. When they finished eating, Maximiliano excused himself and Juliet and Simone drank coffee. Simone drank two cups even though she was in the habit of drinking coffee only in the morning.

"I could use a walk after all that caffeine," Simone suggested.

"How about a run instead? We could cover more ground."

"A run would be even better," Simone said. "Have you been running a lot?"

"Not really. How about you?"

"You know me. I always run," Simone said. "I would lose my mind if I didn't."

As soon as they were outside, Simone felt stronger. "It's perfect running weather," she said, and they were off.

They had to keep their eyes focused on the ground so as not to slip on the squashed grapefruit that lay like decapitated heads all along the sidewalks. Juliet and Simone didn't believe in chatting while running, so they didn't talk much. Juliet pointed out the important sites—the cathedral, the museum, the port. It was obvious that she hadn't been running much lately, but Simone didn't say anything. She just kept a slow, steady pace. When she noticed Juliet was getting tired, Simone said that she was worn out from the long plane ride, so they headed back. Then Simone took another bath in the water that smelled of metal, and when she came downstairs again, Raúl was there.

He was not what Simone had expected. He was old, not as old as their father, but in his forties. And he was blond. He looked German because his ancestors were, in fact, German. "There is nothing German about our family anymore, however, since we have lived in Paraguay for four generations," Raúl said.

Raúl spoke perfectly correct British English with only the slightest accent, pronouncing all his letters carefully. He used a lot of words rooted in Latin such as *ascend* and *perpetual*. "Raúl speaks many languages," Juliet explained. "Spanish, of course, German, Guaraní, the indigenous language of the Paraguayan Indians, and Latin and Greek, of course. He studied with the Jesuits and can actually carry on a conversation in Latin. He's like a priest," she said, laughing, and Raúl smiled.

"So how do you find our little country?" Raúl asked Simone.

"I have not been here long enough to have many impressions," Simone answered carefully.

He smiled, uncrossed his legs, and then immediately crossed them again.

Maximiliano came downstairs with one of his sketchbooks and sat on the floor at his father's side. He waited until there was a break in the conversation and then he asked his father if he wanted to see his latest drawings. Raúl took a long time looking at each one. He asked his son questions and his son answered. To Simone he said, "My son only wants to draw birds."

"He is still very young," she said.

"Yes, but there is something unnatural about his obsession. He has no interest in any other animals. My brother has a farm, and Maximiliano completely ignores the other animals when we visit them. He walks around the property looking up at the trees. Just last week we saw a family of monkeys and he cried and cried, enraged that his beloved birds had to share their trees with such horrible beasts."

Simone appreciated Maximiliano's loyalty to birds, but she did not know how to explain this to Raúl. He did not seem like someone who had respect for things like devotion and loyalty. "I would like to see monkeys," Simone said instead.

"Tomorrow I will take you to my brother's farm to see monkeys," he said, standing up. "And now, if you'll excuse me, I have work to do." He walked over to Juliet, kissed her lightly on the forehead, tousled Maximiliano's hair, and nodded to Simone. Then he was gone.

They ate another light meal—more avocados, a bland soup with yucca, carrots, and a few pieces of beef. Juliet and Simone drank a bottle of Argentinean wine, and Maximiliano taught Simone how to say everything that was on the table in Spanish—*plato, tenedor, cuchillo, cuchara, vaso, servilleta*. He made her repeat the words until she pronounced them just right. When she had learned them all to his satisfaction, he wanted to take her outside to learn the names of trees and flowers and birds, but Juliet said it was too dark outside.

Simone slept for a long time, and when she woke up the next morning, Juliet was just about to leave for work. "Make yourself at home," she said. She, Raúl, and Maximiliano would be back in the early afternoon. "We're taking you to Raúl's brother's farm," she said. Simone had brought *The Collected Poems of Wallace Stevens* with her and took the book down to the living room. She read her favorite poems, poems that she had read hundreds, perhaps thousands, of times before, poems that she knew by heart.

She read them aloud, very softly because she knew she was not alone—she could hear the woman working in the kitchen. The woman brought her a glass of the ubiquitous grapefruit juice.

"*Café?*" the woman asked and Simone said, "*Sí, gracias,*" and after a while the woman brought her coffee and a plate of bland cookies. "Avocado?" Simone said, holding her hands together in the shape of an avocado, but the woman smiled at her the way someone smiles when they don't understand a joke and returned to the kitchen, coming back after a few minutes with another glass of grapefruit juice. She thanked the woman, and the woman smiled and waited until Simone lifted the glass to her lips.

Simone was starving by the time Juliet, Raúl, and Maximiliano returned, but the farm, it turned out, was on the other side of the country, near the Brazilian border, so there was no time for lunch. As it was, they would not arrive before nightfall. Simone figured they would stop along the way, but they only stopped at a gas station, where she bought some nuts, which she shared with Maximiliano in the backseat. He ate the nuts one at a time, slowly, closing his eyes and chewing carefully.

They did not arrive at the farm until after ten, and once they made the turn onto the property, they drove for another twenty minutes before they arrived at the house. "All this is his property," Juliet explained. "You'll see how beautiful it is in the morning—jungle all around us."

There was a guard with a semiautomatic rifle at the gate. He saluted and pressed a button, and the gate opened. In front of them the house was completely lit up as if there were going to be a party. In the driveway they were met by a team of young men dressed like tennis players, in white shorts and shirts. The young men took their bags and led them to the house, where Raúl's brother stood in the doorway, smiling, rubbing his back against the doorjamb. Juliet had explained in the car that he suffered from some kind of skin ailment that made his back itch. When he was sitting, he squirmed in his chair like a child at a piano recital, and when he stood, he stayed near the walls, rubbing against them like a cat. He spoke the same correct and not quite accentless English that Raúl spoke. "Welcome to my home," he said to Simone, stepping away from the doorway to shake her hand.

He led them to the living room, which was decorated in a modern style—chrome and leather and glass, black and white. Raúl's brother's wife, who was Brazilian and much younger than he, was waiting for them, sitting at the edge of a white leather sofa. She was dressed for a discotheque—high-heeled silver mules, a short skirt. She got up to greet them as they entered the room, moving toward them as if she were about to break into dance.

Once they were all seated, a young maid wearing a completely white dress, so that she looked more like a nurse than a maid, brought them scotch. Raúl's brother explained that scotch was cheaper in Paraguay than in Scotland because Paraguay was a duty-free zone. He told Simone that he would be happy to get her whatever she wanted—cognac, cigarettes, whiskey. She thanked him for his offer but explained that she liked to travel light, that she did not want to be weighed down by bottles and such things. His smile seemed to imply that he knew she was making a big mistake that she would later regret.

Raúl and his brother left the room, taking Maximiliano with them. Juliet and Raúl's brother's wife chatted. Simone could tell that Juliet was trying hard to think of things to say and that the wife was answering but wasn't really trying to keep the conversation rolling. The wife kept staring at Simone. When Simone finished her scotch, the wife poured her another one without asking whether she wanted more.

The wife addressed a question to Simone, and Juliet translated. "Do you have children?"

"No," Simone said.

The wife smiled and said something to Juliet, and because Juliet did not translate it, Simone decided that she was not obligated to participate in the conversation any longer, so she got up to go outside.

"Where are you going?" Juliet asked.

"Outside," Simone said. She could tell that Juliet wanted to come with her. "Why don't you come too?"

"You go," Juliet said. "I'm fine here."

Outside Simone could hear the sound of millions of insects, and it reminded her of being in a snowstorm. Eventually she discerned other sounds besides the insects—men's voices, leaves rustling. Something was scrambling around in the bushes. It smelled of meat cooking, of barbecue.

"What are you doing outside by yourself?" Raúl said, startling her, but she didn't jump or flinch. Maximiliano was riding on his shoulders. He was looking straight ahead, sitting up straight, stiffly, and Simone could tell that he was not enjoying himself up there, that he would have preferred to be on the ground.

"Nothing," she said though it was obvious that she was just standing there, that she was not engaged in any activity.

"Well, we'll be eating soon," Raúl said. It was almost midnight.

They stood around a little longer without speaking, and then they all went back inside. Raúl lifted Maximiliano down from his shoulders. The boy's legs were shaking.

An entire side of barbecued beef, including the intestines, liver, kidneys and heart, had been prepared for them. They ate the meat with thick slices of bread and drank six bottles of wine between the five of them. Maximiliano ate scrambled eggs with tomato sauce and was taken to bed by one of the maids immediately after finishing his dinner. Simone excused herself soon afterward and was shown to her room by the same maid who had attended to Maximiliano.

Over Simone's bed was a painting of the Virgin Mary with her heart exposed. The painting was cracked and the colors muted with age. The Virgin's eyes were without expression, like glass eyes, and her mouth was too small and slightly pouty, like that of a thirteen-year-old girl forced to spend the evening with adults. Her hands were flaccid and boneless, the fingers too thin. Simone tried to read but the words floated around the page, so she turned off the light and concentrated on listening to the insects, trying to distinguish individual insect voices from the general cacophony of the night. Every once in a while a human voice interrupted her concentration, but soon she could not distinguish human from insect and she fell asleep.

The next day Simone awoke at six. She thought of waking Juliet, but she did not know how long Juliet had stayed up the night before, so she took a bath and read from a biography of Graham Greene until Juliet came downstairs. As it turned out, Raúl and his brother and his brother's wife had gone back to Asunción shortly after Simone had retired. Simone asked Juliet what was so important that made it necessary for them to drive such a long distance after a heavy dinner with so much wine, and Juliet said it was something to do with the business.

"What do you think of Raúl?" Juliet asked.

Simone did not know what to say because she did not like him, though she could not put her finger on exactly why.

"I like Maximiliano," Simone answered.

"So do I," Juliet said. "He's very smart."

"Yes, that's obvious," Simone said.

They ate breakfast, more avocados and grapefruit juice and eggs. Maximiliano, who had been delivered to the breakfast table by one of the maids, told them about a girl in his class who cried every time she heard the word *flower*, so the teacher had banned the word from the classroom, though she herself had forgotten on a few occasions. "It seems that if you know you can't say a word you find it popping up all over the place," Maximiliano said. "All the storybooks use it."

"Why does she cry when she hears *flower?*" Juliet asked.

"I don't know. She just does," he said, and then he whispered the word very quietly twice, *"Flor, flor,"* as if to test them, to see whether they might cry also.

It was decided that after breakfast the three of them would take a bird-watching walk. Maximiliano had his own binoculars, which he wore proudly around his neck, but he was careful to make sure that both Juliet and Simone got a chance to use them every time they spotted a new bird. He was good at being quiet so as not to scare away the birds. When Juliet or Simone tried to talk, he turned around, put his index finger to his lips, and opened his eyes really wide. After they had been walking for about half an hour, he spotted a toucan high up. He pointed and looked through his binoculars for what seemed like a very long time. Then he handed Simone the binoculars so she could take a look. When everyone had had a turn, Maximiliano called to the toucan, cupping his small hands around his mouth so his voice would travel. "Be careful, toucan," he said, and the toucan flew away.

They came to a broad mango tree, thick and squat and wide like a tree in a Gustav Klimt painting. Maximiliano wanted to climb it, so Simone and Juliet lifted him up to the lowest branch, from where he scrambled into the thick of the tree so that they could no longer see him. They heard him laughing and talking as if he were sitting in a café, chatting with a friend. Because it had rained the night before, there was no dry place to sit down, so Simone and Juliet stood in the sun, waiting.

"How did he get so interested in birds?" Simone asked.

"I don't know. He just likes them."

"If I had a child, I would like him to be like Maximiliano," Simone said.

Before Juliet could answer, they heard a shrill cackle and a flapping of leaves coming from the tree. "Maximiliano," Juliet called, but he did not answer. There was more scurrying, and they saw Maximiliano about ten feet above them, scooting out onto a branch. Squatting on the same branch, leaning jauntily against the trunk of the tree and watching Maximiliano, was a monkey. Maximiliano stopped, gripped the branch tightly, and turned to look at the monkey. He did not speak or cry but held the monkey's gaze. Juliet and Simone approached the tree slowly, and Maximiliano lifted one hand from the branch and put his index finger to his lips the way he had done before when he was worried about frightening the birds, so they just stood there directly underneath him, holding up their arms, ready to catch him if he fell.

The monkey edged toward Maximiliano, then stopped. Maximiliano clenched his hands more tightly on the branch. It was obvious that the monkey was thinking about what to do next. Should he leap on the boy, push him to the ground? Should he scratch out his eyes or bite? Simone could sense that something terrible was going to happen, that the monkey just could not figure out the form that his torture would take.

"Jump!" Simone screamed. Whether he understood the word or just intuitively understood what she was telling him to do, she did not know, but Maximiliano jumped. Simone did not catch him, but she broke his fall, hitting the ground first with him on top of her.

Except for a few minor scratches, Maximiliano was unscathed, but Juliet did not see it that way. "How could you tell him to jump?" she screamed.

"The monkey would have scratched out his eyes or bitten off his hand. Do you know how deadly a monkey bite is? It's like a human bite."

"It was just sitting there! It wasn't doing anything!"

"But it was planning something. Couldn't you feel it?"

"You're crazy!" Juliet said. She scooped him up and walked as fast as she could, back toward the house.

"Wait a minute," Simone said, running after her.

Juliet started running also, though it was no effort for Simone to keep up with her. "The monkey would have scratched out his eyes," she said again.

"How do you know?" Juliet said, still running, Maximiliano's feet banging against her thighs.

"I just know."

"How could you just know what a monkey is thinking?" she said, and Simone let her run ahead and into the house, up the stairs to the bathroom, where she and Maximiliano stayed for a long time. Finally, Juliet came back downstairs. She told Simone that she had cleaned Maximiliano's wounds and put him to bed. "He's very tired," she said.

"Is he sleeping?"

"Yes. Let's not tell Raúl about this."

"If you think that's best. But what about Maximiliano? Won't he tell his father?"

"No, he won't say a word," she said, and Simone knew it was true.

"What if he asks about the scrapes?" Simone asked.

"I'll just say he fell," Juliet said.

Maximiliano slept until late in the afternoon, and when he woke up the three of them ate ice cream, and because it was raining, they sat on the living room floor and played checkers. None of them mentioned the monkey.

By dinnertime Raúl, his brother, and his brother's wife still had not returned, so they ate the remnants of the previous night's barbecue and retired to their rooms. Simone stayed up late listening to the rain and reading the biography of Graham Greene. She had bought it especially for the trip and found it engrossing, even though she had never thought much of his novels, despite the fact that she had read every one of them. She thought that if she could learn to like his books, she would feel the urge to travel, to have adventures in foreign lands. She was not sure why she believed this was something she should do, but she did. Perhaps it was because she and Juliet had spent so much of their childhood dreaming of adventures. Perhaps it was because such things were so important to Juliet.

At some point late in the night, Raúl and his brother and his brother's wife came home. Simone heard them climb the stairs. She heard their laughter coming from down the hallway. Then it was silent again, except for the rain.

The next morning Simone awoke before sunrise and went for a run. She ran down the long, curveless road that connected the farm to the main highway. It was hard running because the road was still muddy from last night's rain. Her calves ached for the last few miles from too much gripping and securing, and by the time she reached the house, she could not feel her feet. They were like weights shackled to her legs, holding her down. Her legs and arms and clothes were covered with orange mud.

When she walked in the door, Maximiliano ran to meet her. He said something, and everyone except Raúl laughed.

"He said that you look like a painter, like a painter who only likes one color," Juliet explained. Then she added, "Where have you been?"

It turned out that Raúl had planned an excursion for the day. He was taking them to Iguazú Falls, and they had all been ready and waiting for over an hour. Simone apologized profusely even though she had not been informed about the excursion beforehand.

"It's too late to go now," Raúl said. It was only 8:30.

Juliet took Raúl aside and they talked in whispers. Juliet put her hand on his shoulder and he moved away. After a while, she took his hand and he did not pull away, though he still did not move closer to her. Simone stood there with orange clay all over her, and Maximiliano sat on the floor looking overly intently at his drawings. There were more whispers and a smile or two on Juliet's part. Finally, Raúl returned to where Simone was standing. "Well, if we hurry, there's still time," he said.

On the way to the falls, Simone sat in the back with Maximiliano. Raúl had come back in a different car, a big, silver Mercedes. It smelled of leather and cigarette smoke, and every time Simone opened her window, he would close it with one quick flick of a button. Maximiliano paid no attention to any of them. He sat with his nose pressed against the window looking out. Simone wondered what it was that made him so calm. She wondered whether it was from watching birds.

They came to the park and walked down the path that led to the falls. There were butterflies everywhere, thousands of them, hovering overhead, as if they were about to descend upon them, suffocate them with their colorful, dusty bodies.

Raúl was proud of the butterflies. "I bet you've never seen so many butterflies before," he said.

"No," Simone answered. "They're kind of frightening."

"Frightening?"

"You don't find them scary, unpredictable?"

"How could anyone be afraid of butterflies?" Raúl asked, looking to Juliet for help.

Juliet just shrugged.

Maximiliano was walking ahead of them. He wasn't skipping or running excitedly the way children do in parks. Rather, he was walking slowly, looking down as if he were trying to keep the butterflies at bay by pretending he did not even notice they were there. Still, they swarmed around his face, and some settled on his shoulders and his back. Simone wondered whether he could feel them, or whether their weight was too insignificant for him to notice. The adults followed Maximiliano through the cloud of butterflies, but the butterflies did not land on any of them though Simone could feel them brushing against her arms and legs.

They came to an open space and there was the falls—a giant wound of gushing red water. Simone had not expected the falls to be red. She had pictured something cooler—white water over rock. Raúl swooped down on Maximiliano, who was bending over to pick up a rock. He lifted his son high in the air and set him down on his shoulders and took off in a full gallop toward the edge of the cliff. Maximiliano did not hold on to his father's head or neck the way children do when they are riding on shoulders. He sat straight, like a knight, gripping with his knees. They reached the railing and looked out over the falls. Simone was sure that Maximiliano had his eyes closed. After a while Raúl turned, and he and Maximiliano waved.

Simone asked Juliet if Maximiliano had been to the falls before. She remembered how Juliet had dismissed the falls as a tourist destination in her last letter.

"We drive here almost every weekend," Juliet said. "Raúl likes the falls. Sometimes we stand at the railing for two hours just watching."

Simone wanted to bring up the letter, but instead she said, "It's like when we used to go to Weehawken to see the view of New York." It wasn't really like that at all since their father didn't take them there every weekend. They only went with guests, and they never stayed for more than ten minutes, though it often seemed much longer than that because no one wanted to be the first person to say he wanted to go.

Juliet laughed. "This is more impressive, don't you think?"

"Only because it's not familiar. I bet Maximiliano would prefer Weehawken," Simone said.

"Maybe, but he doesn't have much interest in large things."

"No, he doesn't," Simone said.

When they got back to the farm, they ate the usual supper of eggs and avocados and drank too much wine. Simone became unusually talkative, telling stories about Mrs. Levinson, about how she kept all her valuables in the refrigerator so she would always be able to find them. Both Raúl and Juliet laughed too hard at the stories, and Maximiliano sat listening carefully. He did not laugh when his father and Juliet laughed, the way someone who was trying to pretend he understood would do, and Simone felt that he understood what she was saying, even though she knew he couldn't. When the maid came in to take him up to bed, he left reluctantly. At the top of the stairs, he turned around and waved.

Soon after Maximiliano went to bed, Simone retired also, though she knew she would not be able to sleep until the wine wore off. She tried to read the Graham Greene biography, but she was too tipsy to concentrate. After a while, she heard Raúl and Juliet talking and laughing as they ascended the stairs. "Shh," Raúl said. "Don't wake the children."

Simone still could not sleep. After the house had been quiet for some time, she heard a door open. She got out of bed and opened her own door quietly. She saw Maximiliano creeping down the hallway toward his father and Juliet's room. She thought perhaps he was sleepwalking, so she followed him but at a distance. When he reached his father's door, he turned the knob, opening the door just enough to slip in. Simone approached the door, but she did not enter the room. From the doorway, she could see Raúl and Juliet naked, lying on the bed facing each other asleep, the sheets in an unruly pile at the foot of the bed. Maximiliano stood close to his father, his back to the doorway.

For several minutes Maximiliano watched his father sleep, and then he lifted his hand, holding it up in the air over his father's head. He held it there for a moment, but then he lowered it again without touching him, and Simone did not know whether Maximiliano had been about to strike his father, to hurt him so that he would wake up startled and afraid, or whether he had only meant to rest his hand on his father's head for a moment, just long enough to feel his warmth, and then leave him to his dreams.

Cold Places

ANTONYA NELSON

From *The Expendables* (1990)

Hersh drew circles with her toe at the end of the tub. She had been instructed by her mother to stay upstairs, so she brought the phone into the bathroom, dialed her brother's number in Lawrence, and talked as she soaked. They talked about the East High play; Hersh had a supporting part. She played the mother, as usual—she always tried for the younger roles, but always ended up in the oldest. Dress rehearsal had finished late and had been an especially good one. Her hair was still knotted on her head, and the heavy pancake makeup sweated into her bath water, turning it dirty pink. She told Lee that she was in the tub and he said not to drop the phone in the water. Then he asked about their parents, whose marriage was off and on.

Hersh told him *that* hadn't changed. "Something's happening, though," she said, "because I have to stay up here." When she'd come home, her mother had stepped from the kitchen, closing the door quickly behind her, as if keeping something from escaping. She told Hersh to go upstairs, that she could eat dinner later, although it was already late. "No whining," she had warned.

"What did you just say?" Hersh said.

"I wish things would clear up," Lee repeated. "One way or another."

"*Which* way?"

"I don't know." He had started to fade out.

"Talk into the receiver, Lee."

"I said, I don't know."

Downstairs, a door slammed and plaster trickled inside the bathroom walls. "Something's weird," Hersh said. She quit moving her foot so she could hear better. Lee was silent. Hersh imagined she heard little blizzards on the line between them. Then there was a click; someone had picked up the phone downstairs.

"Where is he?" a woman's voice said, the unmistakable voice of a drunk. "Where is he?"

"Who's that?" Lee said, loud and clear. "What's she doing on our line?"

"Where *is* he?" the woman said. Nobody answered. "I hear you breathing," she said. Then she hung up. Hersh heard another door slam, more plaster crumbling.

"What's she doing in our house?" Lee asked.

"I'll call you back." Hersh leaned over the tub's rim and set the phone in its cradle, her breasts flattened against the cool, wet porcelain. She waited for a second before she stood.

Wrapped in a towel, she went halfway downstairs, leaving foot-sized puddles on the floors and steps. Her mother met her on the landing, hands held in front of her as if to push her daughter back upstairs. Instead, she dropped them and leaned against the wall. She started crying, slipping one ineffectual hand in her jeans pocket, one in her short, dark hair.

"What, Mom?"

"Diane," her mother answered.

"Oh." Hersh wondered if that name would ever sound like a normal one again. Diane was her father's mistress. Their affair kept being over, and then not being over. Her father would live at home and then at Diane's and then, sometimes, alone at Motel 6.

"Why'd she come *here*?" Hersh hugged her towel closer, scowled uncomfortably under her makeup.

"Who knows?" her mother said. "She just showed up at the door, saying, 'Marlene, we should talk.'"

Hersh didn't meet her mother's eyes. "So where's Dad?" she asked.

"I think he's at the motel. We were both angry with him. It was an odd scene, Hersh." Her mother let loose of her hair, covered her forehead with her palm. "The three of us," she added.

"I heard you," Hersh said. True, her bathroom was over the kitchen, but all she'd heard were the tones, pitched high and low. It hadn't even occurred to her that Diane's voice was one of them.

Her mother raised her hand like a visor to look more closely at Hersh. "I'm sorry for that," she said.

Hersh shrugged, then smiled to reassure her that it was no problem.

In a new voice, her mother said, "How was rehearsal?"

When she'd left school, Hersh felt she could have run all the way home in the snow, it had gone so well. Her drama teacher had sat in the back of the auditorium, speaking into a tape recorder. Onstage, they knew they were making mistakes when they could hear the click of the machine. Afterwards, he'd said, "I'm not going to tell Hersh to bring her intensity level down—you all have to build up to it." He recommended that the cast take her example. "Become, become," he kept shouting. "Look how Hersh has *become*."

"It was okay," Hersh said. She began to shiver, felt goose bumps spreading from her chest down her arms. Her jaw, from talking, from clenching, was fatigued. She had, she suddenly remembered, a French paper to write before bed. "So where's Diane?" she asked.

"She left after your father did." Her mother paused, then, again in the other voice, said, "You look nice with your hair up. Your face is such a nice shape. Heart." She smiled and crossed her arms. "But that gray is terrible."

"It takes three days to wash out, too. And then there's more to put in before the show." Hersh imagined she and her mother could still share a normal night, talking in these voices, sitting at the kitchen table drinking tea and writing her paper.

"Well," her mother said, and her voice shifted, the conversation with Diane returning to her eyes. "I have to look for your father. You go get back in the tub. You're freezing."

Hersh nodded. She went upstairs and into the bathroom. The water felt better than it had before, hotter. Her aeronautics teacher always said you had to know the bad before the good looked good. You have to know the cold of this house in winter, Hersh thought, before you feel the hot of a bathtub. She lay back and rested her head against the rim. She soaked a washcloth and spread it over her chest, something she used to do when she was younger, taking bubble baths. She'd pretend a long line of men were waiting to kiss her. She'd indicate she was ready for the next one in line by raising a bubble-covered finger.

Outside, her mother's Falcon whirred and hacked to life. Inside, Hersh felt at the center of some disseminating structure. Here she was in the bathroom, in their house, in Wichita, in Kansas, the middle of the country. Away from her were her older sister, over to the left, in Denver, and Lee, to the right, in Lawrence. She heard her mother drive off.

What would her sister do if she were here? Hersh pictured Paige coming home and her mother herding her upstairs. Paige, the oldest, five years older than Hersh, would have sneaked back down and listened in on the conversation as if it were her right. She might not have been able to resist entering it. Even if she had resisted, on the landing Paige would have asked precisely what was going on. Her mother would have wanted Paige's advice, and there would have been a lengthy conversation about her father's lack of self-awareness. Hersh wondered why it was she could predict what Paige would do and yet still not do that thing herself. She reached for the phone to call Lee back.

"Well?" he said. She told him what she knew, which wasn't much. They sighed.

"Do you talk to people about this?" she asked.

"The affair . . . ? No."

"Why not?"

"I don't know," Lee said. Hersh pictured him looking at his shoes, elbows on his knees, fist under a red cheek.

"I almost told Lucy," Hersh said. "But I can't tell her who." Diane worked at East High, teaching government. "Lucy has her class next semester."

"Paige had her," Lee said. They were quiet again. Since they'd found out about their parents' problems, last summer, the enormity of it had overshadowed the other parts of their lives. Hersh felt selfish discussing school. Or almost anything else.

"It's like cancer," she said. "We can't talk about our friends or music or whatever because of it. Just like someone dying."

Lee laughed. At another time he might have corrected her: cancer and death aren't the same thing, he would have said. You act as if they're cause and effect.

Suddenly Hersh heard noise on the steps. "Lee," she hissed. She listened again. It was her father, she could tell by the way the steps creaked, his pace.

"Are you sure it's him?" Lee said.

She was sure. Her father walked down the hall and passed the bathroom door. She could almost feel his shadow go by. He went into her bedroom. "He's in my room," she said.

"*Your* room?"

Neither of them could figure it out. Hersh wanted to get out of the tub and lock the bathroom door; it seemed to her the only safe place in the house, the only place no one except her had been in tonight.

"I think he's hiding in there," Hersh said. From what? she wondered. Lines from rehearsal ran through her mind. *You must behave yourself. Anna, don't play like that. It's not dignified.*

"God," Lee said.

"I'm going to go," Hersh said. "I'll find out what's what and call you back."

"Okay," Lee said. He was getting his phone voice, speaking with the receiver at his throat. Far away, Hersh heard, "Goodbye."

She got dressed. She pulled the plug and let the pink tub water gurgle away. Her clothing felt heavy and oily against her clean skin. If her father weren't in her room, she could roll into her heaps of blankets, curl and burrow, discover tomorrow how the night had worked itself out.

Downstairs, all the lights were on, as if a party were about to begin. Hersh walked around—living room, dining room, kitchen—waiting to be startled. In the kitchen, she listened to the ceiling. Her father was still up there. She wondered if he was sitting on the floor. She thought he was probably sitting right by the radiator.

A green thermos Hersh didn't recognize lay on its side on the table. She remembered a poem she'd read about a jar on a hill. She hadn't understood why it was a poem, what made it a poem in a book. She shook the thermos. Empty. *Anna*, her character said, *don't play like that*. She held the thermos the way her character would, like a treasure. *Remember*, her drama teacher said. *You're starving, living on rations*. Suddenly the front doorbell started ringing, again and again. The dog, Dolores, howled from the living room. Hersh considered letting the bell ring until whoever was there gave up, but neither Dolores nor the person would stop. She went to the door.

"*Hush*." Dolores stopped, but continued to swish her tail angrily. Hersh pulled the bolts. There stood Diane, on their front porch with no coat on. It must have been near zero outside.

"Somebody stole my car," she said. She was younger than Hersh's mother, and much smaller. She wore her long red hair straight down her back, where it hung like fringe. The boys at

East High whistled at her. She and Hersh ignored each other in the halls, and Hersh had had to petition out of her class, though she couldn't tell the administrators why. Everybody knows, Hersh thought, but nobody says.

Diane didn't seem to recognize her, just kept talking as if she'd begun before the door opened. "Somebody stole my car, it's gone, goddamnit, I looked everywhere." The snow on her boots melted into puddles on the mat. Her clothing was all snowy and wet, and she slumped like something dead; she looked to Hersh as if she were melting. "Hey." Diane narrowed her eyes, thinking of something. "Your dad took my car!"

If she told Diane her father was in her room, Diane would march up there and get him out. They would go look for her car together. Hersh would lock all the doors after they had left and call Lee with an update. Or, if Diane went up there and her father refused to come out, they would shout at each other. Or she would go in Hersh's room and they would make love, right on Hersh's bed. Really, there seemed to be no end to what might happen if Diane went upstairs. Hersh wondered if Diane had ever been upstairs in their house before, in her parents' room, looking through her mother's things, lying in their bed.

"He wouldn't steal your car," she said, stepping out onto the porch. She decided Diane wasn't coming back in their house, even if she was so cold she melted and then refroze. "He wouldn't do that," Hersh repeated, but she thought, *He could do anything*.

Diane said, "That's my thermos." Hersh looked down and was surprised to see the thermos in her hand. She gave it to Diane, who immediately dropped it on the brick porch. "Oh hell," she said, and began sobbing, her whole body heaving.

In the play, Hersh's character stood for no nonsense. This sort of crying called for a slap across the face and a sharp reprimand. *Stop this at once!* she would say, and shake the crier's shoulders. To Diane, Hersh said, "We can drive around and look for your car." Diane just nodded.

They'd driven two blocks before Hersh realized she didn't know what Diane's car looked like. "It's a compact, yellow, with a dented fender," Diane told her. "Which was not my fault. My son . . ." Hersh looked over, but Diane was staring out the window. "Hard to believe this, hard to believe," she said.

They drove up First, down Quentin, up Douglas, down Bluff. No car. Diane slumped in her seat, boneless and silent, as if asleep. Several times the car skidded and weaved on the ice, but Hersh knew that nothing more could happen. The odds said nothing more could happen in one night. Diane leaned forward slowly until her forehead touched the dashboard. She seemed to be speaking to herself. "He doesn't love *her*; he loves that *house*."

Hersh realized that this could be true. The house was enormous, eighty years old, and full of furniture and repairs her father had made. Even Lee, away at school, talked about how much he missed the house. Everybody in the family had separate rooms and places for themselves. A couple of times in the last year her father had lived in the house but without seeing her mother: he'd stayed in the guest room, altered his schedule to eat alone in the kitchen. Hersh had only recently understood that all this space was a luxury. Her sister Paige once said she thought their parents' problems would have been resolved long ago if they lived in an apartment. She thought space allowed them corners in which they could avoid the issue.

"Where's your house?" Hersh asked Diane. They had covered six blocks without finding her car. The smell of stale liquor was giving Hersh a headache, and she cracked the window. Then she remembered that Diane didn't have a coat, so she rolled the window back up. She tried to think what it was like before she'd found out about her father and Diane. What had she thought about a year ago? About virginity? About her terrible habit of staring at men's crotches? The car slid around another corner. Filthy snow was piled at the curbs.

Diane rested her ear on the dashboard to face Hersh. She told her where her house was; it was closer than Hersh had thought. "Somebody stole my car. Just another goddamned thing to worry about," Diane said. "Another goddamned thing." She reached across and poked the cigarette lighter. When it popped out, she pushed it back in. Over and over. "You know what he told me? He told me you needed him around. That you were buddies, you did things together. But I can tell you don't do things with him. That would be pretty unlikely, a seventeen-year-old and her dad doing things together." She shook her head, looked out at the snow. "Right?"

Hersh thought about it. "Sometimes we make bread," she said. They would shut off the kitchen and turn on Sunday opera. Hersh assembled the ingredients; her father mixed and told her the plot to the opera. "That's about it," she added.

Diane nodded, tired, disgusted. She pointed. "There's my house."

All the lights were on there, too. Next door to Diane's, the curtains were open and Hersh could see some people sitting in reclining chairs facing the street, watching television. She knew their house would be warm, the thermostat set on 80, and she alternated between wanting to be in the room watching TV with them and wanting to yell at them, tell them what was going on outside, next door.

Diane couldn't find the door handle, and to avoid touching her Hersh climbed out of the car and went around to open the door. She worked on moving slowly, practicing for the play. She held the door for Diane, who pulled herself out and then tripped up the sidewalk to her porch, where she turned around. "No keys," she yelled. "And where's my thermos?"

Hersh found the thermos on the floor. When she picked it up, the broken glass lining rattled. "Useless," she said, but took it to Diane, who, in search of her key, had dumped the contents of her purse on the porch. She and Hersh had begun picking through the mess when the door opened. Diane's son Carl stood there barefooted, his corduroy pants low on his hips, his face foggy with sleep. He didn't say anything, just turned around and dropped solidly onto the couch.

Diane gathered everything clumsily into her hands and said, "Come in."

The TV was on, but it was a recorded show and the machine had stopped. A close-up of Dan Rather's face wobbled on the screen without sound.

"Will you wait a second?" Diane said to Hersh, and then shook Carl awake. "Get up, hon," she said. "We have to find the car." He looked at both of them, and then at the TV. He had graduated from East High the year before, just barely. Hersh knew him by reputation only, wild, dumb. He picked up the TV control box and with a little sweep clicked Dan Rather off the screen. His height and thinness and blond hair reminded Hersh of pale tapered candles.

Diane went into another room and started dialing a phone. Hersh stood awkwardly, wondering where her father sat when he came over, which one was his chair. "She's sort of drunk," she said, by way of explanation. Carl shrugged. Suddenly she remembered the gray in her hair. Horrified, she reached up and felt her stiff bun, like a hat, on her head. But Carl wasn't paying any attention.

"That's my car she's talking about, you know," he said. He combed his hair with his fingers. There were red marks on his cheeks from the couch.

"It's not stolen, I don't think," Hersh said.

"Oh, yeah? Where do you think it is, then?" Carl asked, nastily.

"I don't know," she said. Instead of being angry, she felt she could begin crying any minute. She steeled her lips. *Purse them!* her drama teacher said. *Become a hard-ass. This old gal's a hard-ass!*

Diane came back in with the phone. "I'll call till he answers," she said. Hersh wondered where she'd dialed, where she thought he was. They all stood there for a moment, and then Hersh set the broken thermos on the coffee table and said goodbye.

She was halfway down the front walk, on her way home to bed, when Carl yelled at her. "I want to look for it," he said. "Drive me over there, okay?" He ran down the walk carrying his shoes and jacket. The shoes were enormous. In the car he asked where the knob was to adjust the seat. He took up quite a lot of room, and when he set his foot on the dashboard to put on the shoe, his knee went over his shoulder.

"My dad is at our house," Hersh said. "He didn't take your car."

"Who said he did?" Carl said. The night was bright with snow. They could see everything. They slid when Hersh changed lanes, and then again when she rounded Circle Drive. "She's always doing some dumbshit thing," he added.

Hersh liked him a little better for this. She was tempted to ask, "What other dumbshit things?" That would be what her sister wanted to know. Instead, she said, "You know why we can't have an accident tonight? Because so much has happened that it couldn't get worse."

"Come on," he said. "You could have an accident real easy tonight." He laughed. "It's slick as shit. You could wreck in a second." He snapped his fingers. Hersh blushed. If she'd told Lee, he would have understood. What did her father find to say to this boy? Did he laugh at her father's stories? Did he embarrass her father? "I totaled our last car right here," Carl said. He turned to watch the intersection go by. "That was a sad day."

Fine, frozen snow blew in the streets, like dry ice. There were fewer cars out, almost none parked anywhere. It was getting late; house lights were going off. Carl kept wiping his window to clear the fog. Tomorrow, Hersh knew, she would see his fingerprints on the passenger window. Would she tell Lucy? Point to the fingerprints and say, "You won't believe this?" But then she'd have to say who it had been, and that would lead to Diane. She only had Lee to tell. Or she could call Paige in Denver. She pretended

Paige was watching her drive. She tried to relax. "See anything?" she said.

"You'll be the first to know."

Hersh ran through the questions she couldn't ask him (How long have you known? Where is your father? Do you like my father? Why do you live at home? What do you do all day?). "Did you ever go to any plays?" she decided on.

"Plays?" he said. "Oh, at school." He drew his lips back like a horse. "Nope. Your dad talks about them all the time, though. He says you're good."

"Really?" She regretted it as soon as she said it; she sounded like she was gloating. But what was her father doing, talking about her?

"Really," he said. "Ever eaten there?" He pointed at an all-night diner, Hot Sam's. "Great barbecue." Through the steamy windows of the diner they could see three men hunched at the counter. "You make a big mess when you eat, grease and sauce everywhere. I love barbecue."

"So does Lee," Hersh said.

"And who's he?" Carl asked. "The cousin or the brother?"

"Brother," she said.

"So the brother is the university one and the cousin works construction."

"Right." *And the mother runs a bookstore, the father teaches college.*

"I remember Lee," Carl snorted. "We were in shop together sophomore year. He wasn't so bad, but his *friends*. The worst."

Hersh started to defend Lee's friends, then decided to agree because she'd often felt the same way herself. Then she just didn't say anything. They came to a stop sign, but slid through.

Carl said, "You're a better driver than he says."

"What?"

"Your dad likes to tell about riding with you. You listen to the radio too loud. And you kill the engine in first gear."

"At least I haven't had a wreck."

"Only because we're the only car out tonight."

Hersh said, "Look down that street. Is it there?"

He turned and wiped his window again. "Negative." Then neither of them spoke.

What if they didn't find the car? Hersh imagined driving through her neighborhood all night, checking the back streets, dead ends, and cul-de-sacs, eventually garages. Or they could start in the other neighborhoods, downtown. Where would a drunk mistress park? How far could she walk on ice? It was all a mystery to Hersh.

At the next corner, she considered turning the other direction, moving west, toward the highway. What if she and Carl just drove off to Colorado? They'd arrive in Denver tomorrow and if someone asked them what they were up to, how would they explain their relationship? She looked over at Carl and tried to imagine kissing him. He looked at her and wrinkled his forehead. "What?" he said. She couldn't imagine kissing him.

"Hey!" he yelled. "Stop, stop! There it is." He rolled down the window and stuck his arm out. A lone yellow Toyota sat in the Safeway parking lot, its windows showing the scantest bit of snow drift. Hersh felt both relieved and disappointed—which the most? she wondered—that the night had ended. Then she remembered her father in her bedroom, her mother off somewhere else. Her stomach tensed again; the night hadn't ended.

"Well," she said. *Well well well.* Safeway was at least half a mile from Hersh's house, a mile from Carl's. "She walked a long way," she said, imagining Diane on the ice, without her coat, coming to see Hersh's father.

"You can do a lot of things drunk," he said. She pulled up next to the car, and they sat for a second. In the Safeway window were pictures of bright green vegetables on sale. *How dare you steal bread from us,* her character cried, *from the children.* "My license is suspended," Carl said. "Too many tickets."

Hersh sighed. "What do you want to do?"

"I'll drive it," he said.

"You could say it was an emergency," Hersh said.

Carl laughed at her. "They've heard everything. They wouldn't believe it. *I* wouldn't believe it if I heard it. I'd say, 'Come on, punk, in the car, you're history.'" He laughed again. In the parking lot lighting, Hersh saw that his cheek still had indentations from the couch. She saw he didn't even shave yet, just like Lee.

Carl opened his door and had one foot out. He looked at Hersh and squinted. He reached toward her face and she instinctively jerked her head back, hitting the window. "Hey," he said, touching her forehead. "What's this?"

Hersh felt herself blush. She put her hand to her forehead. Stage makeup came off, pancake base, eyeliner. "Wrinkles," she said. "I'm an old lady in the play. Mrs. Frank." They looked at each other. *All this time we thought it was rats.* Just a couple of hours ago she was at school, onstage hugging Tom Filarecki, who played Mr. Frank. He became nervous and sweaty when they had to lie on the pallet together. During rehearsal he'd said lines from their last play and she had had to coach him.

If Carl didn't get out, she was going to cry. He wiped his finger on his jeans. Both of them watched the snow blow against his car. "I hope it starts," he said.

"It'll start," she said. She thought about the night. "It'll probably start."

He slammed the door when he got out, and stomped over to the Toyota. Hersh watched him slap the snow off the windows and climb in. The car started and he roared off across the lot, spinning several donuts before he pulled onto the empty street.

Driving home, she invented omens. If the light ahead stayed green until she had gone through, her mother would be home. If the light turned yellow, her mother would be gone. The light stayed green. If she didn't see another car before she got home, her father would not be in her bedroom; if she saw another car, he would still be there. No cars. She pulled into their driveway, sliding up it at an angle. Her mother's green Falcon was not under the carport, which confused her omens.

Their house was now the only one in the neighborhood with lights on. Her bedroom window was unlit, though. She imagined her father siting by the heater, in the dark, resting his head on his crossed arms. She stepped out of the car and shut the door, listened to the ticking of the engine. She could have stayed out all night; no one was keeping tabs.

The back door was unlocked and the phone was ringing, echoing through the house like a fire alarm. "Diane," Hersh whispered. She picked up the phone, but said nothing, and heard nothing. Then the line clicked and she hung up. She cleared glasses from the table, rinsed them, and walked through the house turning off lights and locking doors. She felt tired, as if she'd cleaned the whole house that night. She went upstairs; there were still puddles of bath water on the steps and her towel was still draped over the phone desk. Still a mess, she thought. The phone cord led into the bathroom.

She opened her bedroom door and listened to the dark. "Dad?" she said. "I hear you *breathing*," she added, but it was a lie. She couldn't hear a thing. She shut the door. *Don't draw attention to yourself*, her drama teacher said, *when it's not your scene.*

Back in the bathroom, she looked in the mirror. Her makeup was smeared where Carl had touched her, more of his fingerprints. Really, she didn't look like an old woman at all, even from the back of the auditorium. She pulled the skin tight on her forehead. The makeup flaked and filled her own—tiny—wrinkles. She picked up the phone and dialed Lee's number, beginning to undress, shifting the receiver as she pulled at sleeves, buttons. Her brother's phone rang and rang. After turning off the light, she got into the empty tub. She didn't run water. Lee's phone kept ringing in Lawrence. Finally Hersh hung up.

The dry porcelain of the tub warmed only briefly where her skin touched; the rest remained cold. Hersh hugged her knees up to her chest, a perfect, still oval. *Don't call attention to yourself,* she remembered. *Don't distract.*

Outside, dry snow flicked against the window, a reminder of the freezing night. When she shut her eyes, she saw Carl's car, spinning on the parking lot. She saw Diane on the front porch, her mother on the landing, both crying. She shivered without being able to stop. This is how it goes, she thought. You come in from a cold place and sit in another cold place.

When the phone rang, she grabbed the receiver before it could finish. She held it to her ear without speaking.

"Hello?" Lee said, far away. "Hello, Hersh?"

"God, Lee, where were you?" She stretched her legs forward, leaned her head back, reclined for a long talk.

Reflections in the Ice

DANIEL CURLEY

From *Living with Snakes* (1985)

Everyone knew about my father's two wives. Some said he married my mother and then the other one. Some said he married the other one first and then my mother. One day, standing beside a hole in the ice where he was seining for shiners, Robert Martin described to me in great detail a wedding with two brides and my father in the middle. But Robert Martin smelled of vanilla extract that day like all other days and was probably confused in his attempt to express his admiration for my father, whose personal atmosphere was Scotch whiskey and who knew how to take Robert's shiners and catch even bigger pickerel than Robert himself. I had, after all, a sort of right to be out on the ice with Robert.

This about my father's two wives may sound very much like bigamy, but, unless I am mistaken, someone has to file a complaint for a charge to be brought, and who would complain of my father? Who could complain of him? He was a successful businessman and politician. His households were models of propriety. He drank good whiskey. He caught big fish. He went to mass at eight o'clock on Sunday morning and to Unitarian services at eleven.

When my mother and I walked out with him of an evening, the other one, if we met her, would bow to the eminently respectable hardware merchant and he would lift his hat to her. When my mother did her shopping in the morning, she bowed if she met the right respectable member of the school board out for a walk with the other one. He was a goodly, godly, respectable man.

And my mother was a respectable woman. She was straight and tall, and her ways were immaculate. She kept her house and her garden and her poultry and me in immaculate order. She had been a schoolteacher, and she kept his books for him and looked after his business correspondence. She was everything a wife and mother should be—and yet I had a sense of being shortchanged each time she offered that cool cheek just barely scented with the good soap she used, her soap.

Fortunately for my health of mind there was the other one. She was not at all like my mother. A glance was enough to show that she didn't come from our town, for she was dark and plump. We always believed she had been a shopgirl in the city, although Robert Martin once told me, for whatever it was worth, that she had been on the stage. However that may be, it is her kisses I remember. Her lips were very full and soft. I am tempted, in spite of knowing better, to say that I have never felt anything softer—I do say it—I have said it before now.

Why she should have been kissing me, I can't imagine. It seems highly unlikely that my mother would have selected her as baby-sitter—there are limits even to civilized behavior. But I was with her sometimes. I am sure of that. Sometimes when neither my mother nor father was there. As if, perhaps, my father had gone off on a trip and taken my mother with him. And there were other times, in the night, when she would come into my room. I think now she might have been at a party at our house. Very unlikely, of course. Perhaps I dreamed it. But the kisses are very real.

In addition to supplying my father with shiners, Robert Martin also helped out in the store whenever he happened to need cash or the weather was too bad for fishing. It would be a mistake, however, to conclude that my father was his patron. If any patronizing was done in that two-man democracy, Robert did it. He worked only when he wanted and as long as he wanted. He came and went as he liked, and my father, a doubly responsible man, stayed in the store summer and winter, rain and shine. On fine days when Robert happened to be working in response to some need of his own—usually vanilla extract—my father would often invent a delivery at the lake and would send him off and then settle himself down to the routine of the store and a quiet afternoon of vicarious truancy.

On these occasions Robert was always back by closing time—he was paid by the day—with a tale which usually involved a flat tire and his shiftless brother, who just happened to be passing with a fine mess of fish and who sent along something nice and fresh for my father's supper. Robert was invaluable to a man as burdened as my father. I know for a fact that one particularly lovely spring—it was the last of my father's life—Robert made a trip on the store's business to a supplier near Moosehead Lake in Maine. He was gone nearly a month—checking specifications, I think it was.

As far as I know, Robert and my father never discussed Moose-head Lake. In fact, it seems to me, now that I put my mind to it, that they discussed very little at any time, although each was known and esteemed in his own circle as a talker and storyteller. Be that as it may, on a foul day not long after Robert's return from Maine my father broke the silence in the store by saying suddenly, "Robert, would you mind spreading the Boston *Post* on the floor? I want to lie down."

Some people say Robert was so simpleminded that he always did whatever he was told without stopping to ask questions. My private opinion was that he was far more sensible than most adults, but perhaps a child's values are sometimes unrealistic. In any case, Robert spread the *Post* on the floor beside my father's desk as if he did it every afternoon of his life. My father stepped to the edge of the paper, oriented himself, and lay down. He straightened his coat, pulled down his vest, adjusted his watch chain, folded his hands on his breast, crossed his ankles, and closed his eyes. He was somewhat in the way in the cramped quarters behind the counter, but Robert respected his rights— it was a true democracy—and stepped over and around him all afternoon. Only when it was time to close the store did Robert speak to him to ask for the key. By then he had already been dead for some hours.

I don't know how much anguish there was over the problem of burying my father. Clearly it is one thing for a man to go to mass at eight and to Unitarian services at eleven and quite another thing for him to be buried twice. Successive funeral services, perhaps. Simultaneous graves, no. However, my father, prudent as always, had foreseen the difficulty and provided for it.

In those days the two churches were on the common, at opposite ends. The Catholic cemetery and the Protestant cemetery both extended northward from the common with a large field the width of the common between them. What my father had done was buy up this field—John Marsh's pasture—and will half of it to the Catholic church and half of it to the Unitarian church, reserving for himself only one plot on each side of the dividing line and stipulating that he be buried exactly on the line with a wife on either side of him. My mother's grave has been filled for a good many years now. The other is still waiting, and perhaps I'll never see it filled, but I am convinced that wherever she has been all these years and whoever she really is she'll come back in the end. But I'm getting ahead of my story.

After my father's death, our manner of life changed completely. It was no longer necessary for my mother and the other one to nod in the street. The bond between them was broken. They might, as widows, be friends, but they need not be even acquaintances. Now that I think back, I can't remember ever seeing the other one after we left the cemetery. She simply disappeared from my sight, from my consciousness.

My mother, on the other hand, grew and multiplied. She went directly from the cemetery to the store and opened for business. She took off her hat as if she were at home and sat down at the desk with the ledgers. She soon saw, however, that running the store by herself was a hopeless task. She needed help. Night after night she sat over her sewing or her ledgers and convinced me she needed help. I tried volunteering the first few times but discovered, greatly to my relief, that that wasn't what she meant at all. I was big and strong for my age, but I was still, after all, a boy. Then she stopped talking about it, and I assumed all was well.

Imagine my horror when I stopped in at the store for something—as a matter of fact it was fishhooks—and saw Robert Martin wearing a suit and even a tie as he worked behind the counter. He was cleanly shaved and very pale. He brightened for a bit as we discussed fishhooks, and he approved my choice of hook for the pond I intended to fish that day, but he was a very sick-looking man as he turned to rummage through a lot of boxes for a special hinge Mat Warren wanted for some cabinet work he was doing in the old Crawford place. I told him I'd bring him something nice and fresh for his supper, but he didn't seem to hear me, so I went about my business, although the day was appreciably darkened by the knowledge that I couldn't hope to find Robert Martin around the next bend of the river or watch him asleep in a drifting boat out in the middle of some pond. To be quite frank, he was at that time the most important person in my life, the first—and perhaps the only—person ever to treat me as an equal.

Naturally my own troubles preoccupied me at this time, and just as naturally I assumed that older people always got their own way, but even so I was vaguely aware that things were going from bad to worse for all of us. At night my mother talked about business and hard times. In the store Robert Martin grumbled that the stock wasn't being kept up and customers were being lost. "You have to put the money back into the business," he said. "We need the money to live on," my mother said.

But after a while she decided that she would take a teaching job for us to live on and let the money from the store go back to the store. She had precedent for this, too. Back before I was born, when my father was just putting the store together, he worked nights at the foundry to keep it alive. If he could do it, so could she, and her faith was only sharpened as she recited to me her memory of him coming up the stairs on his hands and knees at the end of his night's work. But all the while some adding machine in her head kept banging out its totals, and when a certain figure showed up, she closed the store instantly. Somehow she had arrived at an estimate of the cash value of the stock that would allow her to satisfy all creditors, and when that figure came around she didn't waste another minute or risk another cent. From that time on, it was the teaching that supported us. But that is by the way.

It was late summer when she closed the store and began to get ready for her new career. Perhaps she wanted to be alone to make her plans and so arranged to ship me off for a bit, or perhaps some friend of my father's, remembering him at last, wanted to make some final gesture of appeasement. In any case, Robert Martin and I found ourselves spending the Labor Day weekend at somebody's camp—my father had friends everywhere, as my mother more than once observed bitterly as she sat in the evening and tried to will cash out of uncollectible accounts.

"Do you know," she said on one such occasion, "that I once saw your father's best suit lying in the gutter outside Hanratty's Saloon? It would have been bad enough if I had been able to pick it up quietly and take it home and clean it, but the town drunk was inside it—that was Billy Farrell, back before the days of Sham Martin, whom you know." (My mother was practicing to be an English teacher.) "I don't think your father ever forgave me for leaving Billy—God rest his soul—there in his disgusting ragged underwear." Nor had he, I might add. Billy had merely lost his pants on that occasion and could be philosophical about having to go home in broad daylight in his long johns, but my father had lost face—or thought he had—and more than once I had heard him tell the story, ostensibly in praise of my mother's strength of character. But I wasn't fooled for a minute, not even I who was fooled by the appearance of everything. I remember this as the first time I was ever aware that there could be a message behind the words, a code I had never suspected.

The camp that Robert Martin and I had for the weekend was on a small pond down in the area we called the Thousand Ponds. It was the pond in back of the pond in back of the pond everyone went to, so it was well back in the woods. In fact, you might have said it was so far in that it was coming out the other side, except that on that side a belt of swamp cut it off from the highway. At some time, not so long before, the water level must have risen and flooded new land—probably there was a dam somewhere in connection with cranberry bogs. I can remember those dead trees standing in the water, silver-white and ghastly, although I'm not sure where the memory comes from, because I am told that I always got down on the floor of the car when we drove along that road.

The pond itself was deep and the water was only slightly brown. There was even a sand beach where we were, which isn't surprising in an area that is all old seabed. But we weren't there for swimming—and I was just as glad, because from time to time out in the middle of the pond we could see backs and tails of truly enormous snapping turtles drifting on the surface like the scalloped spines of ancient monsters—which, I suppose, in a sense they are.

We were floating in a boat in the middle of the pond out where the turtles had been. The turtles were now appearing over near the derelict trees, but I was still somewhat apprehensive in spite of the fact that really I had complete confidence in Robert Martin. He was standing in the boat, casting about, with no luck to speak of, an undersized pickerel and a very big perch, which I would have been glad to catch but which he threw back. Robert seemed to be fishing as well as my father, relaxed, almost negligent, but very skillful. He was, in fact, using my father's rod. I was glad of that. I wanted the rod myself, of course, but had sense enough to know I wasn't ready for it. So I took pleasure in seeing my father's rod and Robert Martin working together so well. I told myself that Robert's casts weren't going quite so far as my father's nor quite so accurately, but really no one could have been sure.

Robert sat down in the boat and rested the rod carefully on the side. He took a flat pint of Scotch whiskey out of his hip pocket, raised it in salute to me, and drank deeply. "Your father, now . . ." he said. I waited. "Your father was a remarkable man." I waited again. Robert took another drink. I think now that he had been working himself up to some kind of funeral oration. Perhaps my mother had put him up to it. Perhaps it was only his sense of fitness. I concentrated on my float, pretending I had a nibble, because he was clearly at a loss. "Your father . . ." he said again and then went on with a rush. "The first time I really saw your father was in the third grade. Miss Moss was the teacher then."

"She still is," I said. I had good cause to know. She was a tartar and more than once let me know that my father had never been half the trouble I was and that I would never be half the man he was.

"She was young then," Robert Martin said. "God, she was pretty." I kept my doubts to myself. "We would all of us do anything for her. In those days I was a great reader. I could read better and faster than anyone, and I loved to be called on to read aloud. This time I'm talking about, I remember we had a new book we wanted to get at because it was about a cave boy. His name was Bodo. I'll never forget it. The first chapter was 'Bodo's Hammer and Knife.' When Miss Moss asked who would like to read first, I put up my hand and so did your father. She called on him and he began to read. I had never thought much about your father before that, but I can still see him standing side of his desk in his white shirt and brown tie, brown knickers, brown knee stockings. He was holding his book like someone going to sing in church." I had a real nibble this time, but I ignored it and the fish went away.

"I was sick," Robert Martin said, "when your father began to read, because almost the first word was *knife*, and I had read it to myself for practice, and if I had been called on I was going to say *ka-nife*. But your father sailed right through it. I've been pretty embarrassed sometimes in my life first and last, but it's funny that the embarrassment I remember best never really happened except in my own head. *Ka-nife*. I still get hot flashes when I just happen to think of it. Now, *knife*, that's your father."

"Are you sure that's the same old lady Moss?" I said, completely at a loss.

"She was still young in those days," he said. "She hadn't found out yet about boys who say *ka-nife*."

"I never said *ka-nife* in my life," I said.

"I never said you did," Robert Martin said, and he took another drink from the bottle.

And it was just at that moment that the rod—my father's rod— went into the water. Robert had left the lure dangling just above the surface, and something had taken it suddenly and over went the rod. He was after it so fast that with any luck at all he must have caught it before it sank very far. But he came up without it, and no amount of diving produced it. Finally he climbed into the boat over the stern after directing me to the proper place for balance. "Effing turtles," he said, and that was all he said. I knew better than to say anything, but offered to row to the camp and he let me. On the way in, he tried the bottle again and found it empty. He looked around for the nearest turtle and hurled the bottle at it, falling short by something like the length of a football field.

He found some old clothes in a closet and got himself dry and then began rummaging in the kitchen cupboards where he found a large bottle of vanilla extract. Although there was at least one more pint of Scotch whiskey that I knew of, he began sipping the vanilla and brightening from moment to moment. "We'd better eat something," he said. "I was counting on fish, but there aren't any fish, so I'll heat up some soup and we can have the sandwiches your mother made up for us." He set up a card table on the porch where it was warm and sunny.

"Sounds good to me," I said. I didn't really like fish anyway, and neither did my father. He used to hate the bones and would always wind up choking and cursing whenever my mother served fish.

"I would have been mad at your mother—if it was all right to be mad at her—for making sandwiches and showing that she didn't believe we could catch enough fish to eat, but I guess she was right."

"We'll catch plenty this afternoon," I said.

"Plenty and to spare," Robert Martin said. And he told me about the time my father and two other men drank up all the beer while the rest were out fishing. And the time my father's father broke a scab's jaw during a strike at the foundry.

"Now," Robert Martin said, "I'll tell you something nobody else knows. While your father was alive, he and I knew it, and it was really up to him to tell it or not. I don't mind telling it now—speaking only good of the dead, you know." He was deep into his bottle of vanilla now, and he smelled lovely and seemed to be his old self again.

"He and I were fishing in the surf way down on the Cape—at Nauset—your father, I mean—just the two of us. We had a big fire going on the beach. I could show you the place. There was an old wreck there, and I expect some timbers are still sticking out of the sand. It was a lovely night. We had some coffee going and plenty of whiskey. There was a big moon and a strong tide, and everything was just right. Of course your father was getting married in about a week and we couldn't count on many more such nights, but we were trying not to think about that. You know what I mean?" Fortunately he didn't wait for an answer, because I didn't have the remotest idea what he meant except that it was sad to think of the end of such marvelous nights.

"It was around midnight that your father hooked something big. It was fighting hard, and we could see it rolling white on the surface out a ways. I remember thinking, by God, he's really done it this time. He had a hard time of it and was sweating like a horse, but he kept on bringing it in. I was down the beach and up to my waist in the breakers—more than once I was knocked down and nearly swept away. But I had the gaff ready and was all set to jam it home when I saw that what he had caught was a woman. The line was wrapped around her wrist.

"We got her out on the beach and stood looking at her, naked as a fish, because we thought she was dead. Then she opened her eyes and sat up and began laughing. Hysterics, you'll say. But it wasn't that. I've seen enough hysterics in my time to know what's what. No, it wasn't hysterics." He glared at me a moment. "Not at all," he said. "It was a good long, loud laugh.

"'It's plain to see,' she said, 'that a person born to be hanged is just wasting her time trying to drown herself.'

"'That was a foolish thing to try, anyway,' your father said.

"'That's for me to say,' she said. 'But now that you've caught me what are you going to do with me?'

"'There is that,' your father said. 'What can I do with you?' he said.

"I was over building up the fire to warm her, but I could hear it all. None of us had yet thought of one of the blankets for her, so she just sat there with her long hair stuck to her body and nothing else on her except for the seaweed wrapped around her legs that made her fall back down when she tried to stand up. The seaweed, I remember, was just the color of her hair, rich glossy brown like new-opened horse chestnuts.

"'What can I do?' your father said.

"'That's for you to say,' she said.

"'Well,' your father said. He scratched his head. 'I was going to get married next week anyway, and I suppose I might as well marry you.'

"'Truly?' she said.

"'True as I'm standing here,' your father said.

"'How will you tell her you're marrying me and not her?' she said.

"'Nothing of the sort,' your father said. 'I'll marry the both of you.' And she began laughing again. 'I'll need some laughter in my life,' he said. 'That's a good woman I'm marrying but dead serious.'

"'Then how will you tell her you're marrying the both of us?' she said.

"'That's for me to know,' your father said, 'but she has had her mind set on marrying me since we were in the seventh grade and she couldn't change her mind now whatever I did.'

"'Then that's how it is,' she said.

"'That's how it is,' your father said. 'Now take this coffee to warm you and this blanket to hide yourself in, and we'll have some hot fish in a minute, and all will go well as a marriage bell.'

"And so, by God, it did," Robert Martin said.

"Is that really how it happened?" I said. Oh, I was the solemn one.

"I've just told you so, haven't I?" he said.

"But truly," I said. I was bouncing around on my little camp stool, and in my excitement I fell over backward and brought my feet up under the table and sent the soup and sandwiches flying every which way. I felt like an idiot and looked quickly at Robert Martin, expecting to be told I was one, but he was laughing so hard he had to lower himself to the floor to keep from falling too.

"If you don't kill me with laughing," he said, "I'll live to tell your sons about the time their father kicked the lunch over the house and killed the big snapping turtle."

"I'd like to hear that story," I said, still flat on my back.

Unfortunately, I'll never hear that story now, because it was only that winter or the next one that they found Robert Martin in his own net under the thin clear ice of a night. Boys skating peered into the hole and finally saw something that justified all their peering, although at first they thought it was only some weird reflection in the ice. Thank God I wasn't one of them. I see him still, standing beside the hole, gently scattering oatmeal to attract the little fishes.

Maybe, Maybe Not

BARBARA SUTTON

From *The Send-Away Girl* (2004)

I just married the boy next door from thirty-one years ago. He was my neighbor for a year, maybe less, in a town half a state away from where I live now. His family had moved up from Pennsylvania, and then as soon as the neighborhood got used to their license plates they disappeared to Ohio. The father was a claims adjuster, the mother barely seen on account of the venetian blinds that came with their house. Two boys on bikes was the relevant story. Both were a few grades ahead of me, went to a different school, and displayed what I took to be a big-city sharpness. My parents never bothered to speak to the Glenshaws because the Glenshaws never bothered to remove the labels from their new aluminum trashcans. There was definitely something impermanent about them, which must have been the reason for their acute appeal to me.

Who winds up to be your immediate neighbor is one of the chanciest things in life—as much of a crapshoot as picking up the paper and never knowing what you're going to read. On a recent Sunday I happened to read the *Times* obituaries because an article from the front page jumped close to that section. One of the obits was for a guy named Gary Glenshaw, who'd developed some kind of robotics technology and was a famous person within the scientific community—three school-age children, sad ending from a brain tumor at age forty-four. When I got to the "is survived by" wrap-up, I remembered this guy and his brother as having lived next door for a speck of time when I was young. Why on earth did I remember that the father was a claims adjuster? I must've liked the way the words sounded together—I must've invented a complex of meaning. I scrolled through the names and faces randomly packed in my memory to calculate the distance between then and now as thirty-one years.

I paid a lot of attention to my neighbors thirty-one years ago because I was an only child—a condition I came to consider a personal failing. As if to hammer home this character flaw, my parents bought me a swing set with one swing. "Why spend the extra cash?" was my father's rationale. Kids didn't want to play in our yard because you had to take turns on the swing, and the swing set wasn't long enough to allow more than one kid to hang by her knees from the axle bar. We didn't own a barbecue grill; no game with balls, birdies, or wickets was ever played on the grass. Ours was the lonely backyard of old people, mainly because my parents, like vampires or Austrians with rare skin diseases, never went outside during the day. Inside was their domain, where they were forever chiding me for idleness and mopery—the eighth and ninth deadly sins in their book. They were always on my tail, driving me out of the house, and the single swing was the most effortless place to wind up. The swing set wasn't taken down in the winter; the snow liked to drift around it as the cunning rusting process continued underneath. Under the single swing was a deep rut, the distinct parabolic shape of which was molded by my feet. Sitting on the swing with my heels dug into the earth was like saying, "This is the outside, and this is mine."

The Glenshaw family's importance to me stemmed from an incident involving Mr. Glenshaw and our neighboring backyards. The incident occurred in the late fall, and I can even remember what I was wearing that day: cutoffs rolled up to mid-thigh, red wool kneesocks that came over my knees, penny loafers that were water warped out of shape, a purple parka with a strip of red elephants around the chest. I had put on this parka in the kitchen, just as my mother was stuffing a lot of cabbage into a Crock-Pot to stink up the house for days. "Dinner won't be until nine-thirty. Do something useful until then." She didn't say anything about the fact that I was wearing shorts with a parka; this I distinctly remember.

I liked to sit on the swing doing nothing, waiting for smaller ordeals (for instance, slow-cooking cabbage) and larger ones (say, childhood) to be over and done with. I'd twirl around to twist the swing's chains as tight as I could get them; then I'd release myself so that I could spin—slowly at first and then fast, faster, and finally zip! the end of the show with a jerk to hurt your neck, as if you were practicing for a public hanging at a later date. That day must have been typical of so many others—probably not a pink sunset, but let's remember one anyway—a sunset making the hues of everything in the yard deeper, richer, like every object had a grand and noble purpose. Rusted things looked especially good under the sepia glow of those kinds of sunsets, and there were a lot of rusted things in our yard. That wheelbarrow tilted against the house seemed to be rusted into place. What the heck was that doing there? It had nothing to do with my father, who'd have needed an illustrated manual to work the handles. It must've come with the property, like the Glenshaws' venetian blinds and maybe even myself, because whenever my father caught me just standing around he'd ask, "What—you came with the property?"

That evening of the sunset that might or might not have been present, I saw Mr. Glenshaw come out the back door of his house holding something in his hand. I remember first hearing the screen door slam shut and then looking up for a story to go with it. Each neighbor's screen door slamming shut made a different sound, and I could determine what kinds of domestic situations were occurring by the kinds of slams I heard. Mr. Glenshaw stood in the yard after this particular slam, and I could tell that what he was holding was a pie, because a pie is about the only thing you'd hold that way with one hand. Before I had time to consider what was going on, he hurled the pie at the birdfeeder in our yard. It did not seem like a real pie; it made a cracking sound upon impact, and it scared me. The feeder fell over, and then everything was still and seemed to get darker by the second. I took personal offense at this violent act because I had made that birdfeeder in Girl Scouts; it accounted for one whole badge. It was supposed to have had a mansard roof, though in my rendering you couldn't tell this architectural feature. It took forever to get my father to put it on a pole and put the pole in the ground. He complained that it ruined the yard, that it would attract squirrels, that no one in our family had ever liked birds anyway.

"Mr. Glenshaw just threw a pie at our birdfeeder!" I exclaimed, breathless from having raced into the kitchen. My parents didn't seem alarmed, but both changed out of their reading glasses at the same time—open one case, close the other, the two of them in stereo, ad infinitum until I was of voting age. "Why did he do that?" I kept asking them. I felt that there had to be an explanation, that perhaps throwing pies was something an adult did when he lost his job or bought worthless stock.

By the time my parents got to the kitchen window, you could see the darkened figures of the two boys picking up the debris in our yard and putting it into a trash bag held by the smaller of the two; we watched them as they stood up the feeder on its pole and secured it in the ground. My father said, "I should pay them to rake the leaves."

"But why did he do that?" I continued to ask.

"Do we know what their names are?" my mother inquired of no one in particular, but they both looked at me. I shrugged. "Maybe and Maybe Not."

"Don't be a wise-aleck," my father said. "And what the heck are you wearing on your legs?"

"Not much," my mother replied.

The funeral for Gary Glenshaw was to be held at a Methodist church near Mount Kisco the next day. I wondered if someone at the funeral would be able to tell me why the father of the deceased had thrown that pie at our birdfeeder—maybe the father himself, or else the mother or the brother. From this nuclear group, only the brother was mentioned in the *Times* as being a survivor. I tried to remember what the survivor was like as one of the boys next door. I'd had some brief conversations with him, if what kids say to each other can be construed as conversation. When you asked him a yes-or-no question, he'd say, "Maybe, maybe not." That was his schtick the entire time he lived next door to me—"Maybe, maybe not"—and I had thought it an especially clever one, like something said by kids in more advanced parts of the country.

I really don't know why I decided to drive to Mount Kisco the next day, except that this is the sort of behavior that junk psychologists are always urging on recently divorced women ("embrace spontaneity!"). At the funeral I sat in the back of the church like police detectives do in movies. It turned out to be a packed service with a lot of crying children. There must've been an entire middle school in attendance, presumably the classmates of Gary Glenshaw's children. Surrounded by an entire middle school of weeping kids, I regretted this impulsive action.

You don't really need a program to figure out the principals at a funeral. Even in dysfunctional families the heaviest criers sit in the front row, and this family was no exception, although the Glenshaw brother, the survivor whom I recognized right off because he's the spitting image of his father, wasn't crying and sat a few rows back. He looked like the actor Joel McCrea because his father looked like the actor Joel McCrea. That's all I can remember my father saying about Mr. Glenshaw after it was determined that the labels would not be removed from his family's trashcans—"That guy next door looks like the actor in those Preston Sturges pictures." At least I think he was referring to Joel McCrea; with my father you always had to connect the dots, do the math. His motto, if he had one, was "A word to the wise should be sufficient."

I left the church within a stream of penitent children—they were heading for school buses, and I was intending to take my losses (one day of work and a dollar-something in tolls) and head home. But something made me proceed along with the funeral entourage to a cemetery that was much more effortlessly upper middle class than the one that housed my parents. The scene was as bucolic as a movie set because, luckily for us all, movies constitute most people's experience with burial sites. I'm always conflating my only two burial-site experiences with things I've seen in movies—like there being a steady downpour, men holding black umbrellas above their bowler hats, a priest saying things in Latin, someone suddenly taking off on a horse. My parents died within a month of each other, so in my memory it felt like just the one burial. I purchased the same casket twice—Mr. Oloff gave me a big discount on the second one. Initially I thought this was standard undertaker kindness. Later I learned that Mr. Oloff had been sent two of the kind of casket that I ordered for my mother, and the second one, which had been damaged in transit, had been a bone of contention between wholesaler and retailer, so Mr. Oloff already had the second one kicking around in the garage when I called him again.

"Do I know you?" the survivor asked me as the mourners were leaving the gravesite. I had lost track of him during the "ashes to ashes" part, right about when I lost myself in daydreams about my own funeral and its almost certain lack of drama (I'd have to hire a stranger if I wanted someone to take off on a horse). "Or do you know me?" he persisted.

Because I was caught unprepared, the truth was my only option. "You and your brother lived next door to me in 1971," I told him. "I read the obituary in the paper yesterday. I came here because I wanted to find out something. I don't usually do this kind of thing."

"Did the paper say that?"

"Say what?"

"That we lived next to you in 1971."

"No."

"So what did you want to find out?"

"I saw your father throw a pie at our birdfeeder one night, and I've always wanted to know why he did this."

"Sure," he said, as if nothing about my presence or professed motive was out of the ordinary. "I remember that. I can tell you about the pie." He looked around at the departing mourners, ignoring numerous overtures, people beckoning him toward them. "Do you want to go somewhere for lunch?" he asked. "My sister-in-law hates me. If I go back to her house, I might throw a pie. Look—she's staring at us. Look sad for my sister-in-law. Let's wave at her at the same time."

Though I can't say I had come up with any picture of what the boy next door would turn out to be like, this seemed a plausible result—a little flip, a little renegade. I followed his inexpensive rental car to an expensive restaurant that had once been a stable; I was feeling impressed with myself for not being nervous, for having gotten this far without embarrassing myself. I was planning to pay for the meal with a spare credit card that I'd never used; I practiced sentences that made me sound like Diane Sawyer. Although my original intention was to resolve the pie-throwing mystery for my own satisfaction, I was beginning to feel altruistic, thinking that perhaps the odd encounter would make the flip and renegade survivor feel good about people in the weird way a Preston Sturges picture makes you feel good about people, would confirm for him that we are not all so separate and isolated, although I had no idea why I thought myself capable of this.

Inside the restaurant, however, my confidence began to sag because the brother of the late Gary Glenshaw seemed completely different from the way he had been not twenty minutes before. He was much less secure, maybe even unhappy in a more underlying way than bereavement would call for. He was nervous; he kept lifting the saltshaker and tapping it against the olive oil plate. He cut his lamb into smaller and smaller pieces as he went into more and more detail about some topic that wasn't even audible to me. He would ask me a question but not wait for a reply. "Do you read the *Economist* I read the *Economist*." "Have you been to Japan I've been to Japan." "Are you allergic to shellfish I'm allergic to shellfish." His nervousness was distracting and disorienting, although I suppose it didn't matter given that he never let me get a word in edgewise. Did he really care whether I read the *Economist*, visited Japan, or was allergic to shellfish? Both of his parents were dead; that's one thing I learned. One of his former girlfriends was in an AT&T commercial. Five years ago he borrowed from his brother a lot of money that he never repaid. While his brother was dying, his sister-in-law sent him an invoice for this loan with a 15 percent interest rate compounded over the five-year period.

Toward the end of the meal, I was finally able to ask my own question: "Are you going to tell me the pie story now?"

"I don't think I can today," he said with a pained expression, suggesting that I understood the story as an emotionally complicated one—which in some sense was true. After tapping his coffee spoon against the saltshaker he said, "But I'd like to tell you about it tomorrow."

On the drive home I regretted my impulsive actions. I was hoping he'd forget about tomorrow, was wishing I'd given him a false name and a false number. He was certainly an appealing man if a man was what you were after, but romantic prospecting seemed an unwholesome motive under the circumstances. And besides that, many things about him were sketchy. He seemed to have been through hundreds of jobs but had no discernible career—lots of higher education and then a big gaping black hole. He talked about houses he'd owned in Pennsylvania and yet was living out of a suitcase in someone's apartment on the Upper East Side. He had a name, Kyle, but I felt uncomfortable using it.

The next day he drove up the Taconic Parkway to have dinner at a restaurant I like. He looked much better when illuminated by the lights of this restaurant. In fact, he now seemed different in a new way—not flip, not nervous, but quite comfortable with me, like we'd remained Christmas card friends all these years, like yesterday when he seemed so aggrieved was a tiny blip in a larger narrative, like we had a history of these sorts of ups and downs.

"You start," he said.

"Tell me about the pie."

"OK, but first tell me about you, what you do. I was rude last night, blabbering on and on about myself. I can be like that—rude. Rude when you least expect it, or maybe when you most expect it. Anyway, I'm sorry."

I started to say something, and he interrupted. "I remember you . . . so well. I just wanted you to know that."

This was a difficult comment to gloss over because it was such an outright lie. Maybe he thought I was going to buy him meals indefinitely. Maybe he was even more of a cad than my suspicious mind could anticipate, marshaling all of his charms in a campaign to sustain the pie mystery. I don't know why things happened the way they did aside from the fact that these charms of his were quite potent. He spoke with an intimacy that suggested we were coconspirators in some kind of liberation effort. We spent the entire dinner talking about everything but the reason we were having dinner. "Life in the contemporary world" seemed the gist of it. He acted very interested in what happened to my hometown after his family left, which I found hard to believe given all the places they had lived when he was growing up.

"Let's go there now," he proposed in lieu of coffee. He meant our houses in that little city. "Let's drive there. It's just a couple hours. We'll re-create the pie-throwing incident, like we're detectives, and then you'll know why my father did what he did. Let's see if we can find our houses."

I hesitated before saying, "I lived there until I was twenty-one."

"Great!" he replied, not at all chagrined to have overlooked this obvious—perhaps essential—aspect about me. "You're the expert; you be the guide."

Against my better judgment I consented to be the guide. Curiosity had given way to a mild obsession—I now needed to know what the survivor was looking for, and why I had become part of the search.

It was decided that we'd take my car, which did not surprise me—me driving and him talking. It was somewhat amusing to think that the common denominator between this man and me was a place I hadn't seen in ten years. My parents had selected their cemetery in a larger city where none of us had ever lived. Whenever I visit their graves, I do something a tourist would do; I get a map from the Chamber of Commerce.

"Gary and I used to play all kinds of driving games with my father," he told me soon after we set out. "When we were driving back from Arizona once and he was tired, he played a game to see how many exits he could go before pulling off the interstate and checking us into a motel. We kept ticking off the numbered exits because it was like The Highway versus Dad, a contest. He ended up driving all night and half the next day until we were home. No one said anything for six hours at a stretch. Now it sounds crazy."

"Is that why he threw the pie at our birdfeeder?"

"Dad? I don't know. My mother was the one. She was institutionalized when I was fifteen."

"I don't think I ever saw your mother."

"You were lucky."

I was hoping he'd stop there with his mother because I sensed thickly settled issues, but we had just gotten on the Thruway. Proceeding along on the Diane Sawyer path seemed the decent thing to do, however, so I drove headlong into his issues. "You weren't close to her?" I asked.

"I never thought of her as being close to anyone. She was an only child come to think of it, like you. She was close to my grandparents, I guess. From Lake Placid, though I don't know what that means. That she should have been placid maybe? She was never placid. She was afraid of everything. Always jittery, like an electric toothbrush."

"What was wrong with her?"

"I don't know . . . some kind of depression. She'd drink, she'd stay in bed, she'd fall and hurt herself, we'd drive her to the emergency room at four in the morning. This seemed like the only way it went with us. They gave her drugs, I suppose, but not Prozac-type drugs. Hard stuff, in between the shock therapy."

"That must've been hard."

When he said, "You know something funny?" I could tell that what came next would not make me laugh. "She was the one who got me and Gary saying 'Maybe, maybe not.' This was the sign that she was coming out of it, getting in a better mood. Sometimes she'd shock you by showing up in the living room dressed in street clothes. That was my Dad's word for it—'street clothes,' versus the 'bed clothes' she usually wore, that he was always trying to get her to change out of. When you asked, 'Mom, are you OK?' and she'd say, 'Maybe, maybe not,' it was a big relief, like she was giving you the high-five."

"So did she get better?"

"Killed herself. OD'd."

I was hoping he wasn't waiting for an apology—we're always apologizing about death, and it's the people who don't give a shit who seem the sorriest of all.

"She did it when she was let out with my father for a weekend," he continued, looking out the passenger window. People do that in cars at night—look out the passenger window like it's a video screen showing their own personal past. "He could've saved her," he said, "at least that's what we think. It was his choice. He was a smart guy really. He was in insurance. 'They'll nickel-and-dime ya into the ground'—that was his motto."

"Everyone should have a motto," I said with synthetic cheer. For the remainder of the drive we talked about celebrity dogs, rich people in jail, and mobile telephony—this in addition to music, politics, and the decline of Western civilization.

Our old houses looked small to us, which meant that we'd both grown perfectly typical. I estimated that old people lived in my old house, because even though it looked small to me, it looked the same in most respects; his house had been converted into apartments. We got out of the car and stood on the sidewalk. Both yards were fenced, so we decided not to try to sneak onto anyone's property to re-create the pie-throwing incident.

"We're too old for that kind of thing anyway," I said.

"Is that what we are?" he said with a laugh. Then he looked around, as if we had alternative locations to consider. "Do you think they still have that dump around here?"

"They turned it into a playground a long time ago."

"The way of the world," he said sadly, "ruin a perfectly good dump."

Without much fanfare, we got back in the car and sat there.

"Are you cold?" he asked. "Do we need some heat?" I turned on the car and the heater, and he started talking again. He told me that his mother never cooked dinner; the boys made things from cans, jars, and packages—macaroni and cheese, franks and beans, spaghetti and Ragu. Their father would bring home buckets of Kentucky Fried Chicken. Fast food turned out to be the prelude to his story about the pie.

"One day I got home from school early," he began, "cut class I think. I was always truant, always in trouble at that school. Anyway, I came home, and there was this noise in the kitchen. I go out there, and it's my mother dressed in street clothes; she's making something. Cooking or baking, whatever. The oven was on; she was baking something. She told me to 'go play' because she was making dinner. What was I—eleven? Eleven, and she says, 'Go play.' Anyway, you have to picture how this was for me, for Gary when he got home, what kind of big event this was. I hadn't seen my mother cook, ever. It was shocking. She had once been a good cook—that was the lowdown. Good at just about everything was the lowdown on my mother. I suppose I idealized this time when my mother was good at everything—whatever was just out of my frame of memory—one or two years it was, but it might as well have been a million years before.

"By the time Gary got home, she had switched her plan to dessert. She said something like, 'I'm just making dessert. Just dessert. Call your father and tell him to pick something up, what you like to eat. Tell him I'm just making dessert.' She was using an electric mixer; it was too much. What she was making was a lemon meringue pie. That kitchen had small windows, didn't get much light. She didn't have any of the counter lights on; I remember thinking it was amazing she could do this in the dark. We didn't watch, didn't want to make her nervous. It smelled good though. And my dad was so cool about the whole thing— Mr. Nonchalant. She sat down at the table with us; we had the Kentucky Fried Chicken on real plates.

"When it came time, she got the pie from the counter and put it on the table. This pie looked great. No, not just great—'great' would be an understatement. This looked to me like the most beautiful pie in the world. We could hardly believe it. We just stared at it, and then my mother slid it toward my father. 'You're the man,' she said, 'you carve.' My father smiled; 'I'm the man,' he said. 'I'll *cut*.' But when he put a knife to the pie, the knife wouldn't go in. He tapped on the pie, and the most beautiful pie in the world sounded like plaster of Paris. He looked at my mother; she looked confused and then irritated. 'I couldn't find any cornstarch in *your* kitchen,' she said, 'so I used Sta-Prest.' 'Sta-Prest?' my Dad repeated, sounding equally confused. It was Gary, the great mediator, who translated: 'It's that stuff you iron with, Dad. Starch.' My dad just nodded, staring at the pie. None of us knew what to say. And then my Mom said, 'Well, gentlemen, you know what I hope? I hope we all perish in a fire is what I hope. I hope we're dead before Christmas—charred to bits, each and every one.' Then she got up and went to her room.

"After a bit, my dad took the pie and went out the back door. I think it was too much for him—not the dying in a fire part but hearing her say 'in your kitchen.' I mean, it hit me at that moment that she wasn't our mother anymore—she was this totally separate person. All this pretending that we were a functioning family. She was like a boarder, an inmate in our house. And I think Dad was feeling that, too. Gary and I just sat there at the table. A few minutes later my dad came back in and said, 'I knocked down something in the yard next door. Go over and see what happened. Fix things up.' I remember him saying, 'Fix things up.'"

His version of the story prompted me to recall this important fact from my own: after Mr. Glenshaw threw the pie at the birdfeeder, he started sobbing, crying with both hands over his face. Now I can remember the part of the story where I remained seated on the swing and watched him, or maybe watched over him, because I was afraid that someone would catch him out—someone brutal and cruel, like either of my parents or any of my neighbors slamming their screen doors. I felt intense pity for Mr. Glenshaw, although as children we were taught not to pity adults. We were supposed to be shielded from feeling pity for anyone but ourselves. Don't hog the toys, don't have tantrums—that was about it.

"I don't remember you at all," the survivor confessed after what felt like a long period of silence. "I wish I did though. I wish I paid more attention."

I now felt intense pity for this man who, through no fault of his own, grew up to look exactly like his father. I kept hearing the word echo inside my head—*pity, pity, pity.* And what did pity do? Pity only exacerbated the world's excessive sadness. I had to do better than that. But what, exactly, did I think I could do? "Make people laugh" is the way I had always understood altruism— make like a Preston Sturges picture and illuminate the perimeters of this loopy, madcap world. There should've been a joke to crack about the birdfeeder, something like "Your dad sure was a home-wrecker!" But now the survivor himself was crying, crying inside my own car, and all I could think to do was reach over to turn off the heat. I had been a willing accomplice—no, an agitator, an initiator—in this historical reenactment of grief. I had found out the answer, but the answer for me was a painful point of inquiry for him. It suddenly seemed to me that there was no such thing as "personal history," that his life, his father's life, my life, and maybe the lives of a lot of strangers were a continuum, all of it just one long story with an endless number of weekly installments. He kept crying despite his muscular efforts to hold it in, so that soon his face got all knotted up like a walnut shell.

He finally put both hands over his face, just like his father did that day in the yard. This I could not bear. "Don't do that," I said, prying his hands away from his face—first one hand and then the other. I pulled hard like I was husking corn, although I didn't mean for this gesture to be hard. And when I saw his Joel McCrea face in such a state, this thought struck me as a revelation: I could take him home to live with me. It wasn't that I particularly liked him or wanted him or needed him, but I could so vividly picture him standing in my yard wearing swim trunks when it was hot. I told myself that we did have things in common—for instance, both of our fathers had had mottoes. I told myself that there had to be a basis for a lifelong union with this man and his big gaping black hole of a life. Long story short: we were married in a civil ceremony attended by four people (not including us).

So far my wifely project has been getting in the habit of calling him Kyle. I've also been trying to reconcile him with his sister-in-law—though with little success. My initial effort in this regard was writing her a check for two thousand dollars as the first installment of the delinquent loan, but she tore up the check in front of me. "Come off it," she said. I did come off it, and I did have second thoughts about being the wife of Kyle Glenshaw, but only for a minute. I can say with confidence that there was never any question of turning back, that I had no choice in the matter once we'd agreed to go looking for our homes.

On the drive home that night after learning about the pie, I felt a huge relief, like I'd finally come clean on a lifelong lie. The survivor fell asleep in the passenger seat, but I was awake enough for the both of us. I remember being perplexed at how his father could make an entertainment-worthy children's game out of counting highway exits that were already numbered—my father would've been asking, "Where's the game in that? Where's the game?"—but I didn't dwell on this because I didn't want to think about my father. Instead I thought quite intensely about that night of the pie throwing, and in doing so I realized that it presented me with the saddest, most vivid, most beautiful moment of my childhood. The most beautiful moment—and I wanted this moment back, to have and to hold from this day forward. I wanted it, with or without the sepia sunset, like it was some terrifying intoxicant. I wanted it and would pay vast sums for the luxury of having it. I wanted it to stay with me forever, or at least until I was dead—until the "ashes to ashes" part, until they put me in the ground, shoveled in the dirt, and signaled for the guy I hired to take off on his horse.

My Guardian, Claire

KELLIE WELLS

From *Compression Scars* (2002)

When I was six years old, a ring of shingles wound around my mother's waist like a belt, and she stopped breathing when the ends met. *Dr. Avery Schoenfeld's Bedside Guide to Good Health* says death by a girdle of shingles is a myth. It says it is a superstition dating back to the early Greeks. Evidently it is a myth in which my mother believed.

Claire took me in when disease cinched my mother's shrinking waist. Claire lived by myths of her own making.

I hope my mother felt no pain as the skin scabbed round her middle. I hope it was like slipping into a dream. She told me she had dreamt me, my birth. She said it was clean and painless. She was relieved I was a boy, she said, because boys depart from the mother, splinter from God, more quietly than girls. She said I dropped from a cloud, rain dark at the edges with my expulsion, and tumbled down a shaft of wind, wet and silent as a mackerel.

Muddy-brown pin curls decoratively framed my mother's oval face. They were so perfectly circular, they made me dizzy if I looked at them too closely. They looked like they'd been scribbled on with a Busy Buzz Buzz. She had tiny hands that nearly disappeared when she closed them and three freckles in a row above her upper lip, like ellipses, like there was more to be said.

After the burial, I became Claire's full-time charge.

Claire was a beauty operator, which made me think she carved good looks from flawed faces with scalpel and suture, but it was hair she shaped. She worked out of her basement, where she had two pedestaled chairs bolted to the floor. Whenever Claire pumped the chair up so that the customer's head was at a workable height, it made me think of Elmer Fudd and Bugs Bunny in the "Barber of Seville" cartoon. I imagined Claire perched on the heads of the customers, massaging hair oil into their scalps with all four paws. I saw wet-headed women careening toward the ceiling and bursting through Claire's roof. When I told Claire about my vision she said, "That Bugs Bunny. Whatever happened to him? A huge talent."

Claire wasn't like the adults I knew. People in the neighborhood and at the grocery store and the filling station called her "Claire the Loon." She said she was flattered. She loved birds.

Some people thought it a scandal that my mother had made Claire, no blood relation, my godmother. My mother respected a well-crafted pin curl. Claire was always very polite to her and brought her a brisket when our German shepherd was poisoned. My mother and Claire had the same sense of kindness.

Claire's daughter and husband drowned in a boating accident during a fishing trip five years before I went to live with her. The only thing she ever said to me about it was that it made her feel sad for stealing the worms from the robins that had worked so hard at unearthing them that morning. Once she told me she had phantom pains of maternity that made her bowels ache and that she missed the smell of aftershave on the pillowcase. Then she sucked on my toes and stroked my feet and fell asleep.

I was both surrogate spouse and child to Claire.

And I was sweet on her.

She gave me apples she'd picked herself. "They're not from my trees," she'd say, "but God doesn't mind and Johnny Appleseed is dead." And then she'd laugh, her eyes turning to tiny fists, the gap between her front teeth threatening to pull me in. Sometimes they were only crab apples, and we pitched them at cats when they stalked the birds, stealthing along near the shrubbery. Claire said they were called crab apples because if they could talk, they wouldn't have anything nice to say. Claire, my godmother, had spoken with angels.

They were sitting on her kitchen table, dangling their feet when she came in the back door. They smelled bad and had dirty knees and necks. One had white hair, a wrinkled face, and a crusted, runny nose; the other had red hair, red freckles, and wore silver high heels and white socks. They were both small and shifty, ungraspable as beads of quicksilver. They had eaten all Claire's sugar and vomited on the floor. They'd stayed to apologize.

I asked Claire how she knew they weren't just neighbor kids or ghosts. She said she recalled them from her time in heaven. She said as she was waiting to be born, they brought her a box of Good and Plenty and a bottle of grape Nehi with a crazy-curl straw. She remembered them. She said angels are as distinct as snowflakes.

That was when she first saw her father—in heaven. He had been in an airplane that was shot down over the Pacific Ocean exactly one month before Claire was born. He was entering the Kingdom just as Claire was departing. As they passed, he told her to help her mother with the daily chores when she was old enough and to act surprised the first time she saw a picture of him. She said he was thin and young and handsome and made her think of an antelope. When I asked her what her earliest memory was—and I asked her often, thinking it might change—she always grinned and clutched her elbows and told me about making her father's acquaintance in heaven.

Claire believed we carry with us prenatal knowledge that is mostly lost to us at that moment of induction, that first unencumbered pulse, that first slap into the material world. From that moment on, we forget and spend the rest of our lives trying to remember, grasping at dim and darting shadows of distant occurrences. Before we are born, though, we're tiny fibers coiled in a cosmic blanket that connects us with everything, a throw God covers himself with when he's chilled. Claire believed God dwelled on the inside. Inside all things. Inside the body like a benevolent growth, benign but swelling. She believed you could see God in the furrows of a peach pit if you looked hard enough.

And she believed in genetic memory. Claire said she was often surrounded by antiquated objects in her dreams, like buttonhooks or railroad lanterns, things that felt familiar but that she swore she'd never seen before, not even as a child, in a flea market, or on television. This belief was influenced, I think, by a newspaper article about a young boy who dug up a small fortune buried in the backyard of what turned out to have been an estate once owned by his great, great, great, great grandfather. Supposedly, this knowledge had been passed along genetically from generation to generation, like a pocket watch. It had slipped through the seed, through the blood, through the twisted cords of chromosome into this little boy's unsuspecting brain. Claire's conviction about this phenomenon was more hopeful than heartfelt, though she clung to her celestial recollections with the kind of tenacity that comes only from being touched by something pure and unimaginable, something beyond bald data and observable evidence—something no Freudian interpretation could tarnish.

One midnight in May when I was ten, Claire and I lay on our stomachs with the sides of our faces resting in the freshly tilled dirt, listening. I heard nothing.

"Silence," Claire said. She could sniff out skepticism at twenty paces. I was a new soul and so naturally incredulous she said. Silence was all that I heard.

After a while, I felt something, something infinitesimal burrowing in the ground beneath my cheek. I imagined it was a tiny organism invading the dwellings of sleeping nits. At this same moment, I heard a distant chorus of muffled wheezing that seemed to emanate from someplace deep and hollow. I thought this might be a trick of Claire's, like when I could tell she was moving the Ouija pointer. But the sound was too removed, too disembodied and eerily pitched to be Claire. Claire spread her arms and legs out and flapped and scissored them across the earth. She was making earth angels.

"I heard it, Claire," I said. We had just planted our garden by the flat light of the moon. On this night it looked more bilious than silvery, but it was in full bloom and Claire believed this was the best time to sow, because of the gravitational pull on the sap. She believed you could hear the inception of life if you listened closely enough, and Claire's ears were often to the ground. I believed she could hear the rustling of insect wings in Outer Mongolia if she tried.

Claire had a porcelain pallor. Her skin was that shade of white that was so white it almost glowed a moony green. The skin of her doughy thighs was the best. It was so pure you were tempted to drink it.

Claire and I amused ourselves in the evenings with board games. She had a closet full: Mousetrap, Operation, Mystery Date, you name it. Claire would quote the commercials while we played: "Roll the dice, move your mice." "Take out wrenched ankle." "Will he be a dream or a dud?" Claire cut out pictures from the front of Simplicity patterns so that I could play Mystery Date. The girl with blonde corkscrew pigtails, an embroidered peasant shirt, psychedelic culottes, and white knee socks was deemed the least desirable date. Claire had kept all her daughter's toys, among them a Frosty the Snowman Snow-Cone Maker with bottles of flavored syrup, an Easy Bake Oven, and an Etch-A-Sketch, on which we drew pictures of stiff, boxy cows and grinning bears sitting on boulders, warming their feet by small fires.

Claire and I enjoyed playing Yahtzee. She had a special fondness for it because she always won. In her hands those dice were quintuplets; in mine they were distant acquaintances, fellow integers adding up to zilch. Claire said it was because she believed in the power of numbers and patterns and claimed her luck was "all in the wrists." She had wrists that were unusually thin, as though they were an evolutionary legacy left by birds. I imagined her skeleton filled with air, weighted down by flesh, waiting to skin itself and ascend.

Once when I went looking for Claire to play a game of Parcheesi with me, I walked into her bedroom and found her clutching her knees and gulping air. There were pictures spread on the bed around her, spilling out of a Florsheim shoebox. Black-and-white snapshots of a man with a long face and thin waist, and a little girl patting a brown dog, eating cake, wearing shiny Mary Janes, sitting in a tiny pool. And one with Claire between the two, a light glowing behind them as though they were on fire, smiling, happily aflame. Somewhere in the neighborhood, a little girl began to sing scales. "Hear that?" Claire asked, looking at her knees. I patted her bare feet, hoping the child's singing would make her happy. "That's the sound a swan makes at the end of its life. They sing themselves to death." She gathered the photographs into her lap. "Only other swans can hear it, swans on the way out."

The only time I recall Claire ever getting angry with me—and it wasn't anger exactly—was the time in seventh grade when I brought Damita Davis home and we played Yahtzee and ate Vanilla Wafers. Claire looked on from the doorway as I rolled my way to a big victory. My wrists seemed to glow gold; I rubbed them between turns. It was the first time I'd ever won at Yahtzee. After the game, Claire shuffled out of the kitchen in her fuzzy lavender slippers and holed up in the bathroom. She stayed in there for two hours after Damita had gone home. When I finally dared to check on her, all I could see were her wrinkled, white fingers hanging over the edge of the bathtub and a meringue of pinned-up hair floating above the bubbles that rose up out of the tub like a dream. There were candles burnt down to pools of wax on saucers, and it smelled like the time we ironed Crayola shavings between pieces of waxed paper. The empty, wet and puckered box of Mr. Bubble beside the toilet alarmed me, I don't know why. Maybe it was just the sheer emptiness, ten baths' worth of bubbles extravagantly frothed for a single bathing. I flushed the toilet to cut the silence. Claire parted the foam with her hands, peering mystically through like a movie star in a soft-focus reverie.

"What?" she asked.

"I thought you were ..."

"What?"

"Forget it. You're going to be a prune soon," I said.

"Do you love her?" she asked.

"Who?"

"You love her?"

"Damita? No! I think she let me win. I could never respect a woman like that." Claire gathered the bubbles around her again and sank out of view.

Nothing was ever really the same after the séance. At the time, it just seemed like a bitter bite, something she'd swallow and forget. Now I see it must have been a mouthful of disease.

The day of the séance, Claire was nervous and excited—the

way I used to get before the Oak Grove Elementary school carnivals or the field trips to the Agricultural Hall of Fame. She picked red clover and daisies and marigolds and strewed them throughout the house like a fertility goddess. She even floated some bachelor's buttons in the cat's water. She took everything elevated and breakable off shelves and tables—plates, lamps, clocks, candlesticks—and laid them on the floor, as if she were anticipating a quake. She explained that the collision of the spirit realm with the physical world was known to send actual vibrations all through the house and sometimes beyond. Claire was cautious and reverent when it came to consorting with spirits.

We decided we would try to contact my mother, since she was the only dead person we had in common. Claire made me take a bath, wash my hair, and dress up in my stiff suit even though it was hot and the suit made me itch. She had a high regard for those who now knew "the geography of death." Mrs. Moody, a spiritually compatible customer of Claire's, joined us in hope of hooking up with her late brother, Harold. We sat around the kitchen table and grinned politely at one another for a while, pointing at the bird feeder outside the kitchen window whenever anything more colorful than a starling alighted.

Finally Claire told me to fetch my clackers—two translucent lavender balls with flecks of foil inside. Each ball dangled from a string. You held the clackers by a plastic ring and snapped them up and down, clacking them together, faster and faster until they looked like fluttering wings. I hadn't played with them since a kid at school told me a boy in Saint Louis clacked his a little too hard, and they splintered and flew into his eyes. My mother had given them to me on my sixth birthday. I'm sure she'd had no inkling they'd prove to be dangerous. She also gave me a small, plastic Scrooge McDuck that collapsed in a heap when you pressed on his foundation, snapping back into shape when you released it. Claire thought the clackers would be a better spiritual conduit than the duck.

We all held hands. Claire dangled the clackers between our clasped hands, and Mrs. Moody held a flat, soiled rabbit fashioned out of braided pipe cleaners between ours. She had fat little link-sausage fingers that bulged out of an already sweating palm. She smiled apologetically as we locked fingers, but I didn't mind the sweat because she smelled like cookies. We all closed our eyes, and Mrs. Moody started humming "Amazing Grace." She sang the words *but now am found* and *but now I see* aloud and then stopped.

After a few moments of silence, Claire's grip tightened, and I felt her arm stiffen. When my hand began to go numb, I breached séance etiquette and looked over at Claire. I saw a thread of blood trailing from her lip where she was biting it. I saw that Mrs. Moody was looking too. She was staring at her clenched hand, which was white and bloodless and would probably turn the bluish color of her hair before long—hair Claire herself had recently colored and styled. Neither of us said a word. We were afraid to disturb Claire in this state, as though she were sleepwalking among the dead and in peril of being trapped in a limbo world if roused.

As Claire walked among spirits, I thought about my mother's hands; they were soft as flannel. Sometimes at night as I fell asleep, she would rub my feet and talk about movie stars. She told me she had always been a little bit in love with Cary Grant and knew if he met her, he would want to buy her a pair of black satin pumps. She felt certain Dana Andrews paid his bills long before they were due and invested his money wisely. Gene Tierney, she said, would certainly go out of her way to care for limping dogs and fallen birds, despite what some of the vixenish roles she'd played might make you think of her. After these stories, I often dreamt of large and kind and beautiful people who brought food wrapped in tinfoil to our house or gladly drove us, in cars with seats as soft as feathers, anywhere we wanted to go. I wondered if my mother would remember any of this or if she had left her earthly recollections behind.

Claire let out an explosive gasp, like someone long submerged bursting to the surface of a lake. Mrs. Moody screamed, and I kicked over the bowl of plastic fruit at my feet. Claire sat stone still until Mrs. Moody asked in a trembling voice, "Did you see Mrs. Yulich?"

Claire turned her gaze to Mrs. Moody, but her expression remained fixed. "She's dead," Claire said. She turned to me and said, "You're to sleep in your own room tonight."

I can't be sure if Claire made contact because it was never mentioned again, but I think she experienced something on the other side that pained her terribly. Maybe she saw my mother weeping. My mother cried so quietly, you could tell she was crying only by the rounded shape of her shoulders. It always made me wish I could step out of my skin and wrap her in it. Maybe Claire saw my mother crying, quiet as a sick child.

The good days grew less and less frequent after that. Claire gradually phased out her beauty business and withdrew from me too. She forbade me to go in her bedroom unless she wasn't in it, which was increasingly rare. Tiny wrinkles began collecting around her eyes and mouth, as if she hadn't allowed them until now. She began drinking her coffee with heaping spoonfuls of sugar, and she chewed her fingers until they bled. But sometimes she'd sit in the garden and pull weeds and seem strong and steady in her dirty dress and rubber shoes.

One day, after an extended period of brooding silence, Claire snapped out of it just like that, like Scrooge McDuck, as though strings in her limbs had been pulled suddenly taut. It was a Saturday, and I was watching *Lancelot Link* on television. Claire and

I used to sit together on Saturdays and I'd watch her straining face as she tried not to laugh. She claimed the star of the show, a trained chimp, was my first cousin and always remarked on the family resemblance. On this day, she swept into my room like a warm wind and cupped my face in her hands. She began kissing my fingers and wrists and pecked her way up to my closed eyes. It was a startling change, and I was afraid to move. She laughed out loud and drew me to her, patting my back gently.

"Things are going to be different," she said, looking into my eyes, trying on different grins as she stared into them, as if she had just gotten a new mouth and was testing its range. "Let's go to that new Exotic Animal Drive-Thru Paradise. What do you say? I hear they have bears!"

So we packed a picnic lunch and headed for the park, ignoring the silence, the days and months of anxious quiet that had preceded this transformation. On the way there, we sang with the radio, honked at the grazing cows, and kept track of out-of-state license plates, like we used to. Claire even laughed for the first time in a long time when I imitated Buck, the German shepherd that was poisoned, by hanging out the window, licking the air, snapping at bugs, and threatening to jump.

When we got to the park, a man in a safari hat and leopard-spotted scarf gave us a map and told us to keep our windows rolled up at all times because of the bears. He said not to try to feed them no matter how friendly or harmless they might appear.

We traveled down a road identified as Mallard Avenue on the map. We didn't see anything but trees for quite a stretch. Finally, we saw a large herd of sheep grazing near a pond.

"Pretty exotic," Claire said. One side of her mouth was pursed.

They looked like clouds on legs from a distance. As we got closer, we could see their chewing faces, and I said, "Maybe they'd let you fix their hair." Claire had always shamelessly solicited customers wherever we went, though she claimed to target only the choicest coifs.

"Those mops?" she said. "That would require sheer talent, hardy har," We both laughed, a foreign sound. It felt good to laugh together again, a feeling of convalescence or release like we'd just gotten over a malingering cold or out of an interminable winter.

We turned onto Bison Boulevard. The map made it appear as if this were the wildlife hub. We didn't see anything but some ducks and a couple of deer for the first few hundred feet, then we saw brown, white, and black bodies bumping along the road ahead. As they came into view, we could see they were llamas. We pulled off to the side and stopped in the grass. There was a huddle of llamas a few feet in front of us, and they kept turning around and looking at us as though they were gossiping. The group dispersed, strategically it seemed, and one of the rust-colored llamas walked toward our car. It walked over to Claire's side and looked straight in at her. Claire knocked against the window, but it just stood there staring at her, then it pressed its mouth and nose against the window and slobbered on it.

"Think he wants a tip," Claire said, and she rolled down the window and offered him a shelled peanut. He took it gently from her hands with his thick, sticky lips and tongue.

In spite of the injunction to "keep the windows rolled up," we decided to have our picnic at this site, beneath the cloak of a large weeping-willow tree. Claire found the llamas soothing. As we spread out beneath the tree, we could see two peacocks sauntering toward us. We ate grapes, cheese and crackers, celery stuffed with peanut butter, marshmallows, and we each had a can of lukewarm grape Nehi. As the peacocks came closer, Claire threw out a handful of pastel-colored miniature marshmallows. The birds came near us, but walked on the marshmallows without interest, as though they were only cushioned stones, unworthy of scrutiny. They stopped once they got safely past us, fanned out in the sun, arched their necks, and I imagined they were absorbing energy and color through the eyes in their tails. I imagined they'd lift up in the air and spin colorfully like fireworks.

As we stretched out on our backs, three llamas inched cautiously closer and cleaned up the marshmallows. Then they stood there with stiffened ears, looking at us, baring their big teeth, perhaps waiting for second helpings. One of them hissed at us, and Claire hissed back, causing them all to back up. Claire reached into the picnic basket and pulled out a box of powdered sugar. She pushed my T-shirt up around my shoulders and sprinkled the sugar on my stomach carefully, as if I were a cookie. She pulled out some strawberries and rolled them in the sugar. The llamas looked on like big, curious dogs, dipping their noses and sniffing the air as we ate. When we had eaten all the strawberries, Claire licked the remaining sugar off my stomach, and my muscles tensed. She laid her head on the moist circle.

"I can hear your intestines laboring," she said. She traced a winding path along my stomach with her finger. "The food sprouts, grows, takes shape, and we eat it. It changes and is passed along to feed the earth. It assumes a new form, a radish, a pear, and we eat it again. We could be partaking of the organic leftovers of . . . Akhenaton . . . Fatty Arbuckle . . ."

"Who?"

"We could be breaking bread with Christ in a manner of speaking." Claire sat up and gently kissed my eyebrows, my nose. "Do you suppose resurrection disqualifies him?" she asked. "How human was he really, if there was no putrefaction?" She leaned on her elbow and twisted my hair around her finger.

"Life is an endless meal, a banquet, and this moment, this succulent moment, is merely a bite." My stomach lurched. This was an observation Claire had been fond of making, but in her privation the metaphor had not been apt for a long time. I wondered if it could last, if she'd savor that arm-in-arm companionship again, if it would be like before when the warmth we shared—each of us clumsily reckoning with loss—kept the boxed-up memories from haunting her, from making her sit so still and dead, staring at her knees, our intimacy interrupted by phantoms whose sternness she buckled beneath. I missed the feeling of her hand on my stomach.

And then I imagined choking on a bad day, the unpleasant hours sliding down my windpipe, blocking my breath as I struggled to dislodge them. As I lay there thinking, a black-and-white zebra-striped jeep pulled up and parked behind our car. A man dressed from head to toe in khaki stepped out and shined a flashlight at us, as though the beam would hold us in place. It shone through the drooping branches, competing with the threads of sunlight that embroidered our faces. We sat up. Claire positioned her head in the light's path and stared into it.

"You folks are clearly in violation here," the man said, lowering the flashlight. "It states right there on your ticket that you are not under any circumstances to get out of your car. In so doing, you have jeopardized your own lives as well as the welfare of the park and do hereby relinquish your rights as guests. I must escort you out of the park immediately. Your tickets are nonrefundable." The words came out of his mouth rapid and shaky. I could tell it was a speech that he had long waited for the opportunity to make and now that it was over, a look of letdown crimped his face.

"I am not frightened of peacocks or llamas," Claire said in a formal drawl. "Nor they of me."

"You are very near the wild boars' favorite watering hole. They're a rough lot, them boars. They'd just as soon skewer you as look at you," he said.

"*I've* only seen llamas and peacocks and assorted barnyard stock," Claire said, as she stood and smoothed her dress.

"I bet you don't even have any old bears," I said.

"We have bears. Just because you didn't see them doesn't mean we don't have bears. They don't appear on demand. We have bears."

I'd hit a nerve.

"Please gather your things, get in your car, and follow me out of the park."

Just before we came to the exit gate displaying a sign that read THANK YOU FOR VISITING THE EXOTIC ANIMAL PARADISE. HOPE YOU HAD AN UNBEARABLY GOOD TIME, the man in the truck pointed his arm out the window at a dense stand of trees in the distance. "Bears!" he yelled, as we drove out.

That afternoon was the last savory bite Claire and I shared. It seemed the moment we arrived home, the day became instantly something to be filed away in a mental scrapbook. Claire tried hard to hold on to her good humor, but she quickly lost all resolve. The bitter bites came back, consumed her. Or her soul had decided to fast. Sometimes I could see her face straining so to form a smile, thoughtful with effort, as though it were heaving an anvil. I held Claire's slack and thinning body to mine, felt the sharpness of her shoulders, tried to be bone and muscle to her. I imagined pushing my hand inside Claire, straight through her navel and into the nucleus of her history, casting out sad pictures and making more room for her god—the god of a glorious growth you could hear if attuned—to take root. I imagined something cool and small at the center, something untouched by pain or memory or shame, and I clasped it in my hands, a shriveled seed, tried to shore up the last fragments of an ailing spirit.

Some months after the trip to the animal park, she agreed to go to a movie.

Fantasia was playing at the Bijou. Claire moved slowly about the rooms of the house as the steps of grooming came back to her one by one. She dabbed circles of rouge on her dry cheeks and pinned knotted curls back with a pearl-studded comb. She pressed a flowered dress and found a pocketbook the same watery blue as the petals. Claire had grown so thin, the dress hung on her. There was only a faint suggestion of body beneath the fabric. You could see through her skin that even her spirit was withered. Claire's eyes were wide open, wet and restless with longing. I felt sure the movie would bring her back to me, hungry, joyful.

As the coming attractions played, two young girls sat down in front of us. Claire, who had been speaking of the plush comfort of the theater seats, became quiet again. She smiled periodically and nodded at me, twisted her hair, fingered the pearls on the comb. When the movie began, I looked over to see if it registered any expression on Claire's face. She was staring at the back of one of the girls' heads. I reached over and took Claire's hand in both of mine. I smoothed and patted her arm as though trying to tame it. She pulled away and reached into her purse, took out a brush. She leaned forward and freed the girl's hair from the back of the chair. The girl turned slowly around, looked at Claire, then locked her gaze on me. Claire brushed the long blonde strands in her hand. I half-smiled at the girl, as if I had just asked her for a favor. She turned back around and sat perfectly still as Claire stroked her hair. The other girl turned and stared at Claire, who grinned down at the rope of hair in her hands.

The subtle music behind the movie changed abruptly, bellowing deeply and thumping beneath our feet. I heard someone behind me ask, "Where are the words? When are they going to say something?" Claire dropped the hair and stood up. She stared absently at the screen. Popcorn hit her back. She apologized to the people sitting next to us and moved to the aisle, walked toward the screen. People in the audience turned to look at her and began whispering. She walked up the steps at the side of the stage. The audience became audibly hushed. She walked to the center of the screen and raised her hand to it. Mickey Mouse capered about, ankle deep in water, a pail in his hands. He scrambled frantically through Claire's shadow, sweeping the water away. Claire gracefully eased herself to the floor like a falling leaf. A battalion of angry brooms marched above her. Some of the kids in the audience clapped, others giggled, and some threw empty candy boxes at the stage. I caught the worried eye of the blonde girl who was seated in front of us as I walked down the aisle. When I reached Claire, I knelt beside her and put my hand on her forehead. The projectionist stopped the film, houselights came on, and teenaged ushers rushed toward us and stopped short, uncertain. Claire looked at me, at my mouth. She licked her lips. "I can't taste a thing," she said.

After that Claire and I lived together in silence, Claire's hunched figure deforming into a shape of increasing resignation and sorrow I couldn't—or didn't want to—make out. I fed her and bathed her, read her stories from *Life* magazine about the world's transformations and setbacks, and sometimes she'd smile, shake her head. One day, at the instigation of a concerned neighbor, two men and a woman dressed in crisp, white clothing came and took Claire away. They held her by the arms and escorted her into a van. She offered no resistance.

I visited her once—last year, June 29, my seventeenth birthday. It wasn't Claire really, just a facsimile, a loose satchel of cells unable to cage the roaming soul, fled, in search of soiled seraphim. I wouldn't know where to begin looking for the Claire I'd known. In the garden, maybe, clinging to the slick pink and green underside of a rhubarb leaf. In the scraps of earth, the dirt beneath my fingernails. Or maybe drinking a soda with friends in heaven, waiting to be born again. Hibernating like bears in a drive-through paradise, napping in inaccessible places.

A nurse told me she'd become fully unresponsive and they were forced to feed her through a tube. She'd shed all superfluous gestures, one by one. Claire and I sat together quietly, her eyes looking past me, weary with the onus of sight, her gaze resting on my shoulder. I put my finger between her dry lips and pressed against her teeth. She parted her teeth slightly and I waited, hoped for the gentle pressure of her bite. I closed my eyes and listened for distant singing, listened for signs of invisible growth happening somewhere in the world.

CONTRIBUTORS

DANIEL CURLEY was one of the editors of *Accent* and founded and edited its offspring, *Ascent*, from 1974 until his death in 1988. In addition to three novels and several collections of short stories, he wrote criticism, poetry, plays, and three books for children. A posthumous collection, *The Curandero*, was published in 1991.

CAROLE L. GLICKFELD grew up in New York City, the setting of *Useful Gifts*, her award-winning collection of stories about a family with deaf parents and hearing children, and *Swimming toward the Ocean*, a novel that won the Washington State Book Award. She is the recipient of a Literary Fellowship from the National Endowment for the Arts and a Governor's Arts Award (Washington State) and was a fellow of both the Mac-Dowell Colony and the Bread Loaf Writers' Conference. Her stories, essays, and poems have appeared in numerous literary journals and anthologies. Now living in Seattle, where she has taught creative writing, she works on a consulting basis with aspiring writers on their manuscripts when she is not indulging her passion for travel.

AMINA GAUTIER is an assistant professor of English at DePaul University. Her work has appeared in the anthologies *Best African American Fiction* and *New Stories from the South* and in numerous literary journals, including *Antioch Review, North American Review, Iowa Review, Kenyon Review,* and *Southern Review.*

DANA JOHNSON is a professor of English in the Dana and David Dornsife College of Letters, Arts, and Sciences at the University of Southern California. She is the author of *Elsewhere, California: A Novel.*

TOM KEALEY is the author of *The Creative Writing MFA Handbook.* His stories have appeared in *Best American Nonrequired Reading, Glimmer*

Train, *Story Quarterly*, *Prairie Schooner*, and the *San Francisco Chronicle*. His nonfiction has appeared in *Poets and Writers* and *The Writer*. His MFA in creative writing is from the University of Massachusetts Amherst, where he received the Distinguished Teaching Award. Tom has taught creative writing at Stanford University since 2003.

C. M. MAYO is the author of several books on Mexico, including *The Last Prince of the Mexican Empire*, a novel based on a true story and named a *Library Journal* Best Book of 2009. Her collection *Meteor* won the Gival Press Poetry Award for publication in 2018. A native of El Paso, she is a member of the Texas Institute of Letters.

MELINDA MOUSTAKIS was born in Fairbanks, Alaska, and raised in California. She received her MA from the University of California, Davis, and her PhD in English and Creative Writing from Western Michigan University. In addition to winning the Flannery O'Connor Award, her book *Bear Down, Bear North: Alaska Stories* won the Maurice Prize, was shortlisted for the William Saroyan International Prize for Writing, and was a finalist for the Washington State Book Award. Her stories have appeared in *Alaska Quarterly Review*, *Kenyon Review*, *New England Review*, *Conjunctions*, *Cimarron Review*, *American Short Fiction*, and elsewhere. She was named a 2011 "5 Under 35" writer by the National Book Foundation.

ANTONYA NELSON is the author of eleven books of fiction (four novels and seven collections of stories), including *Funny Once: Stories* and *Bound: A Novel*. Nelson's work has appeared in the *New Yorker*, *Esquire*, *Harper's*, *Redbook*, and in many other magazines, as well as in anthologies such as *Prize Stories*, the *O. Henry Awards*, and *Best American Short Stories*. Her books have been *New York Times* Notable Books of 1992, 1996, 1998, and 2000; in 2000 Nelson was also named by the *New Yorker* as one of the "twenty young fiction writers for the new millennium." She is the recipient of the Rea Award for Short Fiction, a 2000–2001 NEA Grant, and a Guggenheim Fellowship. Nelson teaches creative writing at the University of Houston and at Warren Wilson College.

LORI OSTLUND's first collection of stories, *The Bigness of the World*, received the Flannery O'Connor Award for Short Fiction, the California Book Award for First Fiction, and the Edmund White Award for Debut

Fiction. It was shortlisted for the William Saroyan International Prize for Writing, was a Lambda finalist, and was named a Notable Book by the Short Story Prize. Her stories have appeared in *Best American Short Stories* and *The PEN/O. Henry Prize Stories*, among other publications. In 2009, Lori received a Rona Jaffe Foundation Award. She is the author of the novel *After the Parade* and lives in San Francisco.

ANDREW PORTER is also the author of the novel *In Between Days*. His award-winning fiction has appeared in *One Story*, *Epoch*, and the *Pushcart Prize Anthology* and on NPR's Selected Shorts. A graduate of the Iowa Writers' Workshop, he has received a variety of fellowships, including the 2004 W. K. Rose Fellowship in the Creative Arts, a Helene Wurlitzer Fellowship, and a James Michener–Paul Engle Fellowship from the James Michener/Copernicus Society of America. Porter is an associate professor of English and director of the Creative Writing Program at Trinity University in San Antonio, Texas.

ANNE RAEFF's second novel, *Winter Kept Us Warm*, was published in 2018. Her short story collection *The Jungle around Us* won the 2015 Flannery O'Connor Award for Short Fiction. The collection was also a finalist for the California Book Award and was on the *San Francisco Chronicle*'s 100 Best Books of 2017 list. *Clara Mondschein's Melancholia*, also a novel, was published in 2002. Raeff's stories and essays have appeared in *New England Review*, ZYZZYVA, and *Guernica*, among other publications. She is proud to be a high school teacher and works primarily with recent immigrants. She lives in San Francisco with her wife and two cats.

PAUL RAWLINS's fiction has appeared in *Glimmer Train*, *Southeast Review*, *Sycamore Review*, and *Tampa Review*. He has received awards from the Utah Arts Council, the Association for Mormon Letters, and PRISM International. He lives in Salt Lake City.

BARBARA SUTTON's stories have appeared in *AGNI*, the *Missouri Review*, the *Antioch Review*, the *Harvard Review*, *Image*, and other publications. She works as a government speechwriter in New York City and blogs at *Sketches by Baz*.

KELLIE WELLS was awarded the Flannery O'Connor Award and the Great Lakes Colleges Association New Writers Award for her short-story collection *Compression Scars*. She is also author of the novels *Fat Girl, Terres-*

trial, and *Skin*, and the shory-story collection *God, the Moon, and Other Megafauna*. Her work has appeared in the *Kenyon Review*, *Ninth Letter*, and *Fairy Tale Review* and was selected for inclusion in the 2010 anthology *Best American Fantasy*. Wells is a graduate of the writing programs at the University of Montana, the University of Pittsburgh, and Western Michigan University.

NANCY ZAFRIS is the author of two novels, *Lucky Strike* and *The Metal Shredders*. Her stories have appeared in numerous literary magazines, and she is fiction editor of the *Kenyon Review*.